THE KISS

By the Author

THE KISS

by

C.A. Popovich

2022

Credits

Editors: Victoria Villaseñor and Cindy Cresap
Production Design: Susan Ramundo
Cover Design By Jeanine Henning

Acknowledgments

Maybe it was the pandemic and the importance of family it highlighted that prompted me to add a child to my book. I've never written about children, and I know very little about them, so I turned to my psychologist sister for help. Who knew there was something called a toddler bed? I thank her for helping me get the life of a three-year-old woven into the story. And, once again, I thank my editors and all the hardworking folks at Bold Strokes Books for giving my stories a home. Thanks to Sandi for feedback on my first draft. I hope readers enjoy the story and feel the love.

Dedication

To Love

PROLOGUE

Kate Willis took a deep, settling breath and quickly peeked out her daughter's bedroom window searching for moving shadows. She saw nothing amiss and heard no unusual noises, but she edged away from anyone lurking outside and used her body to shield her daughter from view as she tossed the last of her three-year-old's toys and clothes into boxes. Her thoughts raced with hasty plans to flee. Leaving in the early morning hours had worked the last two times, and she prayed she could get away permanently this time. She'd lived with guilt, shame, and fear for so long she'd almost convinced herself she'd never escape. She forced away the fear threatening to paralyze her and concentrated on the task of getting them to safety. If her ex caught them leaving again, she was certain there would be worse repercussions than last time. This time, she'd leave the state and go to her sister's house in Michigan. She choked back tears as she tossed boxes into her car and went to retrieve her daughter. She vowed she'd keep her safe no matter what.

CHAPTER ONE

One year later

"What are the chances?" Kate whispered and moved out of the way of the women streaming into the room. She studied the tables set end to end that formed a large square in the middle of the spacious room while she kept an eye on the woman she'd spent the past half a year thinking about.

Six months after she'd moved in with her sister, she'd gone on a hike with a local lesbian group. Leslie had been one of the hikers, and they'd hit it off right away. They'd laughed, talked, and hunted mushrooms for Leslie's restaurant. And in an unexpected moment of spontaneity, she'd kissed Leslie. It had been the kind of kiss written about in fairy tales, the kind that curled your toes and made your heart race.

And then she'd run. There wasn't a place in Kate's life for that kind of complication, but she'd never stopped thinking of that kiss.

Now, six months later, Kate was part of the organization of a speed-dating event fundraiser. She'd decided to participate, hoping to meet someone to test her resolve to trust again. She never thought she'd run into the one whose memory lingered and had slipped into her thoughts unbidden nearly every day since they'd shared that moment of beautiful intimacy.

She pushed away the memories and concentrated on the moderator who'd begun to explain the rules. Folding chairs lined each side of the tables spaced three feet apart and centered between makeshift dividers placed on the table to separate the couples and offer a semblance of privacy. She snaked her way through the crowd toward one of the seats at the end of a table.

"You will each get five minutes to spend with the potential love of your life before the bell rings and you move to the next woman in line." She continued with details and codes of conduct before wishing the group luck and starting the timer for the first five minutes.

Kate sat across from her first date and glanced at the list of questions she'd made. The term speed date took on new meaning as she'd hardly begun the conversation and the five minutes of information exchange was over. She moved to the next woman and repeated the process while feigning calm as she got closer to Leslie, who was at the end of the line. She dabbed the sweat off her upper lip with a tissue and took a few deep breaths as she slid into the seat across from the woman she hadn't been able to purge from her memory. Would she recognize her? Would she remember? Kate pushed aside the ache of loneliness that had settled in the pit of her stomach since her arrival in the state. The ache that had convinced her to participate in this event, now that her world had seemed to come to rest in a calmer place. Leslie sat across from her and offered a sad smile.

Distrust and uncertainty clouded Leslie's gaze. "You're back, I see."

"I'm so sorry for leaving so abruptly, but I had a huge personal issue to resolve. It turned out I wasn't ready."

"Yeah. Well, here we are." Leslie looked conflicted as she toyed with the sheet in front of her.

"Yes, we are. I'd like a date with you." Kate reminded herself to breathe.

"Will you tell me why you left the way you did?"

Would she? After a year of counseling, she knew she had to be open if she wanted to be close to anyone. "Yes."

"I look forward to it." Leslie stood and walked away when the buzzer sounded.

Over the past year, she'd managed to push aside her mountain of mistrust and this event was an opportunity to risk dating again. She couldn't quit now that she might have a chance with Leslie. Uncertainty churned in her gut and warred with anticipation, and she reminded herself it was only a date.

The only person she'd shared her crush with was her friend Joy. They'd met at the same Meetup hike where she'd met Leslie, and they'd been friends ever since. At least she could keep friendships. She turned in her date choices to the moderator and took her time leaving in hopes of connecting with Leslie on her way out. She only caught a glimpse of her back as she walked out the door.

Kate helped the cleanup crew fold tables and chairs before she thanked the moderator and left. She took her time walking home to her two-bedroom apartment in Ferndale, Michigan. She'd chosen the location to be near her sister and the LGBTQ community center where she volunteered. She enjoyed the satisfaction of helping to raise funds to keep the doors to the community center open. Their many programs and support groups for lesbians, gay men, and LGBTQ youth and transgendered folks were lifelines, and she took pride in her ability to help them thrive. It also gave her a sense of purpose and a place of safety.

She had an hour before she'd pick up Portia from her sister's, so she made herself a cup of coffee and sat at her kitchen table to sort her notes on the various women she'd met. She put Leslie at the top of her imagined triangle, and the others she arranged in order of preference along the sides. She lined the bottom with ones she probably wouldn't consider and ignored a stab of guilt that her divorce wasn't officially final. Kate had feared Wendy's rages after she'd served the divorce papers and she'd still refused to sign. Wendy had no idea where Kate lived now, but she had been to her sister's with her several times, so Kate worried she might look for her at Deanna's. But aside from her not signing the papers, the last year had been quiet, and she could only pray Wendy had moved on. Wendy had never threatened to hurt Portia, but she'd never cared about her either. She checked the time and left to pick up her daughter from her sister's place.

"Mommy!"

All her angst disappeared with one word from her little girl. "Hi, baby. Did you have fun today?" Deanna and Rob had taken her to the zoo with their sons.

"I saw lions and lelephants." Portia's sea green eyes, so like her own, sparkled with delight.

"That's great, honey. Are you ready to go home and tell me all about it?"

"Hi, Kate," Deanna called from the dining room. "You guys want dinner before you leave?"

"I'm sure Portia had lunch, and I'm good. We'll have spaghetti when we get home." Kate looked at Portia who had settled on the floor with a small plastic dinosaur. "It looks like she got a souvenir from her zoo trip."

"Of course. The boys each got something, too. You know how hard it is to get past the gift shop without stopping." Deanna grinned and shrugged.

"Thanks again for keeping her today. The speed-dating event went well. I think everyone had a good time."

"How about you? Meet anyone interesting?" Deanna sat at the dining room table as if they had all evening to talk.

Kate wasn't ready to talk about Leslie yet. It still felt new and fragile. "I'm going to get Portia home. Can we talk about it tomorrow?"

"Sure. But don't think you're going to get away without giving me details." Deanna stood and hugged them both.

"Talk to you tomorrow." Kate put a jacket on Portia and carried her and her new toy to her car. She smiled at her babbling about the animals and snakes she'd seen until she dozed off in her car seat. She gently lifted her out when they arrived home and carried her to a play area she had set up in the corner of the living room.

"How about a bowl of spaghetti?" Kate poured milk in Portia's cup and gave it to her before heating a small cup of spaghetti and some creamed spinach. She might outgrow it, but it was a combination Portia liked now. "Okay, honey. Dinner's ready." She set her in her booster seat at the table where Portia rattled on between bites about the bears and the bear fountain in the zoo. Her favorite turned out to be the kangaroos in the new exhibit. She could barely keep her eyes open by the time she'd finished eating, and Kate followed her to the bathroom for another lesson in brushing her teeth. She helped her with the buttons on her fish pajamas and tucked the covers around her. Portia was already asleep by the time she kissed her good night, and her phone rang as she settled on the couch with a glass of wine.

"So, how did it go?" Joy's enthusiasm made her smile.

"It was fun. I think it brought in a substantial amount of much needed funds for the center, too."

"Great. So, was Leslie there?"

"She was. And she wasn't happy with me. I apologized and promised to tell her why I left so abruptly when we have a date."

"So, you both agreed to a date? They're all secret, aren't they?"

"Yeah. The moderator will get all our picks and there's no guarantee the person we choose will have the same choice, but Leslie will go out with me. To get an explanation if nothing else." Kate shrugged as she spoke.

"I hope it works out for you two. I like you both. So, no word from the ex?"

"No." Kate took a deep breath to suppress her anger at her soon-to-be ex-wife. "She was supposed to sign the papers and mail them to my lawyer last week."

"Well, she has to sign eventually, doesn't she?"

"Not since the advent of no-fault divorces. But if she doesn't, I can file it as a default divorce. I've had her served, and I can offer proof if needed. I need her out of my life so I can move on."

"Well, hang in there. Things will work out as they're meant to."

"I suppose. Thanks for calling." Kate disconnected the call and booted up her computer. She'd told Wendy she could email copies of the signed divorce papers, as she wanted as little face-to-face exposure with her as possible. The violence, the threats, the anger, and possessiveness were in her past. She was finally looking toward her future, and even hoping to find love again. The empty inbox stared at her as her curser blinked. Maybe tomorrow. She closed down her computer and finished her wine.

CHAPTER TWO

L eslie sat on her couch and propped her feet on her coffee table before taking a sip from a cup of green tea. She reviewed the notes she'd scribbled about each of her seven five-minute dates. Only one stood out. She knew she would when she saw her seated at the end of a table. Memories of the softness of her lips and the quiet sigh when they'd broken their connection sent yearning through her chest. She put Kate's card off to the side. She'd be her first choice for a date, and she hoped Kate would keep her promise to tell her what happened. Why she'd run off that day without a word. *A huge personal issue,* she'd said.

She reviewed the other potential dates, trying not to compare them to Kate. There was no comparison. She took her time with each one recalling their voice, the color of their eyes, and the level of interest reflected there. Any one of them would be worth spending at least one date with. She noted the absence of Meetup events on her calendar. Morel mushroom season was long over, and she hadn't been able to muster her usual enthusiasm for the hikes after Kate left that day. They'd only spent an afternoon together, but their connection was strong. She'd never had a kiss that had affected her so deeply, so quickly. When Kate had run, Leslie couldn't help but wonder what she'd done wrong.

She sighed, accepting that at thirty-nine she might end up being alone for the rest of her life. At least she had her family and her friends. The thought reminded her how long it had been since she'd spent time with her friend Alex. Her very married friend who hated mushrooms. She smiled at the memory of the few excursions on which she'd joined her. Her discomfort with the cool spring weather was evident, as was the intense scrutiny necessary to find the concealed mushrooms, but she'd never complained. She made a mental note to call her soon.

She put her date list aside and held her cup in both hands as she took a swallow of her tepid tea. Kate told her she'd explain her disappearance, so she allowed herself to feel the anticipation at seeing her again. It troubled her that she expected anything from someone who'd kissed her as if she were precious and then left without a word. She put her empty cup into the dishwasher and put on a jacket before heading out the door.

"Hey, Mom. You busy?" Leslie called from the door to her parents' house before entering. They rarely locked the door despite her insistence they do. Fortunately, they lived practically next door, their houses completing a perfect triangle with the restaurant.

"We're in the kitchen, honey," her mother answered. "You're just in time for fresh baklava. It's still warm."

Leslie grabbed a couple of potholders and helped her mom retrieve a huge baking pan from the oven. "It smells great." She set the pan on a cooling rack on a large table set against the wall like she'd done so many times before. She'd worked at her family's Greek restaurant since she was old enough to carry dishes. "What's the occasion?" Any food made for the restaurant was cooked in its kitchen, not at her parents' house.

"I had a taste for it, and you know it's your father's favorite. It's best warm, so get out the plates, please." Her mom efficiently cut the pastry into perfect two-inch squares and lifted them out of the pan onto a huge serving tray. Leslie placed two pieces on a plate as her father entered the kitchen.

"Hi, honey. Are those for me?" he asked and kissed Leslie's cheek.

"Yep. How are you feeling, Dad?" Her father had been fighting a cold for a week.

"Much better. I'm staying away from the restaurant for another couple of days and drinking enough hot tea with lemon to float a boat." He grinned and gave her mother a kiss on her cheek.

Leslie relaxed with a piece of baklava, feeling as much at home there as she did in her own kitchen.

"No more morels now, huh?" her mother asked, more of a statement than a question.

"The season's way over." Leslie took a bite of the sweet pastry and moaned. "This is fantastic, Mom."

"Thank you. I see you were ready for some, too."

"I've managed to lose the five pounds I put on, so one piece is my limit." Leslie grinned and wished she had inherited her father's metabolism. He ate anything he wanted and never gained a pound.

"How was your event today?" her mom asked before taking a bite.

"It went well. I met a few interesting women. We'll see if anything comes of it."

Her mother swallowed before speaking. "My book club is reading a book about a woman who's bisexual. You don't think you could be, do you? My friend Esther has an extremely good-looking son who's single."

"Sorry, Mom. I am what I am, and men don't interest me romantically."

"Oh, honey." Her mother stood and pulled her into her arms. "I only meant it would give you a much larger pool of choices. I never want you to feel you have to apologize for who you are. We love you and we'll accept whomever you choose to love."

"Thank you." She hugged her mother and smiled when her father toasted with a piece of baklava. "I realize I haven't done a great job choosing someone so far, but I'm still holding out hope I'll find her one day." She stepped out of her mother's hold and kissed her cheek. "Thank you for being so supportive. I suppose I better get home. I'll see you tomorrow for the Sunday brunch crowd." Leslie went out the way she'd entered.

She fell back on her bed when she got home, thinking about a pet. Coming home to an empty house was getting old. She got up and reviewed the names of her potential dates again and arranged them in alphabetical order. She'd try every single one but start with Kate. She put her dates into her desk drawer and checked the time. Too late to turn in her date choices today. The deadline was Tuesday. She confirmed she didn't have any laundry to do before she undressed and slid into bed with her latest lesbian romance novel.

Leslie startled awake and pulled herself from her semi-dream state. One of the reasons she loved reading romance was the escape to a life of love, but seldom did she experience such intense arousal. She throbbed with an ache she feared only one woman could assuage. A woman she'd only known for an afternoon. She set her book on her nightstand and rolled to her side, hoping for dreams of the perfect kiss.

Her clock radio played soft music and gently drew Leslie from sleep. She had hours of work ahead of her at the restaurant, and she rose to take a shower and dress in her usual work clothes, a white long-sleeved shirt with the restaurant name embroidered in script above her left breast and a pair of black trousers. She watched the news with a cup of coffee for half an hour then headed to the restaurant.

Leslie vacuumed, wiped tables till they shone, and then visually reviewed the room for anything that might be out of place. Satisfied it was ready for the expected wave of patrons, she followed her mother to the kitchen to help with any food preparation or needed supplies.

The dining area soon filled with people, and Leslie spent the first hour they were open taking orders and serving coffee. Her parents had insisted they be open for lunch on Sunday to accommodate the after-church crowd. They rarely missed the early Greek Orthodox mass at the local church and felt it was important to cater to other churchgoers. Leslie had convinced her parents to limit the hours to noon until four, at least, so they got some time off. Her mother had always insisted on being the one to serve the food. She never failed to engage the diners in conversation and, as a result, most of them knew her by name. She smiled at her dad in the kitchen creating omelets and grilling bacon. "You good in here?" she asked.

"Fine." It was his standard answer with a grin that indicated he loved what he was doing. "I feel much better today, so I came in for a few hours."

With half an hour left until closing, Leslie made a pass to check on the diners lingering with coffee and dessert. She stopped at a few tables and turned toward the door as she heard it open. She nearly dropped her notepad when her eyes locked with sparkling green ones. "Kate."

"Leslie?"

Leslie stared for a moment. Kate walked into the restaurant holding the hand of a stunning little girl with green eyes that matched Kate's. Kate had mentioned that she had a sister. This must be her niece. "Sit anywhere you'd like. I'll get a booster seat for you," she said when she found her voice and retreated to the kitchen.

"Are you all right, honey?" her mother asked as she set a tray of baklava on the counter. "You look flushed. Come sit." She pulled out a chair from the small table in the corner of the kitchen.

Leslie plopped onto it. "I'm okay, Mom. A woman I haven't seen in a while just walked in. She needs a booster seat."

"Oh." Her mother rushed to the dining area before Leslie could stop her.

Leslie took a deep breath to settle herself and retrieved the child seat before following her mother. She approached slowly, not surprised her mother had Kate engaged in conversation. The little girl seemed to be doing her best to interrupt, however, and regale her mother with information from a visit to the zoo.

"Here's your throne, Princess." She set the child's chair on the bench seat across from Kate. She grinned when the girl slid off Kate's lap and raised her arms to be lifted. Leslie glanced at Kate quickly and was rewarded with the same slight smile imprinted on her memory six months ago. She gently set the child onto the chair and bowed. "And will you be having our special today, Your Highness?"

The girl looked shy for the first time and stared at Kate.

Kate turned to her and looked serious. "Yes, we'll both be having whatever the special of the day is." Her smile broke through like the sun through storm clouds.

"I'll be in the kitchen if you need anything. It was great to meet you, Kate and Portia. I hope you bring your mom back again soon." Leslie's mother winked and left.

Leslie's breath caught. Kate had a daughter? There was so much she didn't know about the woman she'd been fantasizing about. And damn if she didn't want to know everything there was to find out.

CHAPTER THREE

S o." Kate drew out the word, unsure what came next. This must be the restaurant Leslie had told her about when they'd met. She inhaled and released a slow breath to tamp down her arousal as memories flooded back of the short time they'd spent together and of the kiss she should never have allowed and would never forget. "This must be your parents' restaurant you told me about. A friend recommended it, so I thought I'd try it."

"I'm glad you did. We've been here for thirty years. Most of our menu is Greek food, but we have a fairly diverse offering." Leslie refilled her coffee cup.

"I think I'll have some baklava to go with my coffee, and the special of the day. And could I get a glass of milk for Portia? Do you have time to talk?"

"We close soon. I'll make sure Mom can handle the kitchen cleanup, and I'll be right back with your baklava and milk."

"I'll be here." Kate leaned back in her seat and watched Leslie stride back to the kitchen. She sipped her coffee as the few diners still there finished their meals. Each one stopped on their way out and waved or called out greetings to the kitchen. Kate relaxed, enjoying the friendly atmosphere. She chuckled at Leslie as she approached with a large platter of baklava pieces all cut into perfect two-inch squares. "We probably don't need that much." She took the glass of milk from Leslie and set it in front of Portia.

"Thank you," Portia said softly.

"You're welcome. Mom insisted I bring the whole plate out here for you." Leslie set the platter in the middle of the table as she spoke. "It's her specialty and she loves to show it off. Can Portia have a piece?"

Kate picked out a piece and took a bite. "Oh. It's fabulous. I think she'd love a piece." She took a drink of coffee and slid over on the bench seat so Leslie could settle next to her.

"Here you go, Princess." Leslie cut a piece in half and served it to Portia on a napkin.

Kate laughed at Portia's face when she took a bite. "I think she likes it. She doesn't get much sugar at home so you might have become her best friend." Kate's stomach jumped when Leslie laughed. "Thank you for being so kind to her."

"She's yours. Of course I'd be kind to her."

Kate took a bite to cover her threatening tears and sipped her coffee to swallow the lump in her throat. Apparently, she was still a little more raw than she'd realized.

"So, you wanted to talk?" Leslie turned toward Kate and stretched her arm across the bench behind her.

"I do, but I realized I'd rather talk when we can be alone. Maybe over a glass of wine. I'd like our date to be soon, if you're up for it?" Kate basked in the heat of Leslie so near. She hoped she'd lower her arm and rest her hand on her shoulder. She shivered when the length of their thighs met, and she swallowed a whimper.

"How about the little bistro next to the bookstore tonight?"

She'd take whatever time Leslie would offer, and a bistro sounded perfect. "I know the one. What time will you be available?"

"I'll help Mom and Dad clean up and meet you at the entrance about five thirty. Will that work?"

"I look forward to it." Kate watched Leslie smile and wave at Portia before she slid out of the booth and headed to the kitchen. "Let's go home, honey. Mommy has to change." Kate left money on the table and carried Portia to her car. The trip home took less than twenty minutes and Kate smiled the whole way.

"Nice lady," Portia said in a sleepy voice as Kate lifted her out of the car.

"Yes, she is nice, honey. Mommy is going to meet her later, so Sharon will be over to stay with you. But it's nap time for you, young lady." Kate helped her into her pajamas and set her stuffed bear next to her on the bed before she went to get ready for her date.

She checked the time, knowing Portia would sleep for at least a half hour. Kate called her neighbor to confirm her availability before she got into the shower. She used her cinnamon and lavender body wash and took her time drying off before a full-length mirror to assess her forty-one-year-old body. At least her stretch marks were no longer too prominent. She mentally slapped herself. They were going to a bistro, not to bed. She chose her favorite long-sleeved blouse and black slacks to lay out on the bed before slipping on a robe and heading to check on Portia. She was sound asleep with her fingers wrapped around her stuffed bear.

What was she doing going out with Leslie? She was still waiting for Wendy to sign divorce papers, she was settling into a new job, and she had a three-year-old child. The last time she'd tried dating it had been disastrous. But she was tired of running, and things were quiet now. She sighed and fixed herself a cup of decaffeinated coffee. She owed herself a life with love, one with someone who loved her and her daughter. If only she could get rid of the last of the fear. No, she really had no business dating again, not yet. But she and Leslie could be friends, right? Nothing wrong with that. She rinsed her cup and went to get dressed.

"Thanks for doing this on such short notice, Sharon. I appreciate it. I shouldn't be too late." Kate pulled on a jacket as she spoke to her babysitter.

"No problem. Take as long as you like. We'll be fine. Portia's a great kid."

Kate kissed Portia's cheek and headed to her car. As she drove to the bistro, she considered how much she would say to Leslie. She had to tell her the truth, but did she need to know how long she'd put up with Wendy's abuse and nastiness? Did she need every sordid detail? She swallowed her embarrassment, took a deep breath, and entered the bistro.

Leslie stood and reached for her hand as Kate approached the two-seater table.

"You look amazing."

Heat trailed the path of Leslie's gaze over her body and Kate sank into one of the chairs, already weak-kneed. "Thanks. You look pretty good yourself." She returned the open appraisal, pleased at the slight blush dusting Leslie's cheeks. This had to stop. She needed to apologize, explain, and go home. Complications weren't something she needed right now, even if she really did want more from life.

"Can I buy you a cup of coffee?" Leslie asked.

"Is this going to be a regular thing?"

"It can be our first." Leslie grinned. "But I do want to hear why you left the way you did. I was pretty confused. Did I do something wrong?"

Kate heard the underlying worry in Leslie's voice. "I'm sorry." She was glad for the interruption of the server at their table to take their order. It gave her time to organize her thoughts. She took a breath before continuing. "The day we met, when we took that hike, I told you I lived in Ohio. Six months earlier, I'd had to leave the place I was living in because my ex-wife had become violent. That hike was the first time I'd been around anyone other than my family, and the connection I felt with you was amazing, as well as terrifying. I'd been in a bad situation, and I wasn't ready to feel something for someone else yet."

Leslie watched her as she spoke, her gaze never wavering. "I get it, and I'm sorry you went through that. Thank you for explaining. So when is your divorce final?" She took a drink of coffee from one of the cups the server placed on their table.

"I don't know. Wendy won't sign the papers." Kate sipped her coffee, glad Leslie hadn't asked anything further. "I'm not sure she ever will, and I'll have to find another route."

"So, what are your plans for the future?"

Kate had been asking herself that question for months. She'd changed her phone number when she'd moved out of her sister's house, and Deanna was the only one who knew where she lived. She shivered at the lingering fear of Wendy coming for her.

Leslie reached for her hands and squeezed gently. "Are you all right?"

"Yes. Thank you." Kate clung to the safety of Leslie's gaze. "Memories sometimes take over and I have to pull myself back."

"Shall we have a little dinner? Then would you like to take a walk before you go home?" Leslie slid her fingers over hers as she pulled away.

"Yes. Let's."

Leslie left money on the table for their food and coffee after they finished their meal and held the door open for Kate when they left. "Let's walk through town."

Kate looked at her watch. She'd give herself a few minutes to enjoy Leslie's company.

"I'm glad you agreed to meet me tonight," Leslie said. "I worried I'd never see you again."

"I'm not sure it's a good idea you do." She hesitated but decided the truth was best. "Wendy is off the rails, and she's done some terrible things. She sees rivals for me everywhere. Once, I went to a preschool to talk to some teachers for Portia and Wendy threatened them, insisting I was having an affair with one of them." She bit her lip and shoved her hands in her pockets to keep them from shaking. "I started dating someone about six months after we first split up, and she put the woman in the hospital."

Leslie flinched. "Has she ever hurt you?"

The truth was too much, and she couldn't say it out loud. "Not physically, not yet. And I don't believe she'd ever hurt Portia, but she yells and swears, which scares her." She glanced at Leslie and then back at the sidewalk. "You see why I ran that day. My life is complicated."

"Put my phone number in your phone. You call me if you need help, but call 911 if she threatens you." She grimaced. "Not like you need my advice on that, I imagine."

Kate put Leslie's number in her phone. "I'll give you mine, too, but I may change it again if I think there's a chance Wendy has it."

"Do you believe she'll come looking for you?"

"I wouldn't put it past her, but it's been pretty quiet for the last year, overall. I've filed restraining orders, so that's probably part of it, although she walks through them like the paper they are. I'm probably overreacting, but she didn't take the divorce papers well, so I'm still concerned." Kate gave Leslie her number and checked the area around them out of habit.

"Do you still want to have the date we agreed to?"

Kate knew what she should say. She knew it was a bad idea. "Absolutely."

CHAPTER FOUR

Leslie settled on her couch as soon as she got home and composed a text to Kate.

I'm home. Let me know you got home safely.

She set her phone on her nightstand and considered what Kate had told her. Her own life had been safe. Boring by many estimates. She'd grown up an only child with two working parents and her Greek grandmother. High school had been uneventful. She graduated toward the top of her class and then began working full-time in her parents' restaurant. She'd dated a few women but never came close to marrying because she'd never felt the spark of forever. She wondered now if maybe it was best she hadn't. How could she know if the one she chose wouldn't turn on her like Wendy had on Kate? She sighed and rose to retrieve a bottle of sparkling water from the refrigerator. Her phone pinged with a message.

Thanks for checking on me. I'm home safe and sound. Portia says hi.

Leslie smiled at the text. Kate's daughter seemed like a good kid, but she'd never had any experience with children. It had never crossed her mind to have any, and she wasn't sure how to handle the fact that Kate did. What would it mean if they continued to date? Had she and Wendy had Portia together, or had Portia been there before Wendy? She shook the thoughts from her mind. They hadn't even had their first official date, and there was still plenty to learn. She finished her water and went to bed.

She shot up in bed and her chest tightened. Her mother's voice in her house at four a.m. could only mean something was very wrong. She tossed on her robe and met her mom in the middle of her living room. "What's wrong?" She took her mom's shaking hands in hers.

"It's your dad. I think it's his heart. The ambulance is on the way."

"Let me put some clothes on." Leslie quickly slid into a pair of jeans and a sweatshirt before following her mother out the door and rushing to their house. The ambulance pulled up just as they got to the kitchen where her father sat on a chair clutching his chest. Leslie's breath caught at how pale and weak he looked. "It'll be okay, Dad. The ambulance is here." She supported her mother as they followed the paramedics when they loaded the stretcher carrying her father into the ambulance. "We'll follow them, Mom. I'll drive." She checked their doors were locked before leading her mother to her car. The ambulance was already out of sight by the time they pulled out and headed for the hospital. Leslie focused, staying calm for her mom, even though panic slithered at the edges of her mind, waiting for a moment to slide in.

Leslie took her mother's arm to steady her when they arrived at the hospital, and the desk attendant directed them to a waiting area. "You sit, Mom. I'll see if I can get any information." Leslie found out where her father had been taken and led her mother to a chair outside a curtained area of a large room. She stood next to her mom and rested her hand on her shoulder. The doctor stepped out from behind the curtain.

"Mrs. Baily?" He looked past Leslie to address her mother.

"Yes." Her mother wrung her hands as she turned her full attention to the doctor.

"I'm his daughter, Leslie. Is he going to be okay? Can we see him?" Leslie kept her hand on her mom's shoulder as she spoke.

He pulled the curtain slightly away to allow them to enter the area where her father was propped up on a gurney. Her mother rushed to his side and took his hand. He looked pale and exhausted but smiled when he saw them.

"Mr. Baily has had what we call non-cardiac chest pain. He told us he's been fighting a cold for a couple of weeks. We did a chest X-ray, and it looks like he's got the beginnings of pneumonia which could have contributed to the discomfort, but more likely he's suffering from acid reflux. We'll have a list of medications and diet restrictions on his discharge papers and since stress could be a factor, suggested lifestyle changes. Do you have any questions for me?" the doctor asked.

Leslie's mom fussed over her dad, clutched his hand, and held it to her chest.

"We're relieved it wasn't a heart attack and we'll make sure he follows your instructions," Leslie said.

"My office number is on there if you have any questions." The doctor smiled and left.

They sat with her dad, and he made light of the situation, and the panic finally made its way into Leslie's chest. She couldn't fathom what she would have done had it been the worst. Her parents were her world, her rocks. She took her dad's hand and held it, feeling the strength in it. He rested his other hand on her head, and she saw the understanding in his eyes when she looked up.

After he'd been discharged a while later, Leslie followed her mom and dad out of the hospital and kept a close eye on her father as she helped him into the car. He chatted on about how he was fine and didn't need to go to the hospital for a little indigestion, but she noted the hesitation in his step and minor tremor in his hand as he reached for the car door. The time was coming closer for her parents to cut back and let her take over the restaurant, and today might be the beginning. Her dad's episode was evidence of his aging, and her mother wasn't far behind. It was time for Leslie to finish the last class she had planned, and to hire another server and maybe some kitchen help.

"You relax today. Both of you." Leslie gently guided her parents to their living room. "I'll run up to the pharmacy and get Dad's medication while you two rest." Leslie made two cups of chamomile tea with honey and gave them to her parents before she left.

She sat in her car for a moment to de-stress. She leaned her head back on the headrest and gave in to the desire she'd been suppressing since her mother had shown up at her house. She called Kate's number.

"Hello. This is a nice surprise."

"Hey, Kate. I wanted to say hello." Leslie had no idea why she'd called Kate instead of her best friend. She just knew she had to.

"I'm glad you did. Is everything okay? It's early and you sound a little stressed."

"We just got back from the hospital. My dad had a non-cardiac chest pain event." Leslie took a deep breath and expelled it. "Mom thought it was a heart attack, and I think he did, too. I guess we all did."

"I'm so sorry. Was it acid reflux or did the doctor say anything about esophageal spasms?"

"Huh? Nothing about the esophageal thing. You sound like a doctor." It occurred to her that she didn't know what Kate did for a living.

"I grew up in a family of them."

"Oh. So, what do you do?"

"I'm an x-ray technician. I wanted to have a baby and didn't want to juggle medical school with that responsibility, so I chose x-ray tech."

"Ah. I imagine that would've been difficult, but I definitely think you made the right decision. Portia seems like a good kid."

"It was the only one for me. So, your dad will be okay?"

"Oh yes. I guess Dad has heartburn and maybe a slight case of pneumonia. He's home resting, and I'm on my way to pick up some medication for him. I'm grateful it wasn't a heart attack."

"Yes, that's good. Do you have to work late today?"

"I'm not planning to open the restaurant today. When I get back, I'm going to put up a sign. Why?"

"I'm off work today, and I thought it would be nice to get out for a while."

"I feel like I need to stay close to my dad..."

"Would it be okay if I come over? I'll bring some chicken soup."

"I'd love it, and I think Mom and Dad would, too, but you don't need to bring soup." Why did the idea of Kate being there feel like having someone to come home to?

"Please, let me. I'd feel like I was helping."

"Chicken soup it is, then. Come anytime. I should be back in less than an hour. And, Kate?"

"Yes?"

"I'm looking forward to seeing you."

"Me, too."

Leslie disconnected the call and grinned all the way to the drugstore. She parked next to her parents' house when she returned and saw Kate waiting in her car in the restaurant parking lot. She mentally slapped herself for not letting her know the house behind it was their residence. "Hey there," she called out and waved. Kate got out of her car and Leslie flushed, her pulse rate rose, and she couldn't tear her eyes off Kate walking toward her.

"Hi." Kate held up an insulated bag. "I brought healing food."

"Thanks. This way is my parents' house." Leslie held the door open, delighted when their fingers briefly contacted as Kate passed her.

"Hey, Mom and Dad. Kate brought dinner." Leslie led the way to the kitchen where she put her dad's medication on the counter.

"Kate!" Leslie's mom pulled her into a hug. "Where's Portia?"

"She's home playing with her babysitter. I needed a couple hours of adult time today. So how's the patient?" Kate took the soup out of the bag and set it on the counter.

Leslie motioned toward her dad. "You haven't met Kate yet. She brought some chicken soup. Do you feel up to some with your pills?" Leslie relaxed a little seeing her dad's smile and enthusiastic nod.

"Thank you, honey."

"I'll get you a bowl." She left Kate and her dad discussing the benefits of chicken soup so she could retrieve bowls and spoons. She filled two bowls and took them to her parents and returned to sort her father's pills into the daily holder she'd bought.

She sensed Kate behind her before she heard her whisper. "I made the soup extra bland, so you might need salt." Kate didn't move away after she spoke but reached around her to retrieve a bowl.

Leslie turned and pulled Kate gently against her for a hug. "Thank you," she whispered, then released her, leaving a huge vacuum in her place. She shook off the unexpected feeling and concentrated on her father. Whatever was going to happen between her and Kate was yet to be determined, but there was no denying it was good to have her around again.

CHAPTER FIVE

K ate watched Portia sleep for a few minutes when she got home then closed Portia's door halfway and settled on her couch to contemplate Leslie. She couldn't deny her attraction, but attraction didn't equal love. She didn't know where they might be headed, but she had to resolve her situation with Wendy before she considered anything more than friendship. She replaced thoughts of Wendy with the memories of the evening with Leslie and her parents. They were obviously a close-knit family, and Leslie took good care of them. It was an important trait in her choice of a lover, and she'd presumed she had it with Wendy when they first dated. Portia had only been a year old, and Wendy had happily accepted her. Kate would never regret having a baby alone even though it wasn't her original plan. She'd grown up with an older sister and two younger brothers. Family was important to her, and she wanted it for her daughter. But after they'd married, Wendy transformed into a moody, withdrawn tyrant and she'd seemed to dislike having Portia around to take Kate's attention from her. Kate couldn't do anything right, and Wendy snapped at her for looking at her the wrong way. Her anger grew like a cancer, and her outbursts had made Portia cry.

Kate took her empty cup to the kitchen and slammed it on the counter. Why did she let it go on so long? Why didn't she recognize the signs that Wendy was the kind of person she was? She'd stagger home after late night "work events" reeking of alcohol. Kate feared for Portia's safety when her temper tantrums and threats brought her to tears. She'd hit Kate once and then she'd spent two days apologizing and swearing to quit her late nights. She came home with tickets for Disney World the next day, but when Kate mentioned Portia was a little young for that, Wendy exploded in rage and stomped away complaining about all the money she'd spent for nothing.

Kate closed her eyes and focused, visualizing the ocean and how the waves swept up and back from the shore. She'd learned various coping techniques in therapy, and this one most often worked when the memories assailed her. She put her cup in the dishwasher and checked her email before getting ready for bed. Sleeping alone wasn't so bad when she carried the memories of drunken Wendy pawing at her and snoring beside her.

Kate woke a few minutes before her alarm the next morning and listened for any sounds coming from the baby monitor on her dresser. Portia was quiet so she took a few minutes to lie still and enjoy the fresh air filtering into the room from her partially open window. It reminded her of the breeze that had rustled her hair as she stood in the field with Leslie. Just before the world faded away and all she knew was the feel of Leslie's lips on hers and her breath on her cheek. Had she ever felt anything like it with Wendy? She couldn't remember if she had, and she didn't care anymore. Kate rose and slipped on her robe before heading to the kitchen. Portia shuffled in shortly after her dragging her blanket and stuffed bear behind her.

"Good morning, honey." Kate hugged her. "I'm making oatmeal with raisins today." She set a glass of orange juice in front of her at the table.

"Will we see the nice lady?" Portia took a mouthful of oatmeal.

"Probably not today. I have to go to work, so Sharon will be here with you. We can go for a walk downtown when I get home, though." Kate figured she would be a shopper when she grew up as much as she loved to look inside every shop window they passed.

She put their dishes in the sink and settled Portia in the fenced off play area in the living room before she got in the shower. She checked on her once before she dressed and waited for Sharon. "Good morning. Thanks for being available today. I know you usually have class."

"No problem. I brought my laptop so I can log in to the school computer remotely."

"Portia's had breakfast, but I'd appreciate it if you helped her get dressed. I don't want her to get used to lounging in her pajamas all day."

"No problem. We'll be fine."

"Thanks again." Kate gathered Portia in her arms before she left. "You be good and mind Sharon." She kissed her on the cheek before heading out the door.

Kate strode to her car thinking of Portia's smile and hug and how they were the best things in the world. She unlocked her car door and slid behind the steering wheel, but just as she started the car, she noticed the writing on the passenger side of the windshield. It looked to be done with a crayon or some sort of marker.

Did you think you could get away from me? You're mine! I will drag you back home with or without the kid. You can't leave and think you can fuckin' get away with it. I'll never let you go.

Fear made it hard to breathe, and as soon as she reached the main road, Kate pulled out her cell phone and hit Sharon's number. She answered on the first ring.

"Did you forget—"

"Make sure the doors and windows are locked. Wendy left a threatening note on my car. Call 911 if you see her. I'm afraid she might try to take Portia to get to me."

"I'm locking everything right now, Kate. Don't worry. I'll get my football player brother over here now, and I won't let anyone else in. We'll be okay."

Kate relaxed slightly. Sharon's brother had a football scholarship to the University of Michigan, and he was a great guy. He was also huge. She pulled into the parking lot of the clinic where she worked and took a breath. The brazen act indicated she had somehow found her, and Kate swallowed the lump of panic threatening to choke her. It had only been a matter of time, but God how she'd hoped she'd finally given up and gone away. She sat for a few minutes deciding if she should turn around and go home so she called Sharon again.

"Hey, Kate. We're good here. I've looked out all the windows, but I haven't seen anyone, and Paul's on his way here."

"Okay, thanks, Sharon. I'll give you a call at lunchtime." Kate disconnected the call and pushed aside her apprehension. She took a picture of the windshield with her phone before she drove through a carwash. She didn't want to have to look at Wendy's vitriol any longer than necessary. She prayed she didn't know which apartment was hers. She'd been grateful to find the one she did but didn't like parking her car so far away. Now she was glad for it. She blew out a frustrated breath. She'd move again if she had to, but she was just getting comfortable here, and she loved living near her family. She locked her car and went into work.

She called Sharon at noon. "Everything okay?" she asked.

"Yeah. We've been working on a puzzle all morning, and nobody's been around. Paul's circling the building every couple of hours, but no strangers have shown up."

"Thanks, Sharon. What kind of pizza do you and Paul like? I'm going to buy you one to thank you."

"Paul loves pepperoni and I'll eat anything, but you don't have to do that."

"I do. I'll stop on my way home about four." Kate hung up and called 911 to report the violation of her existing restraining order. She finished her workday, though she was distracted and paid little attention to the conversations going on around her. She scanned the parking lot from the door before she dashed to her car and into the driver's seat. She definitely could not live like this. She picked up the pizzas and went home, always watching her rearview mirror to see if she was being followed. In the parking lot at the apartment, she had to compose herself before leaping from the car and practically running up the stairs. Once she was inside, she closed her eyes. She'd thought this kind of terror was behind her.

"Mommy!"

Kate never tired of hearing Portia's little voice as she rushed into her arms after she handed over the pizza to Sharon.

She cut a slice into small pieces for Portia and left her at the table with Sharon and Paul when she went to her bedroom to make a call to her sister.

"Hi, Kate. What's up?"

"I wanted to warn you Wendy is here. She left a nasty note on my car this morning. I don't know what she has in mind, but she knows where you live and I'm worried."

"Thanks for letting me know. She didn't hurt you, did she?" Deanna's voice rose as she spoke.

"No. I never saw her, so I'm not sure if the restraining order covers what she did, but I called to report the incident anyway. I'll have to move again." Kate ran her fingers through her hair in frustration.

Her sister was silent for a moment. "You're always welcome here. You know that, don't you? There's power in numbers, and we could keep you both safe."

"Thanks. I do, but I don't want to involve you in this anymore than I have, and I'm not about to put your family in danger too. I just wanted to let you know what's going on."

"I had cameras installed around the house for the kids to watch the deer, so it'll be more secure than it was. If she keeps bugging you, get another restraining order."

"Thanks, Deanna, but you know how effective those are. She's always gone before the police arrive and they never arrest her because she says she wasn't anywhere near me. I suppose I can't even prove it was her that left the nasty note. I think my only option is to leave again. I'll let you know what I decide."

Kate hung up, tears heavy in her eyes and her mind already in overdrive, thinking about her lease and the boxes she'd need and where the hell she would go next. On impulse, she dialed Leslie's number. She didn't want to think too much about why, but she needed to hear her voice.

"Hi, Kate."

Now that Kate had her on the phone, she wasn't sure how to proceed. "How's your dad doing?" It was a safe question, and she did want to know.

"He's good. We made sure he rested today, and my mom has revamped his diet. Much to his chagrin. How are you doing?"

The truth was the only way to go. She couldn't have Leslie in the firing line. "I'm a little rattled today. Wendy showed up and wrote a threatening note on my windshield. She must have found me and is in the area. I'm worried about what she might do."

"What can I do to help?" Leslie sounded angry.

"I'm not sure if you can do anything, but it helps to know you're willing." The last time she'd let someone in, that person had gotten hurt. There was no way she'd allow that to happen to Leslie.

"I think we should have our official date soon. It'll help take your mind off her. I hope."

A date was the last thing she should consider, but the pull to Leslie was greater than her fear. "You know it could be a bad idea?"

Leslie made a scoffing sound. "You're worth it, and if she comes around, we'll deal with it." She went quiet. "I can't imagine how scary this is, but I hope you'll let people help rather than turn them away."

Kate finally allowed the tears to fall. She couldn't make that promise. "How about dinner tomorrow?"

CHAPTER SIX

Leslie hung up and considered where they could go or what to do for their date. Kate suggested dinner. They'd already been to the bistro. Maybe another place? She made herself a cup of green tea and thought about what she knew about Kate. She had a young daughter, and she was in the middle of a contested divorce with someone who sounded pretty awful and scary. Beyond that Leslie knew she was kind, considerate, caring, intelligent, and beautiful. She wanted to take Kate somewhere nice or fun, or both, and try to take her mind off Wendy. She wanted romantic, but would Kate? It certainly didn't seem like she was in a good place for romance right now. Maybe they could do something to include Portia, to make it less intense? Her thoughts spun so she gave up for the day. They'd take it slow and see where it went. One phenomenal kiss didn't mean they were destined for one another, did it?

The next morning, she concentrated on work and concern for her father. He'd bounced back from his heart attack scare but still appeared weak and a little unsteady. She checked the kitchen and found him scrambling eggs. "Morning, Dad. Did you sleep well?"

"Like a baby." He grinned.

"Great. I presume you're taking all the medication the doctor prescribed, and you're feeling better."

"Your mom would never allow anything less," he chuckled. "And I do feel better. Don't you worry, honey. I'll be fine."

"Good. Do we have an early diner?" Leslie checked the time.

"What do you mean?"

"You're scrambling eggs like you're ready to make an omelet. Is it for you?"

Her dad looked at her and blinked several times. "We have diners, don't we?"

"It's Wednesday, Dad. We don't open until nine." Leslie hoped her father knew what time it was, but he just stared at her, clearly confused. She made a mental note to sign up for the last class she needed to complete her degree in restaurant management. Her time to start taking over and giving her parents a break was coming sooner than she expected.

"Hello?" Leslie's mother entered the kitchen from the back door. "Good morning, honey." She hugged her and kissed her cheek.

"Morning, Mom. Can we talk in the dining area?"

"Sure. Let me get the cleaning supplies."

Her dad sat down and stared at his hands as though he was trying to work something out. Leslie took the bowl of scrambled eggs and put it into the refrigerator before following her mother out of the kitchen. "Do you know why Dad was scrambling eggs already this morning?"

"No, I don't. We had breakfast before he left."

"I think he thought there was someone in the dining area. Has he been acting off at home?"

Her mother sighed. "Sort of. I think it's the anti-anxiety drug he's on. It makes him forget things, too."

"Maybe we should call the doctor. Do you think he needs them anymore?"

"I'll check with his doctor this afternoon. At least let him know what's going on."

Leslie made sure the dining area was clean and ready for patrons before unlocking the door and removing the closed sign. She turned her thoughts to Kate and their date. She still hadn't come up with a good idea by lunchtime and considered calling her for ideas. Her musing was interrupted by the jingle of the door. She turned to greet the customers and grinned.

"Hey, Leslie." Joy waved from the doorway.

"Hi there. Sit anywhere and I'll be right with you." Leslie was thrilled to see Joy and Nat. They'd often mentioned wanting to stop in, but they lived a good twenty miles away. She grabbed a couple of water glasses and went to take their order. "I'm glad to see you guys. It must've been a ride to get here."

Nat grinned and hugged Joy close. "Not anymore." She grinned mischievously.

Joy raised her arms when Leslie looked at her. "We moved!" She looked ecstatic.

"Awesome. Where'd you move to?"

"We bought a house a few miles from here. It's all ours, too."

"That's great." Leslie hugged her. It would be fantastic having them so close. "So, can I get you anything?"

Nat and Joy ordered breakfast and Leslie went to the kitchen to place their order and check on her dad. "You doing okay in here?" she asked.

"I'm good, honey." He looked at the order slip. "Two omelets with bacon and toast coming up."

He looked much better than earlier, so Leslie went back to the table. "Your order is on the way. I'm happy for you guys. I didn't know you were looking for a house."

"We had our tenth anniversary this year, so we figured it was time. I'm glad we found something in the area we could afford."

Ten years. Leslie pushed aside her threatening envy. Would it ever happen for her? "I am, too. You're good friends. I'm grateful to have you in my life."

Joy stood, hugged her, and sat back on her seat. "Have you seen Kate?"

"I have. She came into the restaurant last week with her daughter. How do you know her?" Leslie thought for a moment. "You know her from the Meetup group."

Joy smiled. "We became friends from that time she did the hike. I know she's going through a divorce, and she's scared. I think she trusts you."

"I hope she does. I like her a lot. It sounds like she has good reason to be scared." Should she tell Joy that Kate's ex was in town? No, it wasn't her place.

Joy smiled and reached for her hand. "Nat and I are having a housewarming party Saturday, and I hope you and Kate will come."

"Me and Kate?" Leslie grinned. "Why do you think Kate will come with me?"

Joy tipped her head and looked at her. "You ask her. I'll be surprised if she says no."

"What time Saturday?" Leslie asked and refilled their coffee cups.

"It'll probably be going on all day. You come anytime."

"I'll ask her. Okay?"

Joy grinned. "Okay."

Leslie worked until closing and prepped for the next day before she checked on her parents and went home. She grabbed a bottle of water and settled on her couch to call Kate.

"Hi. Everything good at the restaurant today?"

"Yep. We were busy for the middle of the week. How'd your day go?"

"Blessedly quiet. Work was good and there was no sign of Wendy, but knowing she's out there and knows where I am..." She sighed. "Anyway, let's talk about something else."

"I've been trying to come up with something we could do tonight, but I'm out of ideas."

"To tell you the truth, I'm kind of beat. Have you had dinner yet?"

"No."

"Would you like to join me and Portia for baked chicken with carrots and potatoes?"

"Sounds yummy. Can I bring anything?" Leslie hurried to her kitchen to check her food supply. She had a can of green beans and some peanuts. Her meals were usually at the restaurant.

"I'm making a salad. If you have any baklava, Portia would be grateful."

"I can do that. I'll change and head over." She stopped by the restaurant and wrapped a few pieces of her mother's creation to take with her.

This wasn't exactly the type of date Leslie had in mind with Kate, but she looked forward to every minute she could spend with her. She anticipated a quiet evening, sharing a meal, and seeing where Kate lived. She parked in the lot next to Kate's building and grabbed the dessert before locking her car. She double-checked the address and began the walk to her door. She took three steps and caught the movement of a figure next to the wall of the building. It was obviously a female, but she moved quickly out of Leslie's line of sight. She wouldn't have thought anything of it if Kate hadn't told her about Wendy's probable appearance. She continued toward the building going the opposite direction of Kate's apartment.

She walked past the entrance to Kate's building and waited a few minutes before going to the back door. She checked the area before she slunk inside and called Kate. "I'm in your building I'll be at your door soon," she whispered, hung up, and walked past her apartment door twice before she returned, checked the hallway, and knocked.

Kate opened the door and pulled her into the room. "You okay?"

"I am. I think Wendy was roaming the parking lot. She... someone seemed to be lurking along the wall near the entrance. I walked past your building then snuck around to the back." She set the baklava on the table and turned to Portia. "Hi there, Princess." She was rewarded with a shy smile as Portia hung on to Kate's arm.

Kate wrapped her arm around her. "Do you remember Leslie from the restaurant?"

Portia turned her face toward Kate and pushed against her.

Leslie grinned and shrugged, but she couldn't get the woman off her mind. "It was probably her, wasn't it?"

Kate nodded and lifted Portia onto a raised seat at the end of the table. "Ready for dinner, honey?"

Portia answered by reaching for the spoon in front of her on the table.

"Let's eat and we can talk later, okay?" Kate looked nervous as she set the chicken and vegetables on the center of the table.

"Sounds good." Leslie sat next to Portia across from Kate. She smiled and hoped she could come up with ideas to help Kate because she sensed she was primed to bolt, and the thought of losing her before they had a chance to find out what they could have together felt like a huge weight on her chest.

CHAPTER SEVEN

Kate put the leftover food in the refrigerator and went to the living room. She smiled at Portia's laughter. Leslie had discovered the toy box Kate kept in Portia's play area and had created a stuffed animal train. She laughed at Leslie's imitation of a donkey and smiled at Portia on the floor clapping. She could almost push aside the worry of Wendy lurking outside as Leslie and Portia moved stuffed animals back and forth. Her pulse jumped when Leslie caught her eye and winked. She double-checked the door lock and joined the fun, all the while trying to figure out her next move.

"Thanks for keeping her occupied," Kate whispered.

"No problem. She's very bright, but you probably already know that."

"I do." Kate smiled at her daughter who was holding her tiger and making growling sounds.

Leslie looked at her watch. "I should probably head home and let you get her to bed."

"It'll only take a few minutes if you want to relax on the couch." Leslie looked conflicted, so Kate spoke quickly. "I'd like it if we could have some time together."

"I'd like that, too." Leslie picked up the stuffed donkey and addressed Portia. "Donkey is sleepy and wants to go to bed now." She handed Donkey to her and stood.

"Come on, honey. It's your bedtime, too." Kate carried her to the bedroom.

Leslie was on the couch looking at her phone when Kate returned. She stood watching her for a moment and wondered why she resisted sending her away. Wendy had somehow found out where she lived. It would only be a matter of time before she figured out which apartment was hers. She needed to tell Leslie to stay away. Stay safe. "I'm having a glass of wine. Can I pour you one?"

"No, thank you. I'd like you to come and sit." She patted the empty sofa cushion next to her.

Kate took a sip of wine before setting the glass on the end table and leaning her head back on the couch. "I should tell you to leave, but I like that you're here. I need to tell you I don't know what Wendy would do if she found me. I don't plan to ever go back to her, and she knows it, but there's no question she doesn't want to accept it." Kate picked up her glass and sipped her wine.

"Do you think she'd hurt you?" Leslie rested her arm around her shoulders.

"Honestly, I don't know." Kate unconsciously leaned into her. "I have an open invitation at my sister's. I'm going to move there again."

"I can only imagine how stressful this must be for you. Let me know if I can help in any way." Leslie looked at her watch. "I'll let you get some sleep, and I'll call you tomorrow. You call 911 if she shows up, okay?"

"I will." Kate stood and walked Leslie to the door. "Be careful driving. We'll talk tomorrow." She reached past Leslie for the doorknob and felt the same pull as that April day with the spring sunshine warming their backs and the sparks of desire drawing their lips together like magnets. She stepped back and blinked.

Leslie stroked her cheek and smiled. "This evening was wonderful. Thank you. Joy and Nat are having a housewarming party this Saturday. Would you go with me?"

Kate hesitated. She should stay away from people so she didn't put them in harm's way. But she couldn't stop living, either. She swallowed her fear and reminded herself of the new restraining order she planned to take out. "Let me know what time, and I'll get a sitter."

"Joy said it would go on all day, so you let me know what time is good for you."

"Sounds great." Kate took Leslie's hands in hers and squeezed gently. "Call me when you get home, okay?"

"Will do."

Kate checked the hallway outside her door and watched until Leslie was safely through the outer door before she closed and locked hers.

She settled on her couch to finish her wine and start a to-do list for moving. Her phone interrupted her review. "Hi, Deanna. What's up?"

"I just called to see how you were."

"I'm doing okay, but Wendy showed up in my parking lot tonight, so I'm moving in with you again."

"I'm so sorry to hear it, but we're glad to have you two. Will you get another restraining order?"

"I will, for all the good it will do. I think I'll move first."

"If she's watching you, maybe it would be better to do it now, so she doesn't follow you. You can come here even if it's only temporary."

"I'll get one tomorrow and make sure it covers your place, and then we can plan a day for the move."

"Let me know if you need help. Rob and I have friends with a large truck."

"Thanks, Deanna, that would be great." Kate disconnected the call and finished her wine before heading to bed, her heart heavy. Moving into her own apartment had felt like a step forward, like she was taking control of her life again. Now, having to move back felt like a leap in the wrong direction, but she couldn't think of any other option that didn't include leaving the state and running once again. That would have to be a drastic step, and it was one she didn't want to have to take.

The next morning, she woke to the sounds on her baby monitor of Portia mumbling something about a donkey. She smiled and rolled to her side for a few minutes to listen and enjoy memories of last night. Leslie had looked completely relaxed playing with Portia on the floor, and seeing them interact had taken her by surprise. She couldn't remember a time Wendy had taken an interest in Portia, much less played with her. She shuddered at thoughts of Wendy and made a mental note to check into a new restraining order at lunchtime. She put on her robe and went to get her daughter.

Kate finished dressing Portia and put her in her play area while she scrambled eggs for breakfast. She showered and dressed after they ate and hurried out the door as soon as Sharon arrived. She scanned the parking lot quickly and locked her car when she got in before taking a deep breath. She couldn't live like this for long. She turned her thoughts to Leslie and their upcoming date. It would be good to see Joy and Nat, and spending time with Leslie reminded her of their kiss. She wanted a repeat, but it wouldn't be fair to her to subject her to Wendy. She'd call the lawyer Deanna had referred her to, set up the stalking protection order today, and hope it would be enough to scare Wendy away. Having a plan calmed her.

Kate's workday went by quickly, and the appointment with the lawyer didn't take as much time as she thought it would. She relaxed a little knowing she had the temporary restraining order and wrestled down the dread of Wendy ignoring it. Kate put a copy of the paperwork in the glove box of her car and one in her purse. The lawyer had advised her to never be without a copy nearby.

She stopped to pick up a pizza on her way home as a minor celebration and to surprise Portia. She checked the area around her parking lot before heading into her building. "I'm home," she called as she opened the door, and Portia ran to greet her. "Hi, honey. Did you have a good day today?" She set the pizza on the table and picked up her daughter.

"We played colors."

"Cool," she exclaimed enthusiastically knowing Sharon would update her on what that meant. Part of her wished she was the one who'd introduced her to whatever it was, but being a single mom with a job was her choice, and she had to make the best of it. "You show me later, okay? I brought pizza for dinner." Portia squirmed out of her arms and hurried to her chair at the table. She paid Sharon and locked the door behind her. "I'll change and be right back,"

Kate said and grinned all the way to her bedroom. She might have picked the wrong woman to marry, but she'd make damn sure Portia grew up knowing she was loved.

Before she went back to the dining room, she called Leslie.

"Hi, Kate. Is everything all right?"

"Yeah. We're good. I wanted to let you know I took out another temporary restraining order on Wendy today, and I plan to move to my sister's this weekend."

"I'm glad you did. I'll admit I'm a little worried about what she might do. This weekend? Will you still be able to go to the housewarming with me?"

"Oh yes. I'm looking forward to it. My sister and brother-in-law have friends with a big truck. They offered to help me, and Sunday worked for everyone. I'll be spending the day tomorrow packing, but it won't take long to pack Portia's things. And I rented this place furnished, so I only have our mattresses, some boxes, and suitcases to move." A sense of melancholy suffused her. "I'm an expert at this now."

"Let me know if I can help. And, Kate, be careful, okay?"

"Will do. Thanks." Kate disconnected the call and turned her attention to the task ahead of her. Keeping Portia safe was her main priority. And staying near family and friends who could help with that made more sense than running and being responsible alone. She just had to remember that if things got any worse.

CHAPTER EIGHT

L eslie put her phone on the charger and reviewed the schedule she'd been working on when Kate called. One of her new hires was due to start in the morning to cover the breakfast crowd, and she planned to supervise her. She still hadn't worked out all the details, but she intended to keep her parents' hours more flexible. Her father's minor hospital scare indicated their advancing age and, as far as she was concerned, they'd earned a life with less stress. Having extra help would give them the option to cut back on their hours if they chose to, but she'd make sure to let them know it was their choice. If they didn't want to cut back, they could adjust the schedule. She guessed they'd ease into the changes and hoped they'd choose to enjoy some time off. She reviewed the applications she'd received for her request for a short-order cook. She'd have her dad take over training to give him say in the process. Leslie wasn't ready to change the menu yet. She'd have enough on her hands convincing her dad to allow a stranger in his kitchen. She set her notes aside and went to check on the few diners finishing their meals.

"How's Kate doing, honey?" her mother asked when she brought a tray of empty plates to the kitchen.

"She's good. I talked to her tonight. She's in the process of moving so we didn't talk long."

"I hope they come back. Kate was so sweet to bring your dad chicken soup. He still talks about it."

"It was sweet of her. She's considerate and kind." Leslie didn't need to go into further detail. It wasn't her place to talk about Kate's business. "Why don't you and Dad head home for the night? I'll close up and see you in the morning."

Her mother had taken a seat at the small table in the kitchen, and she looked tired. "Thank you, dear. Your dad needs to get off his feet." Her mom rose slowly and went in search of her dad.

Leslie finished cleaning the dining area and frowned when she saw the condition of the stove. Her parents had always been meticulous about keeping a clean kitchen and the stove was always virtually spotless. Tonight, there was tomato sauce on the walls and grease splashed over the stovetop. She grabbed a sponge and wiped off the splashes on the stainless-steel back wall and disinfected the countertops. She checked the oven and sighed with relief. She'd have been there for hours if she had to set it to self-clean. She finished mopping and left for the night.

She settled on her couch when she got home and debated whether to call Kate. She didn't want to interrupt her moving plans, but it didn't seem unrealistic she'd call to check on how she was doing. Especially with the new development with Wendy and the personal protection order. She gave in and called her.

"Hi, Leslie."

Leslie let out a sigh of relief. Kate sounded glad to hear from her. Or was she projecting that in her voice? "Hi there. I wanted to check on you. Everything going smoothly?"

"Yes. I'm packing and organizing. Portia wanted to know if the 'nice lady' was coming over again."

"Me?"

"Yes, you nice lady, you." Kate chuckled.

"I'm glad she thinks I'm nice. She's a good kid, and her mom is very special."

"She's too young to know what's going on, but she seems to be okay with moving again. I gave her an empty box, and she packed her toys in it before dumping it on the floor. It's her favorite thing to do now. Packing and unpacking."

"I'm glad you're okay. I worried a little when you told me about the restraining order. You haven't seen Wendy today, have you?"

"No. And I hope I don't. I'll admit I'm scared. I bought some pepper spray today. I'm carrying it wherever I go."

"It can't hurt, but I hope you never need it. Are you going to let me know where to pick you up Saturday?"

"Of course. I'm thinking it'll be about noon. Would that be okay?"

"Sure. I look forward to hearing from you. Sleep well." Leslie disconnected the call and went to bed, thinking about the nature of love and relationships.

The next morning, she went to the kitchen to check on her mom and dad and found them sipping coffee and ready for work. "Good morning." She kissed them both on the cheeks.

"Good morning, honey. What time is the newbie coming in?"

Leslie smiled at her dad's expression. "Her name is Trish, and she's due in a few minutes." She heard the bell on the front door as she finished speaking, and her mother followed her to the dining area.

"Hi, Trish. I'm Leslie and this is my mother, Elena Baily." Leslie smiled and took in the new hire's tidy appearance and confident demeanor.

"It's good to meet you both. I appreciate you giving me this opportunity."

"Come, I'll show you around." Her mother grabbed Trish's hand and proceeded to give her a tour of the dining area and the kitchen.

Leslie grinned at her mother's enthusiasm and watched Trish's reaction closely. She paid attention and treated her mother with respect. The deal was sealed when she stepped aside and opened the kitchen door to allow her mother to pass through first. She noted Trish held up her hand but didn't make contact with her back, as if to steady her if necessary. She waited for Trish to return and showed her where they kept the condiment supplies and how she wanted them arranged on the tables. Trish was a quick learner and open to doing things the way Leslie wanted them. She automatically straightened chairs as they walked to the kitchen, and Leslie wanted her to start work immediately. She stayed and helped Trish for a few hours, impressed with her efficiency and easy interaction with the diners. She'd be a good addition to their little restaurant. She retreated to the kitchen to talk to her mom and dad about hiring Trish and they both eagerly agreed.

Leslie took Trish aside, offered her the job, and requested she work through the lunch hour. Leslie wanted to work in the kitchen with her dad to assess his condition. She'd checked on him off and on since his hospital visit, and he claimed to be feeling better. Her mother still hovered over him and made sure he took his medication. Leslie noted the absence of her mother's endless pans of baklava lately and more of what her dad called boring foods. She relaxed a little at his huge smile and absence of tremors as he expertly flipped pancakes. "Looks like you're feeling much better, Dad."

"I am, honey. Please stop worrying about me. I can handle a little indigestion." He continued working as he spoke.

"I'm glad. Don't forget I have a sous-chef coming in Monday. You can show him what to expect. I'm heading home for a little while. Trish will be here until two, but call me if you need anything." She kissed his cheek and left. Thoughts of Kate she'd suppressed all morning began to surface the closer she got to her house. Was she packed yet? Had Wendy shown up again? She settled in her home office and reviewed the information on the sous-chef she'd chosen for an interview. She checked the time and pulled out her phone to do what she'd wanted to do all day. She sent Kate a quick text message. *I'm thinking of you.* It was simple and didn't put any pressure on what they were building, and it was true. She checked the time and headed back to the restaurant.

"There you are, dear," her mother called to her from the dining area. "Could you please bring in some sugar packets?"

"Be right there." Leslie topped off the sugar supply on all the tables and booths and got to work taking orders and serving food for the rest of the afternoon and evening. She tried unsuccessfully to ignore thoughts of how Kate's packing was going. The strength of the urge to repeat the kiss they'd shared unsettled her. It had been so perfect, could it be repeated? She concentrated on her work and left whatever would happen between them to fate. She wiped tables as they emptied and went to the kitchen for supplies. "How you doing tonight, Dad?" She watched him flip two burgers over on the grill and shift to fry potatoes on the adjoining grill. He looked relaxed and healthy.

"Hi, honey. Do we have another order? It's almost closing, isn't it?"

"Yes, it's not an order. I just wanted to see how you were feeling."

"I'm fine. No more burning or pain. I'm just a little tired. I'll finish this order and clean up, okay?"

"Good idea. In fact, let me finish and you go and take Mom home." Leslie finished cooking the order and took it to the dining area, glad she'd made an appointment for kitchen help. She carried the food out and skidded to a stop when she saw Kate seated at the table.

"Leslie. Look who's here." Leslie's mother grinned and rested her hand on Kate's shoulder.

She warmed under Kate's smile. "I've been packing and needed sustenance. I hoped it wasn't too late to get food."

"It's fine, dear. You relax and eat." Her mother left to go to the kitchen.

"Is your packing going smoothly?" Leslie asked as she set Kate's plate on the table.

"It is. Do you have time to sit?"

Leslie held up a finger and went back to the kitchen. She returned with two steaming mugs. "I found a nice chamomile tea. It'll relax you and help you sleep." She sat across from her as she spoke.

Kate took a sip. "Oh, you're right this is nice. Thank you. I don't think I'll need any help falling asleep tonight. I've been going all day."

"Where's Portia?"

"She was already asleep when I decided to come for food, so I called Sharon to stay with her. This burger is fantastic, by the way." She took a bite and a forkful of potatoes.

"I'll let you eat in peace." Leslie stood.

"No." Kate rested her hand on her arm. "I mean, if you have to go it's okay, but I'd like you to stay if you have time."

"I'll have to lock up pretty soon." Leslie settled back in the seat and wrapped her hands around her cup. "Shall I pick you up tomorrow or do you want to meet somewhere?"

"How about here? It'll save you from having to drive all the way to get me and take me home." Kate sipped her tea.

"Okay. We've got a new server now, so Mom will have help. I'll be ready by noon. I'm looking forward to it."

CHAPTER NINE

Kate sipped her tea and relaxed. Leslie sat across from her and leaned into the corner of the booth. She looked relaxed and sexy, and Kate wanted to crawl on top of her and kiss her silly. She repressed her runaway libido and concentrated on what Leslie had said. "I'll plan to be here a few minutes early. I'm presuming you know where Joy and Nat's house is."

"Yes. Joy gave me a map. It's not too far. I plan to bring a gift box of my mom's baklava."

"I didn't think about a housewarming gift."

"I'm sure they'd understand, especially when they find out you're in the middle of moving. We can give them baklava from both of us."

Kate liked the idea of a joint gift from her and Leslie even though she knew she shouldn't. She finished her tea and checked her watch. "I better get back." She slid out of the booth and Leslie followed her.

"Be careful, and let me know you got home safely, okay?" Leslie asked and reached for her hand.

"I will. I'll see you at noon tomorrow." Kate forced herself to step away from Leslie. "Good night," she whispered before leaving.

She parked at the opposite end of the lot than her usual spot and retrieved the pepper spray from her purse before getting out of her car. She locked it and checked the surrounding area and entered her building from the back entrance. The hairs on the back of her neck stood up as she felt like she was being watched, but she didn't see anyone. The hallway ahead of her was empty and she hurried to her door.

"Welcome home." Sharon called from the dining room where she and Portia sat at the table with a puzzle.

"I hope I wasn't gone too long for you. I appreciate you were available last minute. I kind of thought Portia would stay asleep for you." Kate hung up her coat and sat at the table next to Portia.

"Hi, Mommy. Look." Portia pointed to a pile of puzzle pieces stacked on top of each other.

"Ooh. Very nice." She smiled and glanced at Sharon who shrugged in an "I don't know" gesture.

"She woke up shortly after you left, so we decided to play 'puzzles.'" Sharon stood and hugged Portia. "See you later, alligator."

Portia giggled and mumbled something unintelligible.

"Thanks again, Sharon. Are you still available for tomorrow afternoon?"

"Sure. No problem. I'll be over about eleven thirty."

Kate paid her and locked the door after she left. She watched Portia knock down and mix up the pile of puzzle pieces. She seemed content, so she gave Leslie a quick text to let her know she was home and then settled in at the table to help with the demolition.

She moved pieces back and forth with Portia for a while and decided to see how Portia was feeling about the move. She couldn't understand much of what was going on, but Kate worried about too much disruption in her young life. The vocabulary of a three-year-old wasn't extensive so she worked to figure out how to explain so she'd understand. "Do you like it at Aunt Deanna's house?"

"Yeah." Portia decided tossing puzzle pieces in the air was more fun than trying to fit them together.

"Would you like to go live there with her again?"

Portia nodded enthusiastically, and some of Kate's worry dissolved.

"It's getting late. Let's pick up the puzzle and put it away for the night. Okay?"

"Okay."

Kate settled on the couch with a glass of port wine after putting Portia to bed. She reviewed her mental to-do list for the move and relaxed. She was ready. She'd pack their last-minute items when she got home from her day with Leslie and be out of the building by Sunday noon. She finished her wine and got ready for bed.

She tossed and turned for half an hour before giving up and getting out of bed. At first, she blamed the wine, but she'd only had a few ounces. She was keyed up about the move. She'd lived at her sister's before, but this time felt more dangerous. Wendy had found her, was probably in the area, and could show up any time. And there was Leslie. Sweet, sexy Leslie. What would Wendy do if she found out they were spending time together? If Wendy showed up again, she could be arrested, so Kate held on to that thought, even though she knew how effective the restraining orders had been in the past. She drank a cup of warm milk before lying back down and falling asleep.

The next morning Kate woke to Portia mumbling on the baby monitor. She checked the time and turned to her side to enjoy the anticipation of the day for a few minutes. This was the first time in a long time she had a day she was looking forward to. She got up and put on her robe before going to Portia's room. "Good morning, sunshine." She blinked back tears as Portia reached for her to be lifted out of her bed. Her innocent child trusted her to keep her safe, and she took that responsibility seriously. Portia giggled as Kate picked her up and danced across the room before twirling and gently setting her on the floor. It was their morning ritual and Portia never tired of it.

"We have eggs and pancakes this morning." Kate fixed Portia's plate with a pancake and spoonful of scrambled eggs next to it and watched her pour syrup over all of it. She sighed and let it go. By the end of the day, they'd both be packed and ready to relocate again. Portia had spent two of her short three years of life in a house of tension. Too many days of cowering from Wendy's rants and then having to run from her time and time again had earned her a little extra sugar this morning. Kate finished her breakfast and cleaned up before filling the bathtub. Portia loved bath time, and Kate usually ended up with her clothes soaked by the end of the event. She cut the time a little short so she'd have time to shower herself and get ready for her day. Was it okay to think of it as a date? She wanted to, desperately. She was ready to have someone in her life again, someone to share special moments and quiet nights and passionate mornings with. But it felt dangerous and irresponsible to do it when her life was still so unsettled. She took a deep breath and blew out a frustrated sigh.

Kate checked her reflection in her full-length mirror for the third time. She chuckled at her indecision. She knew Joy and Nat, and their housewarming party would be casual and comfortable. Her favorite black jeans and silk blouse would be fine. Portia was busy arranging and rearranging her stuffed animals, so she wrapped the stems of the flowers she'd picked up for her friends with foil.

Sharon arrived as she was placing them in a bag. "Hi, Kate."

"Hi, Sharon. Thanks again for being available today. I should be home by seven tonight. I'll call you if this party lasts longer."

"No problem. I don't have plans. I've got an exam to study for. You have a good time."

"Thanks. Remember to keep everything locked, okay?" Kate kissed Portia before she grabbed her coat and headed toward her car. She looked around the building and scanned the parking lot for any sign of Wendy before unlocking her car and hopping inside. She drove around the block once and took the long route to the restaurant.

Kate parked at the back of the building and locked her car before heading to the entrance. Leslie stood inside talking to a young woman carrying a pad and pencil. Kate stopped to watch their interaction for a moment and surmised she must be instructing the new server. Leslie looked calm and in charge as she smiled and pointed to a corner of the room, and it made Kate's heart flutter a little. There was nothing sexier than a woman in charge. The woman nodded and turned toward a table full of diners.

Leslie turned toward her and the same heat she'd felt the night at the bistro trailed the path of Leslie's appraisal. "I'm not too early, am I?"

"Never." Leslie reached for her hand. "Want to say hi to Mom and Dad?"

"Sure."

Leslie led her to the kitchen where Leslie's father supervised a young man in a white chef's coat as he worked over the stove.

"Hi, Mr. Baily." Kate relaxed under his welcoming smile. "Are you feeling better?"

"I am. Thank you. I'm sure it was the chicken soup." He winked.

"Glad I could help." She grinned.

"We'll see you guys later. We're going to a housewarming party this afternoon." Leslie kissed him on the cheek. He waved and Leslie's mom rushed to give them a hug before they walked out the back door.

Leslie took her hand as they walked to her car. "Ready to go see friends?"

"I am." Kate retrieved her bag of flowers from her car and sat in Leslie's passenger seat. Holding her hand had felt nice and she hoped she got to do it again. Leslie handed the map to Joy's house to Kate. "So, I'm the navigator?" She chuckled.

"Yep. Thanks for agreeing to go with me. Joy and Nat will be happy to see you." Leslie glanced at her quickly and turned her attention back to driving.

"It'll be nice to see them. I've talked to Joy off and on since I moved, but haven't seen her since early October."

"Wendy hasn't bothered you since the night I was over, has she?"

"No, thank goodness. I hope it's because of the restraining order, but I wouldn't put it past her to ignore it. Another concern I have is that she might not have been served. The others were mailed to her address in Ohio. I'm not sure where she's living now, so it might have been futile to get the order." Kate hated they had to talk about Wendy on the day that was supposed to be about them. She took a deep breath and lifted her chin defiantly. Today would be about fun and living like any single mom on a date with an attractive woman.

CHAPTER TEN

Leslie parked on the side street next to Joy and Nat's house and turned to Kate. She'd been quiet the rest of the ride after she'd asked her about Wendy. "I'm sorry I brought up Wendy. I didn't mean to put a damper on our day out. I promise no more talk of her." She took Kate's hand and kissed it.

"It's okay, but thanks. No more talk of her sounds great."

They followed a group of three women to the house and squeezed through the crowd inside the tiny living room. Four women took up the seats on the couch and both recliners were taken as well as the seats around a dining room table off the kitchen. Leslie took Kate's hand and led her to the kitchen where Nat and Joy stood talking to a couple.

"Leslie and Kate! I'm glad you could make it." Joy hugged them simultaneously as Nat stood next to them grinning.

Leslie noticed the three empty beer bottles on the counter and the half full one in Joy's hand. Clearly, the party had been in full swing for a while. "I brought you some of Mom's baklava." She extricated herself from Joy's grasp and set the box on the counter.

"And I brought some flowers to add to the brightness of your new home." Kate pulled out a beautiful bouquet of mixed blooms.

Nat stepped in and gently led Joy to one of the remaining seats at the kitchen table. "Thank you, both. I'm so glad you made it. Help yourselves to some cheese and crackers and we have beer and wine, and for our teetotaling friend, sparkling water." She put the flowers in a vase and added water before setting them in the middle of the kitchen table. "They're beautiful."

Leslie retrieved a bottle of water for herself and squeezed Kate's hand. "What would you like?"

"Water would be great." Kate smiled and stepped closer to her when she handed her the water bottle.

Leslie caught the scent of lavender and cinnamon she associated with Kate. She barely resisted pulling her into her arms and nuzzling her neck in search of more. She wished the crowd would push into the kitchen so she'd have an excuse to move closer. She took a drink of water and whispered in Kate's ear. "Shall we take a tour of the house? I'm nosey." She grinned when Kate turned and nodded.

"It is a housewarming party after all." Kate took a step toward the living room and Leslie followed.

She held on to Kate's waist as they wedged their way through the crowd. Kate didn't pull away, and Leslie struggled to contain a moan when she was pushed from behind and pressed against Kate's back. She followed her down a hall to three doors, one of which was closed. She presumed it was Nat and Joy's bedroom and pointed to an unoccupied room at the end that looked like a den. She shadowed Kate through the doorway and into the quiet room. Either they'd lucked out, or the crowd hadn't discovered this yet. She sat on the end of a small couch and tugged Kate to sit next to her. "This is better." Leslie leaned her head on the back of the sofa. "I had no idea Joy and Nat knew so many people, but they've been involved in the Meetup group for years."

"Have you known them long?" Kate asked.

Leslie thought for a moment. She counted back the years since she'd begun participating in the hikes. "I guess it's been about eight years now." She took a drink of water and reached for Kate's hand. "It was a lonely time in my life. One Saturday, a diner came into the restaurant for a take-out order. It was obvious she was excited about wherever she was going, so I casually asked her. She told me about the group and about the women she'd met there. I signed up for our local LGBTQ events email and found Joy's ad. I've been attending most of their hikes since."

"My sister told me about it. Joy works at her clinic and mentioned the group to her. That's how I found out about it." Kate squeezed her hand before letting go and sipping her water.

"So, how are the plans for your move going?" Leslie sat back on the couch but didn't touch Kate. She didn't trust herself not to pull her into her arms.

"Good. I'm ready although I'm a little nervous about imposing on my sister again. She has two adolescent boys, and I'll be adding a little girl to the mix."

"I'm sure she wouldn't invite you to stay if she was worried." Leslie often wondered what it would've been like to have siblings.

"You're right. She and her husband had an extra bedroom for us added to their plans when they had their house built, and we lived there for a while before I moved to the apartment in Ferndale. I'm just really—"

Leslie couldn't stand Kate's obvious turmoil. "You are a strong, brave woman, and you and Portia will be fine." She cupped her cheek with one hand and skimmed her lips over hers. It was meant to be a kiss of caring and support, but the same force she'd felt months ago drew her to Kate, and she leaned into the kiss at the same time as Kate wound her fingers through her hair and tugged her closer. Time stopped and the world faded. All her awareness centered on Kate. Her scent, the taste and firmness of her lips, the heat rising between them. She reluctantly brought herself back to the present and broke their connection. She took a deep breath to settle herself. "Are you all right?"

Kate chuckled. "Oh, yes. As long as you are, too."

"I'm totally upside down and inside out." She took another breath. "And please don't ask me what that means, because I have no idea." She grinned. "We should probably go mingle."

Kate looked at her watch. "Yeah. Joy and Nat will think we left without saying good-bye."

"What time do you have to be home?" Leslie hoped she'd have more time with Kate.

"I told Sharon I'd be home by seven. Why?"

"I thought we could go to the living room and visit a little, and then I'd like to take you to a nearby cider mill. What do you think?"

"I think it sounds great." Kate stood and reached out her hand.

Leslie took her hand and tugged her to the living room.

"Hey, you two," Nat said as she entered the room. "I made a pot of coffee. Would you like to join us?"

Leslie waited for Kate to respond. They could save the cider mill for another time.

"I'd like that. Okay with you?" Kate looked at her for confirmation.

"Sounds good." Leslie followed her and Nat to the kitchen. Joy was seated at the table with a hot mug of coffee and appeared to be in a much more sober state than when they'd arrived.

"I'm glad you came today," Joy said.

"Thanks for the invitation. You have a lovely place." Kate leaned against the counter.

"Thank you. We love it." Nat beamed.

"It's a good feeling to have your own home, isn't it?" Kate looked sad.

"Oh, yes. We can do whatever we want to. I'm going to paint the living room next week, and we're going to pick out wallpaper for the kitchen. Joy's going to rent one of those carpet cleaners for the whole house after we're done."

Leslie smiled at Nat's enthusiasm for all the work to be done, but she knew the feeling of having her own house to transform into something to be proud of and comfortable in. It made the work fun. She finished her coffee and relaxed with her friends. She watched Kate laugh and turn her full attention on whoever was speaking. She allowed herself the brief fantasy of her and Kate visiting friends as a couple, but she didn't linger on that long. They'd shared a couple of kisses and spent a few hours together. Incredible kisses and a comfortable few hours, but she could feel Kate's hesitancy, one Leslie understood and wasn't in a position to help with.

"How many people showed up today?" Kate asked Joy.

"We didn't count, but a lot. We had women from the Meetup group and the lesbian hiking group as well as our euchre players."

"I recognized a few of the women from the LGBTQ center," Kate said.

Nat had collected the various crackers, nuts, and cheese from the living room and Leslie figured it would be their dinner when she glanced at the clock. She caught Kate's eye and saw her slight nod. They hugged Joy and Nat good-bye and headed to the car.

Leslie opened the car door for Kate before getting behind the steering wheel. She pulled out onto the street and slammed on the brakes when a car pulled in front of her and stopped. The woman driving sneered at them before she took off, squealing her tires.

"Damn! That was Wendy." Kate hissed out the words.

CHAPTER ELEVEN

Kate wanted to catch Wendy and make sure she ended up in jail. She took a deep breath and slowly exhaled to calm herself.

"Can you call the police on her for ignoring the restraining order?" Leslie asked.

"I will when I get home. There's not much they can do if she's gone, but there will be a complaint on file. I'm sorry."

"Kate, you have nothing to be sorry for. She's an idiot and you're taking care of yourself."

"Yeah. I can't figure out how she knew where I was." Kate didn't speak about her fear for Leslie. Wendy had seen them together, and that may have put Leslie in danger. She'd been selfish to think this was a good idea.

"I don't have any experience with it, but on TV those restraining orders don't work too well."

"I'm going to ask if the police would send a patrol car tomorrow when I move. It's stressful enough without worrying about her being around." Kate turned her thoughts to the last few things she needed to do. Her heart thumped hard in her chest, and it was difficult to breathe. She wanted to get moved and be in the safety of her sister's house before things got worse. And in her heart, she had a feeling they would.

"Would it help if I came over to assist in the loading?"

Kate wrestled down her inclination to accept. Leslie had a restaurant to run. Wendy was her problem, and she'd deal with her. "I appreciate your offer, but it'll be okay. My brother-in-law and my babysitter's football player brother will be there. *She* may not show up anyway."

"What time are they bringing the truck?"

"They're coming at noon. I might ask if they can be there earlier, just so we can get it over with."

"I have a new server now. She can cover the four hours we're open, and Mom and Dad can handle the Sunday crowd. I'd like to help you if you'll let me. It might go faster, and we can get you out of there sooner." Leslie glanced at her before turning her attention back to the road.

Kate considered her offer. It probably would go quicker with an extra person. She sighed. "Damn it! Okay, but you have to promise you'll help and go right home when we're done."

"Promise."

Kate shook her head and grinned. Leslie was determined to be in her life Wendy or no Wendy, and Kate wished she wasn't so pleased by it. She turned her thoughts to the kiss they'd shared on Joy and Nat's couch. She could still feel the tingle like a lingering electrical current running throughout her body. She'd let her help load the truck and send her safely home. And then maybe she'd be strong enough to keep some distance between them…

"Everything okay?" Leslie took her hand as she asked.

"Yes. I'm remembering that kiss on the couch."

Leslie lifted their joined hands and kissed hers. "It was as fantastic as the first one."

"Yes, it was." Kate reluctantly withdrew her hand when they turned into the restaurant parking lot.

Leslie parked and turned to face her. "You're okay with the kiss, aren't you?"

"Oh yes." Kate hadn't seen Leslie look uncertain before. "I would have pulled away or said something if I wasn't. Honesty is important to me. That's one reason Wendy's behavior was so abhorrent to me. She did whatever she wanted with no consideration of my feelings. She lied all the time."

"Your feelings matter to me." Leslie's confident smile was back.

"I sense that, and I appreciate it." She reached for the door handle but turned before opening it to quickly kiss her. She chuckled at Leslie's objection when she pulled away. "I'll see you tomorrow morning." She checked the area around her car before she got in and backed out of the parking spot. She pulled out of the lot and panicked when she noticed a car behind her. She checked again and relaxed. Leslie had followed her, and she wasn't surprised when she stayed behind her the whole way home. She parked as close to the building as she could and stood outside to wait for Leslie.

"I'm sorry. I thought I saw the same car we saw earlier, and I wanted to make sure you were okay." Leslie strode toward her and took her hand before heading to the building.

"Thank you for the escort." Kate squeezed her hand gently and released it to unlock her door. Sharon and Portia sat at the table with crayons and coloring books spread across it.

"Mommy!" Portia hurried toward her and wrapped her arms around her legs.

"Hi, honey." Kate picked her up and squeezed. She'd never tire of the feeling of Portia in her arms. "I brought the nice lady with me."

"Hey, Princess. I've missed you." Leslie sat on the floor and Portia looked confused until Leslie opened her arms and Portia stepped into them for a hug before backing out and looking shy again. Leslie stood.

"Sharon, this is my friend Leslie."

"It's good to meet you. I think I've heard about you from Portia. She's quite expressive and with her limited vocabulary, I believe she called you 'nice lady' and 'candy.'" Sharon grinned.

"My mom makes baklava and Portia had a piece one day when Kate stopped in. I can't believe she still remembers it. I better leave you to whatever you need to do. I'll see you tomorrow. It was nice to meet you, Sharon."

"I'll walk you out." Kate chuckled to herself. Walking her out meant taking a few steps to the door. "Thanks for the nice afternoon, and I'm sorry about Wendy."

"You don't need to apologize for her. She sounds like a disturbed woman, and I'm glad you're doing what you need to do to get away from her. I'll see you tomorrow morning."

Kate watched Leslie until she got through the outer door at the end of the hallway before shutting her door and locking it.

"Leslie's nice," Sharon said.

"Yes, she is," Kate said. And thoughtful, kind, gentle, and sexy.

"I'll be back tomorrow to help watch Portia during the move. Good night."

"Good night and thanks, Sharon." Kate repeated the watch from her door as Sharon left.

She turned her attention to Portia who sat quietly moving her stuffed animals back and forth. She made herself a cup of decaf coffee and a bowl of oatmeal for Portia. She sat at the table with her and arranged her pile of stuffed animals in front of her. "Can you help me count?"

Portia swallowed a spoonful of oatmeal and put the spoon down before reaching for her donkey. She clearly spoke the word "one," and went back to eating.

Kate smiled. They could practice more after the move. She had a busy day ahead of her and Portia would need to adjust to yet another living situation. She finished her coffee and cleaned up the kitchen before putting Portia to bed. She settled on the couch and checked the time. She'd have time in the morning after breakfast to pack the last-minute things and get Portia dressed. She picked up her phone and called Deanna.

"Hi, Kate. Is everything okay?"

"Yes, we're fine. I wanted to know if it would be possible to get the moving truck earlier tomorrow."

"Sure. It's sitting in our driveway. What time would you like us to be there?"

Kate thought for a moment. "Would nine be too early for you?"

"Heck no. We can be there by eight if you want. What's up?"

"Wendy showed up today when Leslie and I were on the way home from a friend's house. I have no idea how she managed to follow us there." She held her hand to her stomach to settle the tremble.

"Okay. Let's get you out of there ASAP. But who's Leslie?"

Kate forgot she hadn't told Deanna about Leslie. "She's a new friend I met at the Meetup hike I attended in April."

"And I'm just hearing about her now?"

"I've been a little busy. Moving, new job, moving again. I've only just run into her recently and started seeing her again. I'm sorry. You'll meet her tomorrow. She's coming over to help with the move."

"Does Portia like her?"

"She calls her the 'nice lady,' so yes."

"I look forward to meeting her then. We'll plan to be there by nine."

"Thanks, Dee. Love you."

"Love you, too."

Kate disconnected the call and checked the time again before calling Leslie.

"Hey, Kate. Is everything okay?"

"Yes. I wanted to let you know I've moved the moving time to nine tomorrow morning."

"Okay. I'll plan to be over by eight thirty."

"Thanks, Leslie. I appreciate your offer of help."

"No problem. Get some sleep, and I'll see you tomorrow."

Kate had one more call to make. She looked up the number for her local police precinct and called to make her report. She sighed with relief after the officer assured her they would send a patrol car to canvas the area in the morning and enforce the personal protection order. They reminded her to call right away if Wendy showed up again. She checked Portia was sound asleep before heading to bed, where she tossed and turned despite all of her meditation efforts. Like an old movie reel on rewind, her mind replayed the day with Leslie over and over. For a few hours she'd felt free of the grip of fear of Wendy. She'd allowed herself to feel the heat of Leslie's fingers on her skin, the tenderness of her hands cradling her head, and the fervor of her kiss. She'd reveled in the sensation of freedom to explore who they could be together and unwittingly given herself permission to push fears of Wendy aside. It was an amazing comfort and one she could never allow herself again. She wiped tears from her cheeks before she finally fell asleep.

CHAPTER TWELVE

I'll give you a call if I'm going to be later than six. Trish will be here, so make use of her. I don't want you guys overdoing it."

"We'll be fine, honey. Give Kate and that little girl of hers a hug from me."

Leslie kissed her mom and dad and loaded the take-out bags of food her mother insisted on giving her, into her car. The drive to Kate's apartment was uneventful, though she was constantly on the lookout. She couldn't imagine how Kate had lived this way for so long. She parked in front of her building in case Kate needed to load anything in her car, but she chuckled at the thought when she saw the huge utility truck sitting at the back door. Two men were already carrying out boxes, so she waited until they passed by before going to Kate's door. It stood wide open, so Leslie stepped inside and put the bags on the counter before searching for Kate. She entered the bedroom and came face-to-face with a gorgeous, slightly older version of Kate. She had to be her sister.

"Hello. You must be Leslie." Her smile matched Kate's.

"Yes. I'm Leslie Baily, Kate's friend."

"I'm her sister, Deanna. Thank you so much for helping this morning. We've only been here about fifteen minutes."

"I'm happy to help. I know Kate wants to move as quickly as possible." Leslie felt Kate's presence before she saw her. She wore a pair of faded jeans and a T-shirt with the name of an orthopedic clinic emblazoned across the front. Leslie's breath caught when she walked across the room and hugged her.

"Thank you for helping. Portia's having a rare temper tantrum, so I've been pretty useless as far as putting boxes in the truck goes." Kate looked tired. "I think she's finally getting tired of moving."

"I'll take those boxes out unless there's a different plan." Leslie pointed to the boxes stacked against the wall next to the couch.

Deanna laughed. "Oh, there's no plan for this. We're a bunch of doctors who could run an OR efficiently, but trying to plan a move means we're bumping into each other like we've all got two left feet. You have at it."

Two men walked in. "Thanks for your help today. I'm Rob, Deanna's husband. This is my friend Pete. He owns the truck we're using."

Leslie took Kate's hands in hers and squeezed gently. "You take care of Portia." She winked and retrieved two boxes to carry out the door. She worked steadily until the only items left in the apartment were Kate's and Portia's suitcases. "Do you want these in your car?" she asked Kate.

"Yes. Thank you again for your help. We'll be able to leave soon."

"No problem. I'm glad I could help." Leslie put the suitcases in Kate's car. "You're all set."

"Thank you, Leslie. We're leaving with the truck now. We'll see you at our house." Deanna followed the two men out.

Kate looked at her with a question in her eyes, and Leslie would have said yes to anything. "Do you have to get back home right away, or can you follow me to Deanna's?"

"Lead the way." Leslie grabbed the food bags she'd brought and held them up. "Mom sent moussaka and baklava. Enough for everybody." Leslie followed Kate and Portia to her car and checked the area surrounding the parking lot. She saw no one outside except them and no suspicious cars. She went to her own car when Kate and Portia were safely locked in theirs and tailed her all the way to her sister's. She parked in the circular drive and looked up in awe. Deanna's house was gorgeous. And huge.

"Ready?" She jumped when Kate appeared next to her.

"Yes. This house is amazing."

"I know. They had it custom built just before their boys were born. Come on. Deanna will be excited to give you a tour." Kate picked up Portia and carried her into the house.

"Welcome. My name's Marta. Are you Kate's friend?"

Leslie smiled at the short woman who beamed from the kitchen doorway. "Yes. Nice to meet you, Marta. I'm the moving helper today. I'm Leslie."

"Come in. I have coffee made, but we have tea if you prefer."

"I'll have a cup of coffee, but first I want to help unload the truck. I brought some food and dessert for everyone." She placed the bags on the kitchen counter and hoped it would be enough when two teenage boys raced into the room. She left Marta to deal with their exuberance and headed back to carry boxes.

"This is the last one," Kate said and set a box on the floor at the foot of the stairs. "I'll carry it up later." She sat on the stair and ran her hand through her already mussed hair.

"You look tired. Marta's offering coffee. Would you like a cup?" Leslie asked. Kate grabbed her hand, and Leslie pulled her off the stair and into her arms. "Oops." She grinned and released her.

"Let's get some coffee and take it upstairs. Portia wants to say hello. I don't think she realized you were at the apartment."

"Okay." Leslie led the way to the kitchen and Marta handed them each a cup. "Thank you." She sipped the dark roast and hummed in pleasure. She set her cup down and retrieved the boxes full of baklava and the moussaka from the bag. "Help yourselves." She set them on the table as Deanna and the two men came in.

"Truck's empty. I think we're done here." Rob turned to Leslie. "The two boys racing around are our sons, Jake and Dale."

"I was happy to help. Help yourselves to the moussaka and baklava I brought." She pointed to the food on the table and turned to follow Kate upstairs.

"Shhh." Kate put her finger to her lips in a *be quiet* gesture. "She just fell asleep."

Leslie followed Kate to a small room across from the bedroom. A desk faced a sliding glass door overlooking a balcony in the back of the house. They each settled in recliners separated by a small wooden end table. "Nice room." Leslie flipped up the recliner's footrest and breathed a sigh of relief. "You'd think I'd be used to being on my feet all day, but this feels pretty good." She sipped her coffee and watched Kate sip hers. "How long will Portia sleep?"

"About an hour. Her naps are getting shorter."

They were silent for a moment, and Leslie wondered if it was okay to ask one of the questions that had been on her mind. She decided to go for it. "I presume you and Wendy planned your pregnancy. Is she stalking you for custody?"

"No. Portia was a year old when I met Wendy. I had decided I was ready for a baby, and even though I didn't have a partner, I went ahead and did it anyway. It was the perfect decision."

"That's a big decision to have a baby alone."

Kate shrugged. "It wasn't for me. I grew up with an older sister and two younger brothers. I think my parents would have had more children if they'd been younger. They're both doctors at the Cleveland Clinic and it takes a lot of their time. That factored into their decision not to have more kids, too." Kate took a sip of coffee and continued. "I always knew I wanted to have kids, but I didn't make good choices in partners, so after I finished college and had a secure job, I checked into donor sperm banks and had a baby on my own. I have no regrets."

"Portia's a great kid. You raised her well." Leslie reached for Kate's hand across the small table between them. "I used to envy my friends with sisters and brothers. Maybe that's what kids do. Envy what they don't have. I was an only child, but I didn't have to compete for my parents' attention like some of my friends did."

"Did your parents ever regret not having more kids?"

"I never asked them, but I don't think so. My grandmother, my mother's mother, moved in with us when I was five. That might've contributed to my parents not having more children. She taught me some Greek, and I taught her some English. I missed her a lot when she died."

"How old were you?"

"Sixteen." She released Kate's hand and pushed the footrest down on her chair. "Shall we go have some food before it's all gone?"

Kate quickly crawled out of her chair. "Hopefully they saved us some."

Leslie followed Kate and admired her grace as she headed down the stairs.

"Shall we sit on the balcony and eat?" Kate asked.

"Lead the way."

Kate led her to a balcony overlooking the backyard and she sat next to her on one of the chairs facing the yard.

"Wow. This is nice. I have a small patio in the back of my house, but nothing like this."

"Yeah. I love it out here." Kate took a forkful of food. "Mm. This is fabulous. Did you cook this?"

"No. Mom made it for you. She said, 'moving is a stressful event and Kate doesn't need to worry about cooking.'"

"I'll have to stop in and thank her." Kate finished eating, leaned back in her chair, and propped her feet up on the edge of the balcony.

"Do you feel relieved to be here?" Leslie asked.

"I do. Wendy knows where Deanna lives, but Deanna has cameras around the outside of the house to watch the deer, so we'll be able to see her if she shows up here. And with so many people around I think we'll feel safer."

Leslie wasn't sure what else to say that she hadn't said. There wasn't advice to be given or wise words to be said that Kate probably hadn't heard a million times already. She checked her watch. "I need to get going." She stood and suppressed the urge to pull Kate into her arms. They hadn't even had an official date yet, but the connection to her was strong. She had to slow down.

"Be careful going home. I'll probably stop in to thank your mom one day this week." Kate stepped closer but didn't touch her.

"I will." She ran her schedule for the week through her head. She had to confirm Trish's availability, and the new cook was scheduled to start the next day. "I'd like to take you out on an official date, but I'm having trouble figuring out when, or if that's what you want or need right now." She shifted foot to foot. Her uncertainty flustered her.

"I'm going to be unpacking and settling in for a couple of days." Kate remained quiet but looked thoughtful.

"Have you turned in your date choices for the speed-dating event?" Leslie asked.

"Oh yeah! I dropped them off on Tuesday, although I'm not sure I'll follow through on any of them, given what's going on right now."

Them. Leslie pushed aside the disappointment. Of course Kate would have several choices for dates. She'd planned on a few, too, until she'd seen Kate again. Now she wasn't sure she could be unbiased. "I did, too. So, think about where you'd like to go."

"Okay. You, too. We'll go somewhere special and do something fun." Kate smiled. "I do want to go out with you, Leslie. Thank you for being so understanding and patient."

Leslie said good-bye to Deanna, Rob, and Marta, but didn't see the boys before heading to her car. She drove the distance home lost in thought and didn't notice the car behind her until it was nearly touching her bumper. She checked her rearview mirror and recognized the hateful sneer. It had to be Wendy. She debated the satisfaction of slamming on her brakes against the hassle and cost of a car repair. Before she could decide, Wendy pulled next to her, smirked, and raced past. She took a deep breath and let it out slowly to settle the anger simmering in her gut, but her white knuckles indicated it wasn't going away. She continued home and double-checked the area around her house before hurrying inside and locking the door. She couldn't imagine how Kate lived with this nightmare, and it bothered her that she wondered briefly if it was wise to get involved with someone who had that kind of negativity swirling in their life. It wasn't Kate's fault, and Leslie was no shrinking violet. If Kate could put up with the hassle and fear, she would stand by her and support her in any way she'd allow her to.

CHAPTER THIRTEEN

The move hadn't taken long thanks to everyone's help, and the tension Kate held in her shoulders slowly uncoiled. She checked Portia was asleep, crawled into bed, pulled the covers to her chin, and let sleep overtake her. For the first time in months, she slept well and her dreams were of soft kisses instead of running from a pursuer.

Kate woke to the sounds of Portia carrying on a conversation with her stuffed bear. She lay listening to her nonsensical babble for a few minutes. Her mind fast-forwarded to a time her little girl would be grown and on her own, and Kate would be alone. She wrenched herself back to the present to avoid facing her insecurities of being a mother. She had hopes and dreams for her daughter, but she knew from her own experience, they might not match the ones Portia chose. The most she could do was love her and teach her to respect herself and others. She rose and reached for her robe, momentarily disoriented. It would take a few days to get used to her new temporary situation. She lifted Portia out of bed and dressed her before putting on sweatpants and a T-shirt. No more wandering around in the bare minimum. "Let's go downstairs and see what's for breakfast."

Portia led the way downstairs but stood at the bottom looking unsure. Kate picked her up and carried her to the kitchen where Marta was busy making pancakes.

"Good morning," she said as she poured pancake mix into the pan.

"Good morning, Marta. Can I do anything to help?" Kate definitely felt out of her element. It had been a while since she'd had anyone else to do things for her.

"You can set the table. These will be done in a minute. The boys won't be down for an hour yet."

Kate set the table and settled Portia in a chair before getting her a glass of orange juice and pouring herself a cup of coffee. "Have Deanna and Rob gone to work already?"

"Yes. Monday is their early day. Here you go." Marta set a plate full of pancakes on the table and Kate set two on Portia's plate.

She checked the time, finished eating, and went to get ready. It felt like a gift that she could shower and change without worrying about who was watching Portia or if she was getting into anything she shouldn't be. Portia sat at the table with two coloring books when she returned to the kitchen. "Thank you again for offering to add Portia to your day, Marta. I can't tell you how much I appreciate it. I should be home by four thirty."

"Don't you worry. We'll have fun today."

Kate kissed Portia good-bye and headed to work. She checked the area around her car at every intersection and sighed in frustration. She had to figure out a way to get free of Wendy. She parked in her usual spot and her phone chimed before she had a chance to open her car door. She smiled at the caller's name. "Good morning."

"Good morning. I hope it isn't a bad time to call. I wasn't sure what time you left for work."

"It's perfect. I didn't know how long it would take me from Deanna's to get here, so I left a little early. What's up?"

"I wanted to let you know I saw Wendy last night."

"Where?" Tension clenched her stomach.

"I was a few miles away from Deanna's before she pulled up behind me and rode my bumper. She glared at me when she passed my car."

"I'm so sorry, Leslie."

"It's not your fault, Kate. Wendy is a disturbed woman."

"Yes, but she's my problem. I feel awful she's turned her wrath on you."

"She's trying to get to you by harassing me. At least she didn't show up at Deanna's."

"Yeah." Kate checked her watch. "I'm really sorry, but I've got to get into work. I'll call you tonight, okay?"

"I look forward to it."

Kate put her phone away and checked the parking lot for any sign of Wendy before going into the building. Her workday dragged despite the steady stream of patients. She finished her last X-ray on a broken arm and left. She checked the parking lot as she walked to her car and stumbled as she got near it. The words "You're mine," written in red paint, stood out in sharp contrast to her silver car. She checked the passenger side of her car and found several scratches that looked like they were made by a key. "Damn it," she muttered under her breath. She wanted to scream and throw something.

She gripped the steering wheel until her knuckles were white and forced herself not to clench her teeth. She took the long route to Deanna's and checked each intersection when she stopped. She'd planned to take several different ways to and from work in hopes Wendy wouldn't find her, but she had and now she had yet another dilemma. Should she try to find another job? She refused to believe this would go on forever, and at some point, Wendy would either be arrested or give up and move on. Kate hoped it would be sooner rather than later.

She shoved thoughts of Wendy aside and remembered she had dates from the speed-dating event. She had no desire to follow up on any of them now with the Wendy situation. If she were being honest, Wendy was a huge problem, but Leslie would be her choice if she were in the position to be able to choose. Leslie probably had several lined up, but Kate's only interest was in Leslie.

What she knew of Leslie, so far, was that she was honest, caring, gentle, and sexy. Most importantly, she cared about Portia. She was the whole package, and she wouldn't be limiting herself by choosing to date her. Wendy had fooled her into believing she cared about her and her daughter, and the fiasco that turned out to be was on her. She'd believed Wendy and had chosen her. Could she trust herself now with Leslie? With anyone? She shook off her wandering thoughts and concentrated on driving. She'd take things one day at a time and go slow with Leslie and, somehow, figure out a way to purge the memory of their kiss.

She parked in the driveway, smiled, and waved at the sweet little face in the front window. Kate would never tire of coming home to her no matter where they lived.

"Hi, honey." Kate picked up Portia and danced around the living room. Her giggles were enough to wipe away all the angst of Kate's day.

"We had a fruit and cheese snack an hour ago. Will you two be okay with dinner at five thirty?"

"That's great. Thanks, Marta." Kate followed Portia upstairs and set her in her designated play area. She began her packing and unpacking toys that would entertain her for hours. Kate sighed and realized moving her four times in her little life had taught her packing and unpacking was a normal event. She watched her for a few minutes and picked up her phone to call the police and make her report. Then she called Leslie. Just to hear her voice.

"Hi, Kate. Are you home from work?"

"I am. Marta's making dinner in a while so I'm trying to chill out, and Portia's playing. Did you have a peaceful day?"

"I did. Our new server, Trish, is working out well. Mom is allowing her to take over most of the dining room. I think she realizes she has more time to visit with the patrons now."

"Good. How's your dad feeling?"

"Much better. I've talked him into cutting down his hours in the kitchen now since we have a new cook. I hate to bring this up, but you weren't bothered by Wendy today were you?"

"I was, actually. That's one of the reasons I called you. I needed a friendly voice. She painted a nasty note on one side of my car and keyed the other side while I was at work. I'm not sure if I should change jobs."

"I'm so sorry you're going through this. I presume you called the police."

"Oh yes. At least the number of incidents are on record."

"Right. I hope that means when they catch her, she'll be put away for a long time." Leslie said.

"I can hope."

"Maybe I can give you something better to think about. Have you thought about where you'd like to go on our speed-dating date?"

"A little."

"Do you like movies?" Leslie asked.

"Definitely."

"There's a small theater nearby having a mini lesbian film festival. I thought it would fun and we could go to dinner first or after. What do you think?"

"It sounds great. It's a date." Kate grinned. She liked the sound of that even as she pushed aside uncertainties about Wendy.

"I'll get the schedule and we can plan it. Okay?"

"Okay. Let me know what you find out, and I'll check with Marta when she can watch Portia." Kate didn't want to hang up, but Marta had dinner ready. "We're being paged for dinner."

"Have a good dinner. We'll talk tomorrow. Good night, Kate."

"Good night." Kate hung up and allowed herself a smile. It felt good to be talking on the phone to someone she had a crush on, like she was a teenager with no cares in the world.

"Hi, you two," Deanna called from the dining room.

"Hi, Deanna." Kate sat Portia in her seat at the table.

"How'd your first day here go?" Deanna sipped a glass of iced tea.

"It'll take me a few days to get into a routine, but I'm grateful to feel safe. Thanks again for letting us stay with you."

"You're welcome anytime." Deanna rested her hand on Kate's and squeezed gently.

"Are Rob and the boys having dinner with us?" Kate settled in the chair next to Portia.

"They'll eat later. He took them to soccer practice tonight. So, how's Leslie doing?" Deanna grinned.

"She's good." Kate filled her plate and cut the lasagna into bite-size pieces for Portia.

"She's special, isn't she?" Deanna's grin was replaced by a serious look.

Kate set her fork and knife down and looked at her sister. "I'm not sure what she is, Dee. I know I like her a lot. She's honest and caring, and she treats Portia well. She's a good friend." Kate didn't feel the need to tell Deanna about her stellar kissing abilities.

"Well, I like her. Especially if she takes your mind off Wendy."

"I don't know what I'm going to do about Wendy. She's shown up a few times despite the personal protection order. She knows enough not to stick around long enough for me to call the police." Kate took a bite of her dinner, but her appetite fled at the thought of Wendy.

"Has she threatened you?"

"I'd call it threatening. She showed up in my apartment parking lot. And she followed Leslie with her car Sunday night. At some point today, she managed to find my car at work and painted a threatening note on one side and keyed the other side. I carry pepper spray now."

"Today! Damn, I'm sorry you're going through all that. I presume you made a police report."

"I did. They're definitely adding up. I can't believe she's so persistent. You'd think she'd get the message and move on." Kate speared her food in frustration.

"Well, hopefully she doesn't know where you live now, and we'll do whatever you need to help you."

"Thanks. I appreciate your support, but if it gets any worse, I will move. I won't put you all in danger."

Deanna squeezed her hand. "We'll need to do everything we can before that happens. You're safer with family around you than you are alone."

"But you're not safer with me here." Kate dashed away the tears and smiled reassuringly at Portia, who looked at her far too seriously for a child so young. "We'll figure it out, won't we?" Maybe if she said it enough times, she'd believe it.

CHAPTER FOURTEEN

"We're all set, then." Leslie made notes on the new schedule she'd designed for the restaurant.

"Thanks for being so flexible," Trish said. "I'll be finished with this semester in January, and I look forward to working full-time after that."

"Mom will never give up her role in the dining area, so I appreciate your flexibility."

"I'd never expect her to. It's your family's restaurant. I'm grateful for the job."

"We're lucky to have you. I'll leave you to it." Leslie went to the kitchen to confirm the new cook's hours and to check on her dad. "Hi, Dad. How're things going here?"

"Paul is doing well. I think you did a good job hiring him."

"Great. I was hoping you'd be okay with him." Leslie felt a huge weight lift away. Her new plan might work. "I have a new schedule I'd like to review with you." She sat at the small kitchen table with her dad and went over her ideas to slowly phase out some of his work hours.

"I like it, honey. You did a wonderful job." He sat back and smiled.

Leslie sensed he had more to say. "I'm glad you're okay with it. I think you and Mom need some time to yourselves."

"We've been talking about taking a vacation. We might be able to now. Thank you."

Leslie held back tears of relief. She'd expected an argument at least, but her father looked relieved. His minor health scare must have worried him more than she realized. She hugged him and went home to review her own schedule and find time for her date with Kate. She looked up the movie schedule and decided to let Kate pick a time and day. She called her expecting to get her voice mail, but she answered on the second ring.

"Hi, Leslie. What's up?"

"Hey, I have the movie schedule, but I thought I'd let you pick a day and time."

"Okay."

"There are five one-hour-long movies on Thursday, Friday, and Saturday. Three being shown starting at two o'clock, and two starting at six. We could grab a bite to eat in between if you'd like."

"I don't work on Saturday. Would that work for you?"

"We're usually busy on Saturday. Would you be home in time to do the six and seven o'clock ones on Friday and then the earlier movies on Saturday?" She winced. Was she being too pushy asking for two days in a row?

"That sounds good. I'll plan on it, but I'll let you know if Marta can't watch Portia."

"Okay. I'll reserve tickets tonight. Are you getting settled in?"

"I am. I feel safe, and I see Portia relaxing."

"Good. Are you home now?"

"Yes, why?"

"I finished going over my new schedule here, and I'd like to take a break. Would you be able to meet me for a cup of coffee at the bistro again?"

Kate seemed to hesitate for a moment. "Sure. Give me about half an hour."

"See you there." Leslie disconnected the call and went to change. She didn't try to suppress her delight at seeing Kate again. She let her mom and Trish know she was leaving before going to her car. She checked the area and drove through the restaurant parking lot before pulling into the street. She turned on her radio and enjoyed the music as she drove. She noticed a car pull out from the parking lot across from her but dismissed it when it turned the opposite direction. She continued to listen to music and allowed the anticipation of seeing Kate to wash over her.

She'd only been on the road for five minutes when someone bumped her car from behind. The car she'd dismissed was directly behind her. "Damn." She turned at the next intersection and went around the block. It had to be Wendy following her, and she wasn't going to lead her to Kate. She grabbed her phone and hit redial.

"Hello?" Kate answered.

"Wendy is following me. I'm going around the block to try to lose her, so I'll call you if I can't shake her."

"Be careful. I'll wait for you."

Leslie pulled into the police parking lot and got out of her car. She hoped Wendy would think she was going inside and leave. She looked up and saw Wendy's car race past. She waited for a few minutes, then took a different route to the bistro. Kate was seated at the same table they'd occupied before.

"Are you okay?" Kate looked spooked.

"I am. I went to the police station. I think it scared her away." Leslie sat across from Kate and kept an eye on the door.

"I am so sorry you had to put up with her." Kate looked close to tears. "It isn't fair to you."

Leslie took her hands in hers. "It'll be okay. She'll screw up one day and the police will catch her." The server brought their coffees and Leslie scrambled for words to calm Kate.

"I'm not sure what to do." Kate covered her face with both hands and tears streaked her face when she looked up. "I'm frightened, and I'm so tired of living like this."

Leslie wanted to tell her it would be okay. Her own tears welled at the sight of Kate so upset. "Let's drink our coffee and talk about the movies we're going to see." She relaxed a little at the slight grin on Kate's face.

Leslie told Kate everything she knew about the movies, pleased to see Kate's spark return. She finished her coffee and reluctantly noted the time. "I need to go home and help close up. You get some sleep tonight and we'll talk tomorrow."

"Please call me when you get home. I'll worry." Kate spoke quietly but looked resolved instead of scared.

"I will." Leslie stood and Kate walked out with her. She checked the area around them and walked Kate to her car before going to hers.

Leslie closely watched every car she passed or passed her on her way home. By the time she pulled into her driveway, she was exhausted. Kate must be totally stressed out. She gave her a call when she got inside. Although she was exhausted, sleep didn't come easily. She kept reviewing the situation, trying to find any angle that might not have been explored, but there didn't seem to be any. Finally, she fell asleep.

She called Kate the next morning as soon as it wasn't too early. Her dreams had been busy and dark. "Is everything okay there?"

"Yes. No sign of Wendy. I hope it stays that way."

"Me, too. I'll let you go, I just wanted to check on you."

"That's really sweet. Thanks for calling."

"No problem. Be careful today, and I'll talk to you tonight." Leslie hung up and wondered what it would be like to wake up beside Kate, to see her beautiful face first thing in the morning. The thought made her smile as she got ready.

"Good morning," her mother called from across the dining area.

"Morning. You're here early." Leslie collected cleaning supplies and followed her mother's lead by wiping tables and chairs.

"I'm going to take your dad to the doctor later for a checkup. He's still coughing and he's almost out of the prescription he got from the hospital."

"What time are you taking him? I'll go with you." Leslie finished her cleaning and put the supplies away.

"The doctor told me to bring him at ten."

Leslie could tell her mother was relieved not to be going alone. "I'll leave a note for Trish and Paul. They'll hold down the fort for us."

"Thank you, honey." Her mother paused and wiped tears from her eyes. "Have I told you how much I love you? I'm so grateful to have you." She wrapped her arms around Leslie.

"I love you, too, Mom. Let's go tell Dad the plan." Leslie drove them to the doctor and kept an eye out for Wendy's car. It was one thing to put her in danger, another altogether to endanger her parents. If she came anywhere near them, she'd take matters into her own hands. The appointment didn't last long, and Leslie made sure her mom had the doctor's instructions for care before she left his office.

"Thank you for coming with us. I get nervous when the doctor starts talking about symptoms and medications."

"At least he's not seriously compromised. It'll just take him a little longer to get over his pneumonia. Keep the instructions on the kitchen counter and you can refer to them daily." Leslie pulled her mother into her arms. "He'll get over this. We'll put his new pills into his weekly pill dispenser, and you can monitor it for him."

"Yes. That's a good idea. Thank you, again, honey."

"I'd like to talk to you both about something else." Leslie paused to organize her thoughts. "I'd like to renovate the restaurant a little." Hopefully, it wouldn't upset her parents that she wanted to make changes, just as she was also trying to get them to work less. She didn't want them to feel like she was taking over.

Her mother looked tired. "I've been telling George we probably need to update things, but he keeps resisting. I think he'll listen if it comes from you."

"I'll talk to him tomorrow. He needs to take his antibiotics and rest today." Leslie drove her parents home and went to check in with Trish.

"How'd everything go today?" Leslie asked Trish.

"Smoothly. We were pretty busy, but Paul did an excellent job keeping up."

"Good. Thanks for helping out today."

"How's your dad?"

"He'll be okay." Leslie didn't feel comfortable discussing his medical information without his approval.

"Good. I like him a lot." Trish grinned.

"He's a good man. Before I forget, would you be able to work this Friday evening and Saturday afternoon?"

"Sure. Friday classes are over at noon, and I'm off on Saturdays."

"Thanks, Trish. I appreciate it." Now she could enjoy her time off with Kate and not worry about the restaurant at all.

"I'm grateful for the hours."

Leslie went to check on her dad. "How are you feeling, Dad?"

"I'm okay, honey. Thank you for going with your mom today."

"Of course, I'd go with her. I'm glad you're doing well."

"I am, and I want to talk to you about the restaurant." Her dad looked conflicted.

"It's okay, Dad. Whatever you want to say."

"I'm proud of you, honey. You'll do an excellent job of taking over when we're gone."

"You're not going anywhere, Dad. You have a slight case of bacterial pneumonia. You'll recover."

"I know, honey, but your mom and I have been at this for many years. You have good instincts. I think you'll do well with the restaurant. Your mom told me you wanted to renovate. I think it's a good idea. I'll go along with whatever you decide."

"Thanks, Dad. I'll do my best." It was like being passed the torch, and she hoped she was strong enough and dedicated enough to carry it proudly. But it also felt a little like the end of an era, and she allowed herself to remember all the wonderful times she'd had with them there. Life was about to change, and she wanted the changes coming her way to be on her terms.

CHAPTER FIFTEEN

K ate tossed the third pair of pants onto the bed and riffled through her closet. She pulled out her favorite blouse then put it back. She'd worn it to the bistro. She finally decided on an appropriate outfit and dressed with the movie theater in mind, since it might be chilly inside. She checked the time and hugged Portia good-bye. "Be good and mind Marta tonight." She kissed her cheek and went to her car. The ride to Leslie's restaurant went quickly, but Kate constantly searched for Wendy's car along the way. She pushed her out of her mind when she arrived and concentrated on Leslie. The cool evening gave way to warmth and soft lighting as she stepped through the door of the restaurant. Her pulse quickened when Leslie stepped into the room from the kitchen and smiled. Her dark eyes sparkled, and Kate felt her gaze skim her face as gentle as her touch. She looked resplendent in black jeans, a cream-colored silk shirt, and a soft looking black leather blazer. Kate longed to slip her hands inside and cradle her full breasts. She tore her eyes away before she embarrassed herself and managed a smile before she spoke. "You look fabulous."

"Thank you. As do you. Ready for the movies?" Leslie walked toward her as she spoke.

"I am. Did you change the lighting in here?"

"Yes. I want to do some updating and redecorating. Maybe change out the seating, I don't know, but I started with the lighting."

"It's perfect." Kate walked the perimeter of the room and allowed her imagination to take over. "I've always loved renovating. I took a couple of classes in interior design after high school."

"I'll consider that an offer to help me redo this place," Leslie said and looked at her watch. "But we better get going now."

Kate took one last look at the room and followed Leslie out the door. She checked the parking lot for Wendy's car and watched the traffic at every intersection. It was getting old.

"Are you okay? You're worried about Wendy, aren't you?" Leslie took her hand as she drove.

"I am worried. She's unpredictable and knows how to avoid the police. I don't know what to do, but I do know I can't live like this."

"If we see her car again, let's get her license plate number. The police can trace her from that, I think."

"That's a good idea." She turned her attention to the movies. "I'm looking forward to these movies."

"Me, too." Leslie squeezed her hand gently.

Kate held Leslie's hand as they navigated through the crowd of lesbians. She relaxed into her seat and turned her full attention to the woman on stage introducing the first movie. Her life with Portia and Wendy had never included enjoying the company of a room full of lesbians. It was one of the reasons she volunteered at the LGBTQ center now. She leaned slightly toward Leslie enjoying the heat from her body and the excitement of the event. She smiled when Leslie rested her arm over her shoulders, and she allowed herself a short fantasy of being totally free from the threat of Wendy. The first movie engaged her complete attention and was over too soon. She clapped with the rest of the audience and grinned at Leslie standing and clapping next to her with a huge smile. "Thanks for this," Kate said.

"Thanks for coming with me. I hope the second movie is as good."

Kate scanned the room and saw two women she recognized from the center. They leaned into each other for a passionate kiss, and a wave of desire washed over her. Desire from the kisses she and Leslie had already shared, and how many more she wanted. She squirmed in her seat and waited for the next movie to start.

"Are you all right?" Leslie whispered.

"Yes. I'm fine." Kate turned her attention to the screen when the movie started and quickly became engrossed in the story. The film was a love story with an explicit love scene, and Kate suppressed a groan. She glanced at Leslie, pleased to see her take a deep breath and expel it. The movie lasted longer than the first one, and Kate enjoyed it as much.

"That was great," Leslie said. "Both of them were superb." She grinned. "And that last one was sexy."

Kate felt the heat rise in her face. "It was. I'm glad we came to see them." Kate took Leslie's hand as they walked to the car.

"Tomorrow's will probably be just as good." Leslie unlocked her car.

Kate rested her head on the headrest and smiled at the feeling of the pleasant evening. "This was the best date ever," she whispered.

"It was, wasn't it?" Leslie took her hand and kissed it.

"Maybe tomorrow we can meet with some of the women for a while after the last movie. Would that be okay with you?"

"Sure. I'd like that."

Kate closed her eyes and replayed the movies in her mind. It had been so long since she'd lost herself in a story played out in a movie. She enjoyed losing herself in a romance novel, but a movie had live characters she didn't have to create in her mind. The respite from concerns about Wendy had energized her, and she wished it could last forever.

"Here we are." Leslie stroked her cheek.

Kate took her hand and held it. "Thank you again for the fabulous date. I had no idea I was so keyed up. I needed to unwind."

"I'm glad you feel better. It was fabulous." Leslie stepped out of the car and walked around to open her door. "Do you have time to come inside?"

Kate checked the time. "I do." She followed Leslie to the building.

"Would you like a cup of tea before you leave?" Leslie dimmed the lights and locked the door.

"That would be nice." Kate didn't want the evening to end, and she sensed Leslie felt the same way. She took in the room while Leslie was getting their tea and wished she had a pad of paper to write down ideas. She moved tables in her mind and added small two-seaters along the back wall. She saw it as a romantic area perfect with the new lighting. It wasn't anything to do with her, but she couldn't help herself. She sat at one of the booths to wait for Leslie.

"Here you go." Leslie set two cups on the table and sat across from her.

"Thanks." She took a sip and spoke again. "I have a couple of ideas about your renovations, if you'd be interested? I don't want to step on your toes, obviously."

"Great. I'd appreciate any ideas you have. Mom and Dad told me I pretty much had free rein to do what I wanted, but I plan to involve them in any final decisions."

Kate finished her tea and enjoyed Leslie's company for another half hour before checking the time and leaving. She drove home lost in memories of the best evening she'd had in a long time. Leslie's swift brush of her lips across hers as she was leaving was far less than she craved, but enough to reignite the simmering desire left over from the sexy movie. She was constantly on the lookout for Wendy as she drove, hoping this wouldn't last for the rest of her life. She sighed with relief when she pulled into Deanna's driveway and went into the house.

Portia was sound asleep when Kate checked on her. She watched her sleep for a few minutes before she sent a text to Leslie to let her know she was home. She smiled at the fond memories of the evening and hoped for dreams of sweet kisses as she crawled into bed.

She woke at her usual six a.m. and was surprised Portia still slept soundly. She hoped it was because she wore herself out playing the day before. She lingered for a few minutes in the memories of her date with Leslie and the anticipation of the day ahead. She put on her robe before heading downstairs.

"Good morning," Marta sat at the kitchen table. "Coffee's ready."

Kate poured herself a cup and sat across from her. "Thanks, Marta. For the coffee and for watching Portia yesterday. She's still asleep, so I figure you must've worn her out."

"She had fun riding her tricycle and coloring. She's a coordinated kid. So, how was your date?" Marta looked at her expectantly.

"We had a great time and saw two good movies. I'm looking forward to this afternoon's event." It was a bland description of a night that had been wonderful, but she didn't want to share it yet. It was special and she wanted to keep it to herself for a little while.

"I'm so glad. You deserve to enjoy yourself, and Leslie seems like a great person."

"She is. After my disaster with Wendy, it's nice to be able to trust someone. Leslie is honest and reliable. Thank goodness for therapy, or I might not allow myself to care for someone ever again."

"Well. It sounds like she could be someone special, and I'm happy for you." Marta stood and began pulling eggs and bacon from the refrigerator.

Kate went upstairs to check on Portia and found her sitting in her play corner talking to her stuffed animals.

"Are you ready for breakfast, honey?" Kate sat on the floor next to her.

"Dance, Mommy." Portia raised her arms.

Kate picked her up and twirled throughout the room relishing Portia's squeal of delight. She set her on the floor and led her downstairs to the kitchen.

"Good morning, sunshine," Marta said while filling a plate with bacon and scrambled eggs.

"Thanks, Marta. You always make the best breakfasts." Kate helped Portia eat. "Do you know, Portia, Marta took care of me when I was your age. She cooked for me and took me places and helped me color, too."

Portia looked from Kate to Marta and back again, clearly taking that in.

"Thank you. There's nothing I'd rather be doing." Marta beamed and sat at the table with them. "What time do you have to leave?" she asked.

"Not until noon. The movies start at two. Thanks again for offering to entertain Portia for me." Kate caressed Portia's hair. "I have to admit to feeling a little guilty about leaving her while I go have fun on my own."

"She's no problem. We'll do more coloring and drawing. And life is about balance, Kate."

"That's for later. Right now, it's bath time." Kate stood and Portia raced past her to the stairs.

CHAPTER SIXTEEN

I'm glad you had a good time with Kate last night. We're looking forward to seeing her today." Leslie and her mother wiped tables and readied the dining area for the day.

"She'll be here before one." Leslie checked the tables and refilled missing condiments. She made a few notes on updates she wanted to make and smiled at memories of Kate reviewing the room. Her eyes sparkled as she mentally rearranged tables and chairs. "How's dad feeling? I noticed he's not here yet."

"He's taking it easy, but he feels much better, and he'll be here soon."

"Good. Make sure he makes use of Paul today." She perused the room, satisfied it was ready and then unlocked the door and put the *open* sign out. Leslie heard the door open shortly after she turned to head to the kitchen.

"Sorry, I'm a little late." Trish hurried into the building.

"No problem. Nobody's here yet," Leslie said. "I was going to the kitchen to check on things." She found her dad wiping the counters. "Hi, Dad. Mom says you're feeling better."

"Much. I'm almost done with my antibiotics." He continued his task.

"Good. How about the anti-anxiety pills? Are you done with those?"

"Yes. I didn't like the way I felt on them, so your mom called the doctor and took me off them. I feel more like myself now."

"I'm glad you're doing so well. Just don't push yourself if you get tired. Paul will be here all day to help you." Satisfied everything was in order, she went home to shower and change for her date. She took her time in the shower to imagine Kate's naked breasts pressed against her back, her hands smoothing lavender body wash over her shoulders and across her breasts and down to the sensitive spot on her abdomen just above her pubic hair. She quickly squelched her wandering thoughts. Their two kisses were enough to hint at what more could be like, but she wanted more time to explore the deeper feelings of connection. She wanted what her parents had. Nearly fifty years of marriage and still in love. She dried off quickly and went to her bedroom to decide what to wear.

Leslie logged on to her computer after she dressed to check on her next assignment for the restaurant management class she'd enrolled in. She reviewed the notes she'd taken on the fine dining information and allowed her imagination to incorporate them into her plan. She'd never change the relaxed family style atmosphere her parents had generated, but upgrading a little might allow them to increase prices somewhat. She shut down her computer and went to the restaurant to wait for Kate. Her breath caught when Kate walked through the door. She wore the same faded jeans she'd worn the day of her move and a soft looking chocolate sweater. She squashed memories of her sexy shower scene as she tracked her motion toward her. Before she could speak, her mother raced past her.

"Kate. It's good to see you." Her mother enveloped her in a hug.

"It's good to see you, too, Elena. How's your husband?"

"He's doing well. Come on." She grabbed Kate's hand and tugged her to the kitchen.

Leslie followed them and winked at Kate when she turned with questions in her eyes.

"George, it's Kate," her mother said.

Her father turned from the grill to wave. "Hello, young lady. I hope you two enjoy the movies today."

"Thank you. If they're as good as yesterday's we will. I'm glad to see you're feeling better."

"Thank you. I am, too. You two have fun." He turned back to the grill.

Leslie stood in the kitchen doorway watching the exchange. "You ready to go? she asked. She swallowed the surge of emotion at the gentleness of Kate's spirit.

"Yep. Take care, you two, and don't work too hard," Kate said.

Leslie opened the door for Kate and followed her out to the parking lot. "Thanks for being kind to my parents."

"Hmm. I remember you said something about Portia being mine, so of course you'd be kind to her." Kate grinned. "Your parents are great people."

"They are." Leslie slid behind the steering wheel and pulled out of the parking lot. She relaxed as they got closer to the theater without any strange cars following them. Leslie took one of the last parking spots and led the way to their seats.

"I like these seats." Kate took her arm and leaned into her.

Leslie pulled her arm from her grip and wound it around Kate's shoulders.

"This is better." Kate snuggled into her and sighed.

Leslie drew her closer and enjoyed the warmth radiating off her body. "This is nice," she whispered in her ear and kissed her lightly on the soft spot below it. Kate shivered but didn't pull away. The movie started and Leslie settled in to watch. She quickly became engrossed in the story. The acting and the gorgeous women in the movie captivated her. She shifted in her seat when the love scene didn't leave much to the imagination, and she glanced at Kate who leaned away from her and took a deep breath. Leslie reached for her hand but withdrew it at the last minute, telling herself to slow down. She turned her attention back to the movie which ended too quickly for her liking.

"That was a good movie," Kate said.

"It was. I didn't want it to end." Leslie stood to stretch, and Kate joined her. She looked over the heads of the women in the theater. Some stood, a few made their way into the aisles to talk, and many stayed seated wrapped in each other's arms. "I'm grateful we have events like this to enjoy. It wasn't long ago that we couldn't imagine a public theater filled to capacity showing lesbian films."

"You're right. We have much to be grateful for." Kate took her hand and kissed it. "Thank you for inviting me."

A woman took the stage to introduce the next movie and the crowd settled into their seats. Leslie kept her hands to herself throughout the show. It was as good as the first movie with no love scenes, and she drew in a settling breath. The lure of Kate next to her stirred her enough without sexy scenes in the movie. "Want to get pizza next door before the last film?"

"I love pizza!"

Leslie smiled at Kate's enthusiasm and took her hand to lead her out the door. The crowd had begun to settle in their seats when they returned from dinner. Leslie held their drinks while Kate slid past her, and she swallowed a moan when her body brushed hers. She held Kate's hand through the last movie delighting in how perfectly their fingers intertwined. The same woman who introduced the movies came on stage to close out the festival, and Leslie shook off a sense of disappointment that it was all over.

"This was wonderful." Kate grinned and clutched their joined hands to her chest.

"Yes, it was. I'm glad you agreed to go with me." Leslie was willing to stand in the lobby holding Kate's hands all night. Several women lingered to talk and review each movie with enthusiasm. Leslie checked her watch after twenty minutes of socializing, and Kate nodded and started for the exit. Leslie followed her to the car and they both sat quietly for a few minutes enjoying the afterglow of the event.

"I'm going to talk to the LGBTQ center and see if we could arrange a movie event. That reminds me. Do you like to dance?" Kate asked.

Leslie started the car and turned toward Kate. "It's been a while, but I do. Why?"

"We're going to have another fundraising event, and I suggested a dance. I think it'll happen soon." Kate grinned.

Leslie pulled out of the parking lot and tried to remember the last time she'd danced and with whom. She gave up and replaced the thoughts with the vision of her holding Kate close as they moved across the dance floor. She turned on the main road back toward the restaurant when a car pulled behind her, riding her bumper. "Damn, that driver is too close." She considered pulling onto the shoulder when she realized it was probably Wendy.

Kate turned to look behind them and confirmed her fear. "It's Wendy." She pulled out her phone and called 911.

Leslie hoped the police would show up right away and catch her. She slowed down to give them time, but Wendy turned on her brights and trailed them for a short time before she pulled next to them, glared, and then raced ahead out of sight. "She's gone." Leslie took a deep breath to calm herself. She turned to Kate who looked scared to death. "Did the police answer?"

"Yeah, but since she's gone, I'll call them back when we get to the restaurant to file a complaint." Kate rested her head on the head rest and closed her eyes. "I'm so sorry."

Leslie reached for her hand. She pulled into the parking lot and climbed out of the car to check around it before opening Kate's door. "Come on. How about a cup of hot chocolate?" She led Kate into the restaurant and seated at a table before she went to the kitchen. She found Kate on the phone when she returned, so she waited for her to finish.

"I reported her. I told them what happened, and they said to call if I see her. They're going to send a patrol car to cruise by. If she shows up maybe it'll scare her away. Thanks for the hot chocolate."

"Let's hope she'll give up. Doesn't she have a job in Ohio?"

"She did. Who knows if she still does? She was drinking a lot, so maybe she lost her job." Kate sipped from her cup. "I hope the police get here soon. I told them what kind of car she drives, but I don't know her license plate number."

"She's gone now, so tell me about this dance you're proposing." She'd do anything she could to chase the anxiety from Kate's eyes. Reminding her of the good things in life was important.

Kate smiled at the diversion. "I think the event area in the building is large enough for quite a few people. I'm going to get info on DJs. I think it'll be fun."

"As long as I can dance with you, I'm in." Leslie smiled and pushed away thoughts of Wendy.

Chapter Seventeen

Kate completed her report to the police officer about Wendy and the restraining order and shook off the last of her worry. "I'm going to head home now. Thank you for a wonderful day and evening." She slid out of her seat and waited for Leslie to stand before she grabbed the front of the sexy leather blazer and pulled her in for a kiss. She lingered on her lips and gasped when Leslie tugged her closer and their bodies pressed together. Leslie cupped her face and slid her fingers into her hair to kiss her harder. Every cell in her body cried for more of her. She complained when Leslie leaned away, breaking their connection, but Kate knew it was for the best. It was too soon for what her body screamed for. She waited until her breathing returned to normal before she spoke again. "I'm going home now." She stepped back on shaky legs and turned toward the door.

"Kate?"

She turned back and seized the doorknob to keep from racing back into Leslie's arms. "Yes?" Her heart beat loudly in her ears.

"Call me when you get home okay? I need to know you're safe."

"I will." Kate hurried to her car before she lost total control and they ended up naked on the floor. She took a settling breath and sat quietly for a few minutes before starting her car and leaving the parking lot. She relaxed a little when she saw the patrol car circle the building and park near the entrance to the lot. Her anxiety rose the farther from the lot she drove, and by the time she arrived home a tension headache had taken hold. She closed her eyes for a few minutes once she was in her sister's driveway. Wendy knew about Leslie and her restaurant, but she hadn't found her at Deanna's, yet. Not that she knew of, anyway, but there was no telling when and where she'd show up next.

She turned her thoughts to Portia and a smile eased her headache. The house was quiet when she entered so she went directly upstairs to her room. She checked the time and realized it was later than she thought. Portia usually went to sleep by eight and it was close to eight thirty. She checked on her sleeping child and quietly went to the den to call Leslie.

"Hello. You must've gotten home okay." Leslie sounded relieved to hear from her.

"I did. I was glad to see the patrol car sitting by your parking lot when I left. It was all clear driving home."

"How's Portia?"

"Sound asleep. I don't know where everyone is, but I'm kind of glad for the peace and quiet."

"I missed you when you left." Leslie's voice dropped an octave.

"I miss you right now. Let's plan another date soon."

"What about all the other dates from the speed dating event?" Leslie asked.

Kate hesitated. She had no interest in dating anyone but Leslie. Maybe Leslie didn't feel the same. Kate didn't play games. She'd be honest and hoped Leslie would as well. "I'm not interested in dating anyone else, but if you are I don't want to stop you."

"I'm sorry. Teasing is a mean thing to do, and that's what I was doing. I don't want to date anyone else either. I'm looking forward to the next time we can get together."

How wonderful to be with someone who didn't play games either. "I'd like to stop at the restaurant with Portia tomorrow. I know she'd like to see you, too."

"I'd like that. I've changed the Sunday hours a little. We'll be open from ten to five." Leslie sounded like she wanted to say more but remained quiet before she said good night.

Kate went back to the den to read and unwind before going to bed. She managed to read a page before her mind wandered to Leslie. She understood feelings of attraction. She'd even felt it with Wendy when they'd first met, but the emotion poking its way past her attraction to Leslie troubled her with the cloud of Wendy hanging over her head. Falling for someone when there was a real possibility she'd have to move again wasn't a good idea. She gave up on more reading and went to bed hoping for dreams of Leslie's kisses.

"Mommy?"

Kate rolled over, drawn from sleep by Portia's anxious voice. She hurried out of bed and picked up her whimpering daughter. "What is it, honey? Did you have a bad dream?"

Portia clung to her with tear-filled eyes. "I woke up and missed you."

"Oh, baby, I'm right here. I'll always be here for you." She danced around the room until a smile replaced her sad expression. "We're going to see the nice lady later, so let's sleep some more. Okay?" Kate tucked Portia in beside her and they both fell asleep.

Portia was still asleep when Kate woke and donned her robe to go downstairs. Marta was stirring something in a large pot. "Good morning."

"Morning, Marta." Kate poured a cup of coffee from the ever-present coffeemaker. "Do you get up at three to make coffee?" she asked, grinning.

"No. It's one of my weaknesses, so I usually make a pot first thing. I'm making oatmeal this morning, so you bring Portia down whenever you're ready."

"Thanks." Kate took her coffee to the room overlooking the backyard for a few minutes of alone time before Portia woke up. The brilliant fall colors along the edge of the property reminded her of time passing. Portia would be four soon and they were living with her sister and she was being stalked by her ex. She refused to allow herself to spiral into self-pity. She'd imagined such a different life for herself by the time she was this age. She replaced her uncertainty with gratitude, finished her coffee, and went to check on Portia. She found her sitting on the floor talking to her stuffed animals. Her vocabulary was growing, and again, Kate sensed time flying. She settled on the floor with her and began the game of talking animals. She glanced at the clock after half an hour. "Marta made oatmeal this morning. You ready for some?"

Portia stood eagerly and Kate followed her downstairs. Wasn't it only a couple of months ago she couldn't navigate the stairs?

"Good morning," Marta said. "You ready for breakfast? Everyone else has come and gone."

Kate ate a small bowl of oatmeal and watched Portia finish hers. She drank another cup of coffee to keep Marta company for a little while before taking Portia upstairs.

"We're going to see the nice lady now."

"Nice lady." Portia started toward the door.

Kate grabbed their jackets and followed her down the stairs and out the door.

As she drove, she maintained constant vigilance for signs of Wendy and parked as close to the building as possible. There were a few diners already seated when she set Portia on the booster seat and sat across from her. She held Leslie's gaze as she approached the table but managed to refrain from grabbing her and pulling her in for a kiss.

"I'm glad you made it." She turned to Portia. "Hello, Princess. What can I get for you today?"

Portia tipped her head down and looked at Kate.

"She's bashful today," Kate said. "Maybe a piece of baklava will help."

"Paul makes a great omelet if you're interested."

"Sounds good. We'll split one. Thanks." She watched Leslie walk away and turned to Portia as she waved to someone outside the window. "Who are you waving at, honey?"

"Momma Wendy."

Panic rose in her throat and Kate looked where Portia had been waving but didn't see Wendy. She pulled the window blinds closed and watched the door.

"Everything okay?" Leslie set a plate filled with a large omelet on the center of the table.

"I think Wendy is outside. She waved at Portia." Kate couldn't keep from staring at the door, expecting Wendy to charge in.

Leslie went to the door and looked outside, then returned to Kate's table. "I don't see her." She sat next to Kate. "Did you see her again last night?"

"No. If I see her when we leave, I'll call the police." Kate clenched her fists in frustration. How could she explain the situation to her innocent child? She cut the omelet in half and cut small pieces for Portia.

"I'll be right back." Leslie went to the kitchen.

Kate picked at her food and waited while Portia enjoyed her eggs. Trish refilled her coffee cup, and she wrapped her hands around it. She nearly ran to Leslie when she saw her return.

"I went out the back door and walked around the building. I didn't see her, but there is a message in red paint on the garbage bin in back of the restaurant." She sat next to Kate.

"What did she write?" Kate asked.

"Just the word MINE. I'll wash it off soon. Do you have to get right home after you eat?" Leslie asked.

"No. Why?"

"I'd like to invite you over for tea or coffee. I have juice for Portia."

"Over where?"

"To my house."

Kate blinked. She'd never asked Leslie where she lived. "We'd love to."

"Great. Whenever you're done eating. I'm going to check on my dad in the kitchen. I'll be back." Leslie brushed her fingers over Kate's hand before she left.

"We're going to the nice lady's house today." Kate wasn't sure Portia understood, but it would be a good learning lesson for her. She finished her half of the omelet, desperately trying to hold on to the idea of doing something as normal as going to someone's house for coffee.

Leslie returned to the table. "Are you ready?"

"Come on, Portia." Kate lifted her off her seat and set her on the floor. She took her hand and waited for Leslie. "Shall I take my car?"

Leslie grinned. "You can decide when we get outside."

Kate followed Leslie through the kitchen and out the back door. She turned right and pointed to a small house on the edge of the parking lot. "You probably don't need to drive."

CHAPTER EIGHTEEN

It's not huge, but it's all mine." Leslie unlocked her front door and pushed it open to let Kate and Portia pass through.

"It's cozy." Kate held Portia's hand and stood in the middle of the living room.

She was proud of her small three-bedroom home. "Thank you. I think so, too, but it's nice to have another opinion. Have a seat." She pointed to the couch as her anxiety rose. Her ex-lover, her parents, and Joy and Nat were the only ones who had ever been in her house. What did Kate's idea of cozy mean? Too small? If she was used to houses the size of Deanna's, this would feel like a cottage. "Would you like a tour?"

"Absolutely." Kate grinned and Leslie's apprehension fled. Kate and Portia followed her room to room, and they were back in the living room within minutes. Portia released Kate's hand, scurried to the corner of the room, and threw herself onto a large beanbag chair. She giggled as she rolled off and jumped up to repeat the experience. Kate picked her up and carried her to the couch. "Sorry," Kate said.

"No problem. She's welcome to play anywhere. I keep my office door locked, so she can't get in there. That beanbag chair was my father's. He never admitted to all the things he was into, but he was a child of the sixties, and I suspect that chair has seen some interesting things."

Kate grinned. "I'd love to hear its stories." Portia slid off the couch and dashed to the beanbag. "I'm afraid she's found a favorite spot in your house already."

"Good. I hope you do, too." Leslie sat next to her. "Can I get you a cup of coffee? Portia a juice?"

"I think we're good. That omelet was great this morning." Kate rested her arm across the back of the sofa and lightly caressed Leslie's neck. "This certainly is a nice spot."

Leslie quivered at the touch and glanced at Portia still absorbed with the beanbag chair. She quickly turned her head and kissed the underside of Kate's wrist. "I'm getting a cup of green tea. Sure you don't want anything?"

"I'm sure, thank you."

Leslie returned to the couch with her tea and propped her feet up on her coffee table.

"How long have you lived here?" Kate asked.

"About ten years. I bought it after I finished getting my degree in finance."

"Did you choose finance because of the restaurant?"

"Yes. I'm working on a degree in restaurant management, too."

"So, no lovers in between?"

"I had one I thought was serious. It was over a year ago now." Leslie took a deep breath. She'd pushed aside most of the memories of Judy and hated she thought of her now with Kate seated so close.

"I'm sorry to bring up bad memories. I know what it's like to be disappointed in love."

"Yeah, I have to admit some culpability since most of my time was spent in the restaurant or studying."

"Speaking of restaurant, are we keeping you from getting back?"

Leslie checked her watch. "I have some time. Trish and Paul are working out well, and Mom will call me if things get out of hand."

"Well, I think my little girl has decided this is her new nap area." Kate pointed to Portia curled up asleep on the beanbag chair.

Leslie watched Portia sleep for a few minutes amazed by her peaceful posture lying halfway off the chair. "Does she always sleep like that?" She turned to Kate.

Kate chuckled. "Sometimes. She obviously feels comfortable here."

"I'm glad." Leslie settled back on the couch.

"Have you done more planning for remodeling?"

"Yes. Would you like to see it?"

"Definitely." Kate looked excited.

Leslie went to her office and came back with her laptop. "I found a great program for designing the dining room." She showed Kate the favorite design she'd come up with.

"I like it. Have you thought about placing a few two-seater tables along the back wall? I think it might attract first date couples or anniversaries. With your new lighting, I think it could be a nice romantic area."

Leslie used the program to move tables and add a partial wall sectioning off the area. "How's this? It'd be more private."

"I like it." Kate grinned. "You're pretty good at this."

"Thanks. I have a lot of planning to do to make all this happen and Mom and Dad need to agree."

Kate cupped Leslie's face with both hands and pressed her lips on hers.

Leslie set her laptop on the coffee table with one hand and leaned into the kiss which didn't last nearly long enough for her liking. Awareness of her surroundings faded, pushed aside by Kate claiming her. Kate pulled away and reality crashed in. Kate was here with Portia, and they'd be leaving. She straightened in her seat and cleared her throat. "You make me forget everything except the feel of you in my arms."

"I feel it, too." Kate stroked her cheek and smiled when Portia's grumble interrupted their moment. Kate went to pick her up and carried her back to the couch. "We'll go home soon, honey. Say thank you to Leslie for inviting us to her house."

Portia wrapped her arms around Kate's neck and buried her face in her chest before mumbling something unintelligible. "She's tired," Kate whispered.

"I'll take that as a thank you." Leslie grinned. "You're welcome, Princess. Come back any time. I'll walk you out." Leslie followed Kate and Portia back to the restaurant so they could say good-bye to her mom and dad.

Before heading back home, she pulled out her power washer and washed off the garbage bin.

Leslie's footsteps echoed as she walked through the empty living room after Kate left. She loved her house and had never felt lonely there, but the deafening silence as she strode to the kitchen stunned her. Kate's and Portia's presence for only a short time filled a void she wasn't aware of but didn't know what to do about. She took her laptop to her office and tweaked the room design she'd considered the most efficient before she printed out a copy and took it to show her parents. The restaurant was filled to capacity and several people waited in the lobby.

She found her mother readying a table for four and followed her to the kitchen. "Your idea to stay open until five was a good one, honey. We've never been this busy on a Sunday." She grabbed silverware and rushed back to the table where a couple and a child now sat.

"I want to show you something," Leslie said when her mother returned to the kitchen.

She put the paper she'd printed on the table and reviewed it with her mother. "Kate had an idea that might work. It means adding a few two-seater tables along this wall."

"Show your father tomorrow." Her mother went back to the dining room.

Leslie followed her and bussed some tables, and she stopped to chat with a patron or two. She worked steadily until five o'clock. She helped her father clean the kitchen and sat at the table with her plans. "Do you feel like looking at this now, or do you want to do it tomorrow?"

"Can we talk in the morning, honey? I'm beat tonight." Her father looked tired, and Leslie kicked herself for burdening him.

"Sure, Dad. Mom looks tired, too. You guys go home and get some rest. We'll talk tomorrow." Leslie finished cleaning, hung the closed sign on the door, and went home to her empty house. She found her phone where she'd left it on her kitchen counter and read the missed text message.

We got home safe and I miss you. K

Glad you're safe. Just closed the restaurant and Mom and Dad are pooped. I may hire another server. I miss you, too. Another date this week? L

Leslie put her phone on her charger and settled on her couch to watch the news, but her mind wandered to when she'd be able to spend time with Kate again. She smiled at memories of Portia playing in her living room and Kate's kiss. She sent Kate a text.

Would you and Portia come over for dinner on Friday? L

She didn't have to wait long for a reply.

That sounds nice. We can be there by five thirty. K

Perfect. See you then. L

Leslie put her phone away and went back to the restaurant to try to catch her parents before they left. She couldn't stop thinking about how exhausted they both looked. "Mom? You still here?" she called from the kitchen.

"We're here, honey." She came out from the storage room.

"I want to talk to you guys about something." Leslie stopped to gather her thoughts.

"Can it wait until tomorrow? We're both exhausted, honey." Her mother sat next to her father who'd settled at the small kitchen table.

"It won't take long. Paul will be in the kitchen all day tomorrow and Trish and I will handle the dining room. I'd like you two to take a few days off."

"The way my feet feel right now, we say yes." Her mother looked at her dad and they both nodded.

"Good." Leslie hugged her mom and dad and went home to revise the work schedule. She checked the time and called Trish.

"Sorry to call you on a Sunday evening, but I need to revise the work schedule a little."

"No problem. I'm usually up until ten. What do you need?"

"My mom and dad will be off tomorrow, so I'll help you in the dining room."

"Sounds good. I'll be in by eight."

"One more thing. You mentioned a cousin who was looking for work. Do you think she could stop in to talk to me?"

"I'm sure she will. Carla's a good worker. I think she'd work out well for you."

"Thanks, Trish. See you tomorrow." Leslie hung up and tapped a pen against the table. She had coursework to do, scheduling to work out, and she wanted to do something nice for her parents. But all she could really think about was Kate.

CHAPTER NINETEEN

A re you sure, honey?" Kate asked Portia.
"I saw Momma Wendy." Portia repeated her statement and pointed to the window on the side of the house. "She waved."

"Okay. Let's get your pajamas on." Kate had worked later than usual and came home to Portia's questions about Wendy, and whether she was going to be living with them again. "It's past your bedtime." She waited until Portia was asleep before going downstairs to talk to Deanna.

"Hey. Portia asleep already?" Deanna asked.

"Yep." Kate's thoughts raced. "She told me Wendy waved at her through the window today. She might've been trying to find out if we're here, but it sounds like she knows." Kate began pacing.

"It'll be okay. I'll ask Marta to keep an eye out for her. If she comes back, she'll call the authorities and they can arrest her."

"Thanks, Deanna, but I hate that Marta has to worry about that. Do your cameras record?"

"No. Sorry. They're inexpensive ones to watch the wildlife around the house. There's a monitor in the kitchen, and you know Marta won't mind helping you."

"I know. I'm going to have to think about what to do." Kate went back upstairs to consider her options. She hated the thought of moving again, but she wouldn't stay and subject her sister's family to Wendy. She grabbed her phone and called Joy.

"Hi, Kate. It's good to hear from you."

"Hi, Joy. Sorry to call this late but I need to ask you something."

"No problem. What's up?"

"You told me you had a friend who had a small duplex for rent. Could I get her phone number?"

"Sure. Are you moving again?"

"Wendy showed up here today and I'm worried, so I'm considering it. Thanks for her number." Kate wrote down the number and went to check on Portia who was sound asleep. Her thoughts bounced from grabbing Portia and driving as fast and as far away as she could until she felt safe and taking the time to plan an escape. Her parents would welcome them with open arms, but Wendy knew where they lived and would probably figure she might go there. The hollowness in her gut at the thought of being so far from Leslie took her unawares. They needed to find a place Wendy wouldn't suspect. She'd check out Joy's friend's duplex and decide. She considered how Portia would take another move and groaned. She was unquestionably the worst mother in the world. She pushed aside her jumbled thoughts and went to bed.

The next morning Kate woke early and went downstairs to talk to Marta.

"You're up early," Marta said as she poured coffee into a mug.

"A little. I wanted to tell you about Wendy."

"Deanna told me yesterday, honey. I'm sorry you're going through such a hard time. Let me know if I can do anything."

"I have a restraining order against her, but she knows where Deanna lives so if you see her lurking around, I'd appreciate it if you'd call the police."

"Oh, you better believe I will."

"Thank you, and I'm so sorry to put you in that position."

"It's no problem if it helps you get her out of your life." Marta set a full cup of coffee in front of her. "I know you're probably tempted to run again, darling. I understand that. But remember that you're always stronger with people who love you surrounding you than you are alone."

Kate gave her a quick hug, but she wasn't sure that was true. If it put the people she loved in danger, then it wasn't worth it. But the thought of a move far away from her family broke her heart. And she couldn't deny her growing feelings for Leslie and her frustration at the inability to keep her safe from Wendy's wrath. Maybe it would be best to leave the state. Her head spun with conflicting thoughts, so Kate went to check on Portia and found her halfway down the stairs. She watched her navigate the steps for a few minutes. She was growing faster than Kate could keep up and she was about to uproot her again. She picked her up when she reached the bottom of the stairs and twirled in a circle before dancing into the kitchen. Portia's smile and giggles erased some of her anxiety.

After breakfast, Kate dressed and made sure she carried her pepper spray to her car. There was no sign of Wendy, but Kate couldn't let down her guard. She took a different route to work and kept a close eye on every intersection and cars behind her. She arrived early and took time to call Leslie.

"Good morning."

"Hi, Leslie. I needed to hear your voice this morning."

"What's up?"

"Wendy showed up yesterday and waved to Portia through a window at the house."

"Oh no. I'm sorry she found you. What can I do?"

"Just talking to you helps. I'm still planning to make it on Friday, but we'll be moving again." Saying the words out loud made her stomach turn.

"Let me know if I can help. I'm making some changes here to give Mom and Dad time off, but you're important to me. I'll make time for you."

"Thanks." Kate hesitated and took a breath. "You're important to me, too. I'll let you know what happens. Take care."

"You, too."

Kate clutched her pepper spray and went into work. She used her lunch hour to contact the name Joy had given her and arranged to meet her after work. She ignored her racing thoughts and concentrated on driving to the address the woman had given her. A security light lit the whole parking area behind the building. She noted the security coded entrance and followed the woman inside the building. She offered the security deposit as soon as they entered the two-bedroom unit and she saw the couch and small dining room table. She drove home feeling more relaxed than she had in a long time. That much security would provide more peace of mind, at least when they were home, and the location was far away from the route she was taking to work. Hopefully, Wendy would look for her in the opposite direction. She pulled into her sister's driveway and scanned the area around the house before getting out of her car and rushing inside.

"Welcome home, Kathryn," Marta called from the kitchen.

"Hi, Marta." She'd miss coming home to her. She'd miss the safety of the family atmosphere so like her childhood. She flinched at the stab of shame for the situation she'd put herself and her child in. It had to change. "No visitors today?"

"No, honey. You relax. If she shows up again, we'll have the police here right away."

"Thank you. I love you." Kate didn't try to hold back her tears as she pulled Marta into a hug.

"I love you, too." Marta held her at arm's length. "Portia's upstairs playing with a dollhouse Rob brought home for her."

Kate chuckled. "Of course he did." She loved her brother-in-law despite his somewhat sexist views. He treated Deanna well, and Portia would grow up to be who she was meant to be with or without a dollhouse. Kate laughed out loud when she saw Rob seated on the floor next to Portia explaining the importance of backup batteries for sump pumps.

"Mommy!" Portia ran to her, and Kate picked her up and hugged her.

"Did you thank Uncle Rob for the gift?" She smiled at Rob when he stood.

Portia nodded.

"She did," Rob said. "I hope you don't mind."

"Not at all. It's important she learn about sump pumps." Kate barely managed not to burst out laughing.

Rob shrugged. "Next week we'll discuss different types of roof shingles. See you, little one." He kissed her cheek and left.

Kate danced across the room until Portia giggled then she set her on her bed. Could she uproot her again when she was settling in? This had to stop soon. "Mommy's going to change clothes now. You play with your new house, okay?"

Portia slid off the bed and began piling her stuffed animals on top of her new dollhouse.

Kate changed quickly and returned to find Portia still on the floor trying to balance her stuffed donkey on the house. She watched her for a few minutes striving for words she'd understand to explain why they were moving yet again. She decided it could wait another day. She had plans to make. "Ready to go downstairs for dinner?" Portia nodded and picked up her ever-present teddy bear as they headed to the kitchen.

"Dinner will be ready in fifteen minutes. Deanna's in the den," Marta said as she stirred something cooking on the stove.

Kate went to the den and sat in the chair she'd occupied many times.

"You look stressed." Deanna tipped her head and stared at her.

"Yeah. I secured a flat today. We'll be moving again soon." She watched Portia settle in the corner next to the fireplace.

"You don't have to do that, you know. We have cameras outside and the police on speed dial." Deanna looked at her seriously.

"I know, and I appreciate it, but I don't know what Wendy is capable of anymore, and you have to go to work and have a life. You can't sit home and watch for her or worry about her lurking around. I can't bear the thought of you and your family being at risk because of all this. I've got to find a way to get rid of her, but until I do, I don't want to endanger anyone else."

"I wish you'd stay, but you do whatever you need to and let us know how we can help. You know we're always here for you."

"Thanks. For now, I'm staying local because I don't want to leave you. But there may come a time when I have to find somewhere I really don't think she'll find us." Kate sighed and felt the weight of the world on her shoulders. How many more times would she allow Wendy to chase her away? Marta's call to dinner interrupted her thoughts.

The next morning, Kate headed to work with a plan. She'd looked up daycares in the area and picked out a couple she'd contact at lunch time. She parked in her usual spot and gave in to her desire to hear Leslie's voice.

Leslie answered immediately. "This is a nice way to start my day. Good morning."

"Morning. I need to go into work in a minute, but I wanted to say hello." She'd been missing Leslie since she and Portia had left her house.

"Will you still be able to make it to dinner Friday?"

"Yes. I'm looking forward to seeing you." Kate didn't mention the physical craving she couldn't shake whenever Leslie was near.

"Me, too. Do you like beef stew?"

"Sounds good to me, and I think Portia will like it. I guess I better get to work. I doubt I'll move before Friday, but I'll let you know." Kate smiled at the sense of relief created by the short conversation. She checked the parking lot and clutched her pepper spray as she walked to the building.

CHAPTER TWENTY

The pumpkin Leslie had been working on for half an hour still looked lopsided. She'd gotten the idea from a magazine and thought it would be fun to carve a few for the restaurant. There was still time until Halloween, but she'd noted many houses had begun decorating. She knew the pumpkins and corn stalks would bleed into November and Thanksgiving until the snow fell and lights would be added to meld with Christmas. She hated that most people combined the holidays and called it the holiday season. Her parents had always made a point to celebrate Thanksgiving and Christmas separately. Halloween was for kids and candy, Thanksgiving for turkey and pumpkin pie, and Christmas for church, lights, and decorated evergreen trees. She decided to leave the crooked faced pumpkin as it was and pretend it was intentional. She put it aside in her workshop which was half of her garage and began working on the next pumpkin.

Her thoughts strayed to Kate as they did most days now. She couldn't imagine moving so many times. Portia must be a resilient kid to be so easy-going after being displaced so often. She put aside the third pumpkin for Friday. Maybe Portia would enjoy helping to carve it.

She checked the time and went to ensure things were going smoothly at the restaurant. Trish and Carla were busy taking orders, so she went to the kitchen. "Hey, Paul. You doing okay here alone?"

"Oh yeah. So far so good. Thanks for asking." Paul's grin nearly matched her dad's in exuberance.

"Okay. Let me know if you need anything." She went to the dining area to refill coffee cups and water glasses and confirm everything was going smoothly before leaving to check on her parents. She took a deep breath and gathered her thoughts before knocking on their door. Her intention was to give them time off to rest or do whatever they wanted, but the restaurant was their life. She needed to assure them they were still needed and important to its success.

"Come in, honey. We're watching the news," her mom called from the living room.

Leslie grinned at the scene when she saw them cuddled together on the couch. "You look comfortable. Anything important going on?" She sat in the recliner next to the couch.

"Nothing new. How're things at the restaurant?" her father asked.

"So far so good. I hope you're enjoying some free time. You look like you're feeling better."

"We miss the place, but we agree this was a good idea for a little while." Her mother settled closer to her dad as she spoke. "It's a nice change to be able to watch the news together with our coffee in the morning."

"Good. I just wanted to check in with you and make sure you were doing okay. I know you're used to working hard and keeping busy every day. I wanted to be sure you knew you're missed and that I'm looking forward to you returning to work." The thing with Kate's ex had her a little spooked, and she wanted to make sure her parents hadn't been affected or approached.

"We know, honey, and you don't have to worry. We'll be back, but we appreciate the short break."

Leslie relaxed. Her concern that she'd pushed her parents away and upset them evaporated. "I'm carving a few pumpkins for Halloween, and I'm putting your pumpkin pie on the menu starting this weekend."

Her mother grinned. "I've already started making the crusts."

"Great. I know I'm looking forward to them."

"Have you seen Kate lately?"

Leslie's pulse jumped, and she took a breath. She hadn't mentioned Wendy to them and didn't plan to involve them. Partly to protect Kate's privacy, and partly to avoid upsetting them or giving them anything to worry about. "She's coming over for dinner Friday."

"Say hello to her for us. She's so sweet."

"I will." She relaxed for a few minutes to enjoy time with her parents. The changes she'd made to give her parents time off affected her as well. She missed their morning meetings to discuss the day and work together to ease the lunchtime rush. "I'll check on you tonight. Call if you need anything." She made one circuit through the dining room to check on things and went back to her pumpkins. She finished cleaning her work area and turned out the lights before heading back to the restaurant. She reached for the restaurant door and flinched at the voice behind her.

"You keep away from her or you'll regret it!"

Leslie turned and caught sight of Wendy's back as she hurried away from the building. She followed her to see what kind of car she was driving but couldn't read her license plate as she raced away. She checked her watch and noted the time and place, and as much about her car as she could. She decided to walk around the building to make sure everything was secure and swore when she saw the broken window on the supply room. She checked inside the room and found nothing missing but there was a message scribbled across the wall.

You will be sorry. You'll find out when you least expect it. She's mine!!

She picked up her phone to call Kate and left her a message when she got her voice mail. At least she'd know what was going on if she checked her phone. She tried to push Wendy out of her mind and took a picture of the wall before she went back to the restaurant. She helped Trish and Carla until closing at eight and then relieved Paul in the kitchen for cleanup. She'd just finished when Kate called.

"Hi there. You got my message?"

"Yes. I'm so sorry, Leslie." Kate's voice broke.

Leslie couldn't stand to hear the anguish in Kate's voice. "It'll be okay, sweet…Kate. She yelled at me and left a threat on the storage room wall then left."

"We need to put you on the restraining order. I'll do it tomorrow if I can't get through tonight."

Leslie flinched at the idea of needing something like that. "Okay. Does it cover the restaurant?'

"I'll make sure it does." Kate sounded steadier.

"Good. I'm not going to say anything to Mom and Dad unless I have to. They're enjoying some time off right now anyway."

"God, what a mess!"

"What kind of wine do you like?"

"Huh?"

"You said something about a glass of wine once, so I'll get a bottle for dinner tomorrow."

"That's sweet. I like a merlot."

"We'll have a nice meal and relax, and you can forget all about Wendy."

"You make it sound easy."

"I know it's not, but I'll do what I can to distract you." Leslie cringed at the way it came out, but didn't say more.

"Okay. I'll see you tomorrow. Good night."

"Good night, Kate." Leslie locked all the doors before going to clean off Wendy's note on the wall. She didn't want anyone to see it and be frightened. She made sure everything was safe and went to check on her parents. She found them still snuggled on the couch. "Hi, you two. I wanted to say good night." Her mother stood slowly and eased a pillow under her sleeping father's head.

"I'm glad you did, honey."

Leslie followed her mother to the kitchen. "Is Dad feeling okay?"

"Yes. He's taking full advantage of this little break from work. I wanted to talk to you about that."

Leslie pulled a chair out for her mother and made them both a cup of tea before sitting opposite her at the table. She sipped her tea and waited.

"You're a good daughter and we love you very much."

Leslie heard a *but* coming and held her breath.

"We always planned for you to take over the restaurant when we retired, and I want to be clear we are not retiring yet, but we talked things over and we want to sign the restaurant fully over to you. You have new ideas. Good ideas. And we see you care about the place as much as we do. Would you let us do that for you?"

Leslie released the breath she was holding. "Of course, Mom. I'm honored you trust me with it. Is there a reason you want to do this now instead of waiting until you're ready to retire?"

"We don't see a reason to put it off. We've been thinking of a vacation and we're not getting any younger, so we figure, why wait."

Leslie considered her mother's words and couldn't deny the truth in them. They'd worked hard their whole life and deserved to enjoy the fruits of their labor. "I remember when Yia-yia was alive, and you and dad took care of her as well as worked hard to make the restaurant a success. I learned what dedication and hard work could achieve." Tears welled when Leslie thought of her grandmother.

Her mother took her hand from across the table and gently squeezed it. "I still miss her, too."

"I guess I'll go and let you get back to your couch." Leslie grinned. "Thank you for your trust in me. I'll do my best."

"We know you will. We'll be in tomorrow to help out. Sitting on the couch all day isn't who we are, but it was a nice diversion. I'm going to get your father into bed and see if he's frisky after his nap."

"Frisky?" Leslie sputtered.

"We've got a few years on us, but we're not walking around with one foot in the grave." She winked and left the room.

Leslie made sure her parents' door was locked when she left. She chuckled at the thought of them being "frisky" but didn't deny the thought sounded pretty good when Kate came to mind. She put on her flannel pajamas and crawled into bed. She couldn't settle her racing thoughts about the changes to the restaurant and her life, but mostly her thoughts about Kate. She had little experience dating and no frame of reference for the feelings that erupted when they spent time together. She understood physical wanting and need, but kissing Kate ignited repressed longings. She'd put all her energy into helping the restaurant prosper and given up on finding the kind of love her parents had. With one kiss, Kate managed to bring optimism back. Their relationship might only be friendly in the long run, but she clung to the possibility of more. She tossed and turned but sleep eluded her. She began to doze off when her phone chimed. Her first thought was of something wrong with her parents.

She didn't look at the readout and her heart rate soared. "Hello?"

"I wanted to say good night."

Kate. Leslie relaxed. "I'm glad you called." She didn't admit to her recent thoughts.

"Should I apologize for waking you, because I'm not sorry."

"No apology needed. I like hearing your voice. And I was awake."

"Thank you. I really just wanted to hear your voice before I went to bed. Sleep well."

"You, too, and hugs to Portia." Leslie fell asleep smiling.

The next morning, Leslie woke to the sound of tires screeching in the parking lot. She rose and looked out the window as Wendy's car sped out of the lot. She dressed quickly and hurried to the restaurant to confirm that all the windows and doors were locked. She didn't see anything amiss until she went behind the building where the garbage bin resided. The words, *She's mine!* in red paint was scrawled across the front. She walked around the building to be sure nothing else was damaged and there were no other messages from Wendy before she took a picture of the desecrated bin. She couldn't help thinking that Wendy was rather unoriginal in her repeated choice of words. And having to wash paint off things all the time was tiresome. Once again she was reminded that Kate had lived with this for far longer and her heart ached for her.

CHAPTER TWENTY-ONE

K ate unpacked the box with dishes and silverware and set the small table. Her decision to move had disturbed Deanna, but she was done worrying about Wendy showing up at her house. It was bad enough her life was disrupted; she didn't want theirs to be. Her family was too important to her to flee cross-country and have Portia grow up a stranger to them, so she hugged everyone good-bye and gathered Portia's toys and their clothes and met the delivery truck with their beds on it that day. She poured herself a cup of coffee and a glass of milk for Portia and put a tuna sandwich on each of their plates.

"Mommy?" Portia stood in her bedroom staring at the box that contained part of her toddler bed.

Kate's throat tightened. How many times would her little girl have to move? "That's your bed, honey. I'll put it all together after we eat." They finished their sandwiches and Kate answered more of Portia's why questions as she set up her bed.

"Why are we here?"

"We live here now, honey."

"Why?"

"Well, we were only at Aunt Deanna's and Uncle Rob's until I could find us a good place to make our own."

Portia remained quiet but hugged her stuffed donkey tightly.

"Let's make you a toy box, okay?"

Portia clapped and began to pick up her stuffed animals seemingly content.

Kate used an empty box and cut off flaps and used duct tape to extend one flap to create the top. She made a note to herself to pick up some paint so they could decorate her creation. "What do you think?"

Portia began to hand her stuffed animals and dolls to fill the box.

When the box overflowed, Kate decided she needed a bigger box. She sighed, certain once again that she was the worst mother ever, and wrapped her arms around Portia until she squirmed away. "I love you, honey."

"I love you, Mommy."

Kate held back tears. Her little girl was beginning to speak in full sentences, and she swore she'd grown two inches since she'd moved from Ohio. She left Portia playing in her new bedroom and cleaned up the dining room table. She settled on the couch that had obviously seen better days and called Leslie.

"Hi there." Leslie's voice held a smile.

"Hi. I wanted to hear your voice." Kate realized it was the middle of the day and Leslie was probably busy at the restaurant. "I won't keep you."

"No problem. I'm hanging out to help if I'm needed. So far, I'm deemed unnecessary."

"We moved out of Deanna's house this morning."

"When you get here tonight, I'll get your new address."

"Would it be okay if we came early? I ended up taking the day off to move."

"You come anytime you're ready. I've got the stew ready to cook, but do I put your wine in the refrigerator?"

"I like it chilled, but not cold, so if you put it in the fridge for a while and take it out about an hour before we get there, it would be perfect." Kate regretted the explanation as soon as the words were out of her mouth. Leslie had invited them to dinner and was thoughtful enough to buy her wine. It didn't matter if it wasn't the perfect temperature. "But it's not important. Room temperature is fine."

"Okay. Let me know when you leave."

"I will, and, Leslie?"

"Yes?"

"I'm looking forward to seeing you."

"Just hurry over."

Kate checked the time. "We'll be there in an hour." She looked around the empty living room. How much should she invest in this place? Would she have to move again? Since leaving Wendy, she and Portia had essentially become homeless. At least, it felt that way. She ignored her growing melancholy and checked on Portia who was busy moving her stuffed animals from the bed to her new toy box and back. She went to her bedroom and put away her clothes then booted up her computer and ordered a small television and a stand to be delivered the next day. She decided that would be enough until she went back to Deanna's for the few items she had in her basement. She checked Portia was occupied with her toys and hurried to take a shower and change. She searched through Portia's clean clothes and found an appropriate outfit for her to wear to dinner. "We're going to Leslie's for dinner tonight. What would you like to take with you?"

Portia surprised her by pointing to the pathetic toy box Kate had made.

"You want to take the box or only what's in it?"

"I want the box."

"Okay. Maybe Leslie has some paint to make it pretty." Kate loaded the box into her car and tossed in a few of the stuffed animals before strapping Portia into the car seat. She reset the security pad and headed to Leslie's.

Kate checked every car they passed on her route and her rearview mirror obsessively. By the time she reached Leslie's she was ready for a glass of wine. She held Portia's hand until they got to Leslie's door and rang the bell.

"Welcome." Leslie opened the door and stepped aside.

Portia ran past her to throw herself onto the beanbag chair.

"Sorry." Kate started toward her, but Leslie stepped in front of her.

She rested her hand on her arm. "It's okay. Let her play."

The heat from Leslie's touch sent shivers up her arm. She stepped into the warm and cozy room wondering again if Portia was doomed to grow up as a vagabond.

"Thank you for inviting us." She wanted to press against Leslie and kiss her. She took a step back.

"Thank you for coming over. It gets lonely eating alone although I usually eat at the restaurant. I've got milk, juice, and water for Portia. Are you ready for a glass of wine?"

"I think I'll wait until I have some food in my stomach." Who knew what she'd do to Leslie with wine warming her empty belly.

"It'll be ready in ten minutes. I've already set the table." Leslie took her hand and led her to the couch.

"By any chance, do you have some paint?"

Leslie looked at her as if she didn't quite understand the question. "I do."

"I made a toy box for Portia today and it needs painting. Can I bring it in and show you?"

Leslie laughed. "Certainly."

Kate hurried out to get the pitiful looking box and brought it inside.

"I like it." Leslie picked it up and waited for Portia who'd raced over to see why she had her new toy box. "Shall we go to the workshop so you can decorate it? I'll turn the stove off, and we'll go."

Portia nodded and Kate took her hand to follow Leslie to her garage. The area Leslie called her workshop was a sectioned off portion equal to half of her two-car garage. The shelves above the workbench were filled with various cans of paint. She set Portia's box on the bench and Portia on a raised chair.

"What color do you like?" she asked and pointed to a shelf.

Portia looked at Kate and back at the shelf and finally pointed to a can on the far end. "This one?" Leslie asked. Portia nodded and Leslie opened the can and handed her a paint brush then brought down several other colors along with several brushes.

Before Kate could intervene, Leslie wrapped an apron around Portia and stepped behind her. "You go ahead and make flowers or whatever you want. It's your toy box."

Kate watched as Portia brushed red over the front. Leslie gave her a clean brush and showed her how to use a new brush for each color which ended up being several. Kate's heart ached at how good it felt to watch her daughter happily working away with someone Kate had feelings for. If only things could be that easy. Portia's sad looking box turned into a colorful masterpiece by the time they were finished.

"Good job, Princess." Leslie held up her hand to show Portia how to high-five her then removed her paint covered apron and lifted her off the chair. Leslie winked at Kate. "It's all water-based paint."

"Mommy, look." Portia pointed to her box.

"It's beautiful, honey. You did a great job. Let's go have dinner so the paint can dry."

Kate watched Portia skip back across the garage floor to the door to the house. Seeing her daughter so happy had her wiping away tears. She was growing fast, and she had joy in her life. Kate vowed to make sure that didn't change.

"Here is your wine." Leslie filled a wine glass and handed it to her. Their fingers brushed, their eyes met, and Kate's breath caught.

"Thank you," she whispered.

Kate picked up Portia and set her on the tall chair at the table then sat at the one next to her. Leslie set a pot of stew on a trivet in the middle of the table and filled their bowls.

"I have warm rolls and salad. Help yourself."

Kate put butter on a roll and handed it to Portia, surprised by her quiet "thank you." Maybe she wasn't a horrible mother after all. She put a small serving of salad in her bowl and filled her own.

"This looks great. Thanks for inviting us."

"I'm thrilled you could make it. So, tell me where you've moved."

"It's a small lower flat not far from Ferndale. I like that it has a security light in back where I park, and there's a security code needed to enter both the parking lot as well as the building itself. I'll give you the address and you can come over for dinner one day."

"It sounds great. I hope you feel safe there."

"I do, so far." She didn't want to talk about Wendy with Portia sitting so close.

There was a moment of silence as they seemed to search for something to say. "I hired Trish's cousin this week to help in the restaurant. She's working out well. I'll probably get a cook to help Paul, too."

Kate's stomach knotted with fear for Leslie's father, and she set her fork down. "Are your parents all right?"

"Oh, yes. They're taking a little break. Dad is feeling much better, but I think my mom is getting bored."

Kate relaxed and watched Portia pick out pieces of carrots from her bowl, but apparently, she liked peas. Spending time with Leslie felt comfortable, and Portia seemed content. At least at this moment in time, life was good.

CHAPTER TWENTY-TWO

The dishes were in the dishwasher, the table cleared, and Portia was back on the beanbag chair, softly chatting to her teddy as her eyes drifted shut. Leslie refilled Kate's wine glass and made herself a cup of green tea before she settled next to her on the couch.

"Thanks for the great dinner," Kate said. "I'm going to have to get back into the habit of cooking again now that I won't have Marta's help."

"You're welcome anytime, but I admit I rarely cook. I usually eat at work or with my mom and dad. This was a nice change." Leslie clutched her mug afraid if she set it down, she'd pull Kate into her arms. "Is Portia going out for Halloween this year?"

Kate groaned. "I suppose she'll want to. She was a little too young last year, but her cousins have been chattering about it already so she's aware of it."

"You're welcome to bring her to the restaurant. We all dress up and have special treats for the kids. My mom loves it." She hesitated, wondering if she was being pushy. "In fact, I have a pumpkin I saved for Portia to help carve."

Kate smiled. "Thanks, that's incredibly sweet. She hasn't carved one yet. I doubt my nephews would be interested in having a little girl following them on Halloween, either. I know she'd love a pumpkin, but I think her toy box project was enough for tonight."

"Come back tomorrow?" Leslie knew she was pushing but couldn't seem to stop.

"Maybe. I'll let you know. I have a television being delivered sometime after four." Kate finished her wine and took her glass to the kitchen. "Do you mind if I make a cup of tea?"

Leslie sprang off the couch. "You relax. I'll get you one." She stood close to Kate in the kitchen aware Portia was engrossed in play in the living room. She caught her slight grin before Kate pinned her against the counter and pressed her lips to hers.

"I've wanted to do that since we got here." Kate leaned away and spoke softly.

Leslie gave in to her need to feel Kate. She wrapped her arms around her and held her tightly against her. She brushed her lips over her neck grateful for the counter holding her up when Kate tipped her head back in supplication. She nuzzled and kissed, careful not to leave any marks. Kate's whimpers fueled her desire, but the small voice filtering into her lust-filled brain broke their connection.

"Mommy?"

Kate stepped back and Leslie wanted to know if the blush across her cheeks and neck extended over her breasts.

"Right here, honey." Kate gave her a small smile and shrugged slightly before putting more distance between them. She let Portia lead her from the kitchen.

Kate and Portia were rolling off the beanbag chair as if it were a hill when Leslie entered the living room with two cups of tea. She sat and watched for a few minutes while she sipped her tea and wished she were in Portia's place. Kate whispered something in Portia's ear and stood. Leslie didn't look away as Kate strode toward the couch, and she lost herself in the fantasy of Kate straddling her lap, her breasts swaying as she caught a nipple in her mouth. She flicked it with her tongue and stroked the underside of her breast with her fingers. She struggled to breathe by the time Kate reached the couch and settled next to her.

"She's quite the athlete," Leslie said.

"Yeah. Right now anyway. We'll see if it lasts as she grows up." Kate looked at her watch. "I suppose we ought to get home. Such as it is."

"Can you finish your tea before you go?" Leslie intentionally hadn't mentioned Wendy all evening. Kate needed a break from that mess, but now she wondered if she should tell her about her visit to the restaurant. Kate felt safe now, so she didn't need to disrupt her serenity with that news.

"Definitely. Thank you for tonight." Kate lightly brushed her lips over Leslie's and took a drink of her tea.

"I'm glad you came over tonight. I like having you both here."

"I hope you'll come to visit us one day. There's a good chance we'll have carryout, but there's a great Chinese place nearby." Their conversation was interrupted by Portia crawling into Kate's lap. "I think someone is ready to wind down for the day."

"I'll get Portia's box out of the garage for you."

Portia heard her name and jumped off Kate's lap to get to her. "My toy box."

"Yep. Come on. Let's go see how it turned out." Leslie waited for her, surprised when she took her hand. Leslie set the box on the floor for Portia to see. "You did a great job. Do you like it?"

"Pretty," Portia said and pointed.

"Yes, it is." Leslie carried the box into the house and Kate agreed the red, green, blue, and yellow paint-splattered box was beautiful. "Be careful driving and let me know when you get home, okay?"

"I will. Thank Leslie, Portia." Kate rested her hand on her shoulder.

"Thank you." She surprised her again by hugging her.

"You're very welcome, Princess. I hope you come over again soon." Leslie walked them to their car and checked the area around the restaurant once before going back inside her house to wait for Kate's call. It came within twenty minutes.

"Hello."

"Hi, Leslie. We're home. Thank you, again for a lovely evening."

"My pleasure. I hope you come over again soon. Did Portia put her toy box in her room?"

"As soon as we got here. She loves it. Thank you for helping her."

"It was fun. If you think she'd like to carve a pumpkin let me know. I could bring it to you and we could carve it and put it on your porch. If you have a porch."

Kate laughed and Leslie loved the sound. "I do have a porch and that would be awesome."

"Let's plan on it. Let me know when."

"Okay. Sleep well."

"You, too. We'll talk tomorrow." Leslie reminded herself to power wash the garbage bin. She decided early the next morning would be soon enough and went to bed hoping for dreams of Kate's sweet kisses.

The next morning, Leslie rose early and dragged her power washer to the back of the restaurant. She took another picture of it first, cleaned the garbage bin, and chuckled at the irony. This was something she'd needed to do for a long time but kept putting off. "So, thanks, Wendy," she mumbled.

She put the power washer away and took the gourds and pumpkins she'd collected to the restaurant. She placed them along the window ledges and set the corn stalks in the corners of the room before heading to her parents' house.

"Good morning," she called from their back door. She decided to make a lot of noise when she remembered her mother's frisky statement. She hoped she didn't find them chasing each other around the house naked. She went to the kitchen and poured herself a cup of coffee before rattling pans and pretending she was looking for a pot.

"What's all the noise out here?" Her father stood in the hall fully dressed.

She sighed with relief. "Sorry, Dad. I was looking for something for scrambled eggs."

"I'm heading to the restaurant now. I can make you some when I get there. Your mom is in the shower."

"Okay, thanks. I wanted to see how you were feeling."

"I'm fine. I've enjoyed a little time off, but it's time to get back to work."

"I'll see you there." Leslie left the way she came in. She wiped tables when she got to the restaurant and helped Trish check for condiments. She put the carved pumpkin on the counter next to the register and added an LED candle inside it. She stood at the door to scan the room.

"It looks great." Trish rested her hand on Leslie's shoulder as she spoke.

"Thank you. Do you think the corn stalks are too much?"

"Nope. I love it all." Trish smiled. "We're dressing up, aren't we?"

"Sure. It'll be fun. Don't wear a costume too scary for the kids."

"No problem. Scary costumes are mean. I'm going to be a 1950s waitress."

Leslie laughed. "What a great idea. Maybe we should all do that. I'll talk to my mom, and if you don't mind, can you ask Carla?"

"Sure. This is going to be fun."

"It is. Do you have a place where you're getting your costume?"

"Yes, why?"

"Could I impose on you to pick up four of them? I can get you sizes and I'm buying."

"No problem and thank you."

"Oh. If they have any, could you get two outfits for the guys? I think Dad would get a kick out of it." Leslie found her mom arranging a plate of cookies for a table of six. "Hi, Mom. I have an idea I want to run by you. Trish is dressing as a 1950s waitress for Halloween, and I think it would be fun if we all do it. What do you think?"

"I like it. Let me know where to get a costume and I'm in."

"Trish is going to pick them up for me. She needs to know sizes. Also, what do you think of my fall decorations?"

"They're great. You have a good eye." Her mother hugged her and carried the plate of cookies to the dining room.

Leslie took one pass through the dining area and greeted a few people before heading home to create flyers for their Halloween event. She worked until she had a preliminary leaflet and gave in to her craving to call Kate.

"Hey, it's good to hear your voice."

"Hi there. I wanted to tell you about our Halloween plans. If you're interested in coming to the restaurant on Halloween, we've got something special planned."

"I'm going to take Portia to Deanna's neighborhood for a short trick-or-treat, but we could stop by for dinner before we go. What's the plan?"

"You'll find out when you get here." Leslie liked the feeling of planning something for Kate and Portia. Being in a child's life was fun. But what would happen if she got close to her and then they moved again? Maybe out of state. Pushing the unwelcome thought away, she went to get more decorations.

CHAPTER TWENTY-THREE

"M ommy?"

"Be right there, honey," Kate called from the living room. She pointed the remote at the TV and turned on the cartoon channel. Portia came around the corner as Kate turned toward her bedroom. She grinned at her mismatched outfit and held her when she raced into her arms. "Are you okay?"

"I woke up and you were gone."

Kate's chest tightened. She had to stop this constant moving. Portia was a resilient kid, but she could only take so much disruption in her short life. "I found Peppa Pig." Portia's smile eased some of Kate's worry. She left her seated on her Disney princess chair watching cartoons.

She called Sharon, now that she needed a babysitter once again. Leaving Portia with Marta and family had been such a luxury.

"Hi, Kate. Is everything okay?"

"It is. I wanted to say hello and let you know I moved again."

"Oh no. Did Wendy find you?"

"Yes. She showed up at Deanna's, so I found a small flat and moved a few days ago. It's not far from your building, and I wanted to ask you if you'd be available for sitting with Portia?"

"I just started my last semester and it's a light one. I could use the income. What've you got in mind?"

"I found a great daycare for her while I'm at work, but there are events coming up I'd like to attend without her." Kate gave Sharon her address and wrote down her schedule. She hung up, relieved to have her as an option. When this nightmare had begun, she'd been determined never to leave Portia alone, but her therapist had helped her see that it wouldn't be healthy for either one of them, and she understood she had to have a life outside of being a mother sometimes.

She settled on the couch to review the calendar for the LGBTQ center. It wasn't difficult to pick a day and time for a dance, and ignoring the anticipation of having Leslie in her arms was impossible. She put her notes away and watched the cartoon pig dance for a few minutes before going to the kitchen to make breakfast. She found Portia sound asleep on the couch when she returned with a bowl of oatmeal. "Time for breakfast, honey." She set the bowl on the end table and gathered Portia in her arms. Her phone rang and Portia squirmed to her side.

"Hi, Deanna."

"Hey, sis. You move and forget about us?"

"Sorry. I've been busy working and settling in. We're still planning on Halloween night."

"I'm teasing. I do miss you, though, and Marta says hi."

"I miss you, too. And Marta was a lifesaver for me and Portia. I called my former babysitter, so I can make time for the LGBTQ center."

"You can always drop her off here, you know. Marta would be thrilled."

It was a nice idea, but going back to Deanna's with any regularity would keep them in harm's way. "Thanks, Dee. I'll keep that in mind."

"So, you're feeling safe there?"

"I am. I haven't seen Wendy since I moved."

"Good. Let me know if you need anything, okay?"

"Thank you. I will." Kate disconnected the call and made a decision. "Would you like to go for a ride with me this morning?"

Portia hopped off the couch and went to the door.

"Hang on. We need to get dressed, sweet girl."

Kate gathered her notes and calendar and retrieved their coats before going to her car. She put her in the toddler stroller when they arrived and entered through the back door of the LGBTQ center. She checked the empty activity room where she intended to hold the dance and watched Portia look at the ceiling but remain quiet. She expected there would be many questions later. She made a few notes about the room and envisioned decorations. "Ready to go?"

Portia looked at the ceiling again. "Big." She pointed upward.

She'd never seen a high ceiling before, so Kate pointed to the ceiling and said, "*Tall.* It's a tall ceiling. Okay. Let's go." Kate could tell Portia had questions and she'd address them the best she could. "We're going to see the nice lady." Kate hadn't planned anything except going home, but once the words were out of her mouth, she knew she wanted to see Leslie. She loaded Portia and her stroller in her car and headed to Leslie's.

Kate parked in the back of the restaurant and took Portia's hand as she led her to the building. There were a few people at tables, but most of the dining area was empty. She checked her watch and realized it was later than she thought. Her pulse jumped when Leslie ambled toward her from the kitchen smiling.

"It's good to see you again so soon," she said.

"We were out so I thought we could stop and get a bowl of soup."

"Sit anywhere, and two bowls of the soup of the day coming up."

Kate relaxed in her seat and waited for Leslie to return. She smiled at Portia pointing to the pumpkins and gourds on the window ledges. She probably would enjoy carving a pumpkin. "Elena. It's good to see you." Kate stood and hugged her when she came to their table.

"And hello to you, Portia. I hope you like my special vegetable soup. And here is a special treat for dessert." Elena put a plate with baklava in front of her soup bowl. You two enjoy and I hope I see you on Halloween. It's going to be fun." She went back to the kitchen.

Now her curiosity got the best of her. She would definitely bring Portia back to see what Leslie had planned. She hoped it included her in a skimpy Halloween outfit. She finished her soup pleased to see Portia enjoy hers. She sipped a cup of coffee and hoped Leslie would have time to visit. Her hopes were fulfilled when Leslie came to her table and sat next to her.

"How's your new place?"

"It's good. We're settling in."

"Good. Do you have time to stop by and work on that pumpkin?"

Kate turned to Portia. "Would you like to learn how to carve a pumpkin?" Portia wrinkled her brow and looked between them.

"If you don't like it, we'll stop. Okay?" Leslie asked.

Portia reached for her baklava and took a huge bite.

"I guess that's her answer." Kate chuckled. "We'll be over as soon as she's done eating and I finish my coffee."

"I'll see you later then." Leslie reached under the table and gently squeezed her thigh before leaving.

Kate gulped down her coffee and wrapped Portia's leftover dessert in a napkin. "Let's go, honey." She left money on the table and took Portia's hand as they walked to Leslie's.

"Welcome." Leslie opened the door. "I think she's grown two inches since last week." Leslie hugged Portia.

"Thanks for confirming my suspicion. I'll have to buy her new clothes soon."

"Beanbag?" Portia asked.

"Of course." Leslie laughed as Portia ran to the beanbag chair.

"We're going to carve a pumpkin, huh?" Kate sat on the couch and sighed when Leslie sat next to her.

"Yep. Whenever you're ready. I already cut the hole in the top and cleaned it out. I thought Portia would like to help cut out the face."

"Let's give her a few minutes to enjoy the chair."

"Okay. Come into the kitchen. I want to show you something." Leslie took her hand. As soon as they were out of the view of the living room, Leslie leaned into her, pressed her against the counter, and kissed her.

Kate melted into her arms. "Mm. I like what you're showing me." She rested her arms over Leslie's shoulders and took a deep breath to settle her raging libido.

"Mommy?" Portia's voice pulled Kate from her intended exploration of Leslie's mouth.

"Guess I need to go." She placed a quick kiss on her lips and slid out of her embrace.

"I'm right here," Kate said as she went to the living room. "Are you ready to carve a pumpkin?"

The frown on Portia's face indicated her struggle to understand.

"Leslie is going to show us how to do it." She took Portia's hand and followed Leslie to the garage.

Leslie cut out triangle eyes and a smiley mouth as Portia watched and clapped when it was finished. Leslie added an LED candle, put it in a large plastic bag, and handed it to Kate. "It's a little heavy, so your mom will carry it for you."

"Thank you," Kate said as they walked to her car. She set the bag carefully in the back seat next to Portia's car seat. "I'm definitely planning a dance at the center. Will you go with me?"

"Just tell me when," Leslie said.

"I'm hoping for next Saturday. I'll know this week if everyone agrees, and we can get enough volunteers to make it happen so quickly."

"Sounds great. Be careful driving home and let me know you got there, okay?"

Kate wanted to kiss Leslie, but she hesitated. Portia had already had so many adjustments and trying to explain Leslie's role in their lives would only confuse her, especially since she didn't know yet herself what they might be to each other. She smiled and waved as they backed out of the parking spot. She turned to pull onto the main road and slammed on her brakes as a car stopped directly in front of her. Wendy jumped from her truck and stomped toward her car, the sneer in her expression something from a horror movie.

Kate took a quick glance behind her and backed the car up enough to turn around and head out the side exit. She kept an eye on the review mirror as she forced herself to stay within the speed limit. She pulled onto a side street and called 911. She knew the report she made was to make herself feel better. Wendy was probably long gone, but she quickly called Leslie to tell her in case

Wendy was still around. She checked on Portia in the back seat and took a couple of settling breaths before taking a roundabout route home. She settled Portia in her room when they arrived and allowed the fear and frustration from Wendy's intrusion in her life to wash over her. Her stomach ached from worry over her situation. She'd run from her abuse but hadn't escaped. She swiped away tears and paced in her living room trying to force answers to her dilemma to materialize. Did she want to subject her daughter to a life of running? She absolutely didn't want to spend the rest of her life living in fear. She took another deep breath. She'd take life one day at a time and protect Portia at all costs. But at some point, it had to end. She wouldn't raise her daughter in a world of fear. She wouldn't.

CHAPTER TWENTY-FOUR

Leslie made three circuits around the building before she was sure Wendy wasn't in the vicinity. She went to the restaurant to help Trish and Carla but found very few diners. She'd review the receipts for the day to confirm the worth of the extra hours on Sunday, but by the looks of the dining area, they weren't. She found her mom and dad seated at the small kitchen table. "Hi." She leaned on the wall next to them. "It's pretty quiet today."

"Oh, it wasn't earlier. It started to lighten up about an hour ago."

"Maybe it was a mistake to stay open longer on Sunday. What do you guys think?" She was taking over the restaurant, but she'd always appreciate their input.

"We feel it's important to be open for the folks after church, but maybe staying open later isn't necessary. Maybe people still like to have Sunday dinner at home." Her mother shrugged.

"I'll review the receipts tonight and we can talk about it. Okay?"

"Of course. Any time. You're doing an excellent job. We trust you completely." Her mother stood and wrapped her in a hug.

Leslie walked across the parking lot lost in thought. She'd been second-guessing her decisions about the restaurant ever since her parents turned it over to her, but the pressure she was putting on herself was her own doing. Her parents had worked their whole life to make a go of the restaurant, and their success was due in large part to their love for the place. She loved them and respected their dedication. She never questioned her dedication to keeping the restaurant profitable; she questioned her ability to keep the homey relaxed atmosphere that drew so many of their clientele. Many had been friends of her parents for years. Now their children and grandchildren returned to experience the ambiance of the place they'd heard about all their lives. It was a lot to live up to and Leslie needed to balance that with the changing demographics. She'd just walked in the door when Kate called.

"Are you home safe?" Leslie asked.

"We are. It was pretty scary. I'm not sure what Wendy would have done if I hadn't gotten away."

"I checked the area after you called, and she was nowhere to be seen. I called in a report anyway."

"Good. I'm so sorry, Leslie. I don't know how to get rid of her."

Leslie felt her own tears well when she heard Kate's voice hitch. "It'll be all right. She'll make a mistake and they'll catch her." She knew she wanted to convince herself as much as Kate.

"I refuse to let her ruin my life. I'm going to confirm the date of the dance tomorrow. My choice is Saturday evening, and we have plenty of volunteers to make it happen. Will that work for you?"

"I think so. I'll talk to Trish and Carla tomorrow and let you know."

"Okay. Portia says hi. She's excited now that the pumpkin is on the porch. She understands it means something fun but isn't sure what. Anyway, you sleep well. We'll talk tomorrow."

"You, too. Good night, Kate." Leslie put her phone on her charger. She went back to the restaurant and noted the absence of diners. She checked the time and saw they'd be open for another half hour.

"Hi, Leslie." Trish came from the kitchen with sugar packets. "You just missed Carla. She took off early since we weren't busy."

"Good. Not that we're not busy, but that she could take off. Has it been slow all day?"

"Oh no. Earlier we could barely keep up. Your mom was surprised. It only slacked off after three."

"Thanks for letting me know. I might've made a mistake staying open until five." She went to the kitchen to have dinner with her parents.

"So, how's Kate and her little girl doing?" Her mother dished pieces of eggplant and braised lamb on plates and salad into separate bowls.

"She's good. I showed Portia how to carve a pumpkin today."

"How fun. Kate is special, isn't she?"

Leslie hesitated. She hadn't completely analyzed her feelings for Kate herself, so she had no idea what to tell her mother. "She is special. She's kind and thoughtful." Leslie set silverware on the small table and forced herself to ignore the feel of her kisses and tender touches. Her mother didn't need to know about that.

"I think she likes you."

"She does, and I like her. I think we could be good friends."

"She seems to be doing a good job raising Portia."

"She's a good kid."

"Maybe you two could date."

Leslie smiled at her mother's hesitancy. "Maybe we will." She laughed when her mother stood and hugged her. She wasn't about to burden them with the knowledge that she'd became part of a stalker's sights.

"You deserve to have someone special in your life."

Her father came into the kitchen and sat at the table. "It's good to see you." He kissed her cheek.

"Leslie and Kate are dating," her mother blurted out.

"That's good." Her father poured salad dressing on his salad.

"Your daughter has someone special in her life. It's a big deal." Apparently, her mom wasn't satisfied with her dad's low-key reaction.

Her dad looked up at her. "Are you happy, honey?"

"I am."

"And she treats you well?"

"She does."

"Then it's a good thing. I'm happy for you. And it will be nice to have a little one around, too."

Leslie hugged her dad. "Thanks."

They finished the meal and Leslie put the dishes in the dishwasher. She'd put soap in the dispenser when her mother called her back to the table.

"We have something to tell you." Her mother sounded excited.

"Okay." Leslie sat next to her.

"Our fiftieth wedding anniversary is coming up and we want to do something special." She glanced at her dad across from her and he grinned. "We've saved a little money for a nice vacation."

"That's great." Leslie pictured her parents relaxing on a beach in Florida.

"We've bought our tickets and made reservations. We'll be leaving on the first of November."

"I'll make sure everything's covered here. Bring me back a refrigerator magnet from the Keys."

"Oh, no, honey. We're not going to Florida. We're going to Hawaii." Her mother beamed and rose to stand behind her father and wrap her arms around him.

Leslie absorbed the news. "Hawaii. That's fantastic. If they sell refrigerator magnets, bring me one of them." She hugged them and began mentally planning for their absence. "How long do you plan to be gone?"

"We'll let you know once we get there." Her dad smirked a little. "Right now it's a one-way ticket. Not that we don't plan on coming back, obviously, but we want to stay until we get bored and want to come back."

"I tell you to take a few days off and look what it leads to!" She laughed and hugged them both, then Leslie left shaking her head. She made sure the building was locked up and carried a bag of garbage out the back door. She lifted the lid to toss in the bag and heard the voice behind her.

"I warned you to leave her alone. She's mine!"

Leslie spun to face Wendy but froze when she saw the knife in her hand.

"You need to move on. Kate wants to start a new life and you need to leave her alone. You can find someone else who wants to be with you." Leslie hoped she sounded fearsome while her hands shook, and her legs threatened to go out from under her.

Wendy looked side to side and swayed for a moment. She appeared to be drunk, and she leaned against the wall as she stared blankly at the ground.

Leslie slid her phone from her pocket and dialed 911. She quickly spoke into the phone and told the dispatcher what was going on. She prayed the police would get there before Wendy came out of whatever trance she was in and left. Maybe keeping her talking would delay her exit. "I know you think she's yours, but there's someone else out there for you. Someone who knows how special you are."

"I *am* special, and I want Kate. She's mine, and I won't let her go." Wendy swayed and braced herself against the garbage bin. "I'll be back to get her, and you better not be in my way." Wendy clumsily swiped at her with the knife before stumbling slightly and hurrying to her car.

Leslie watched Wendy's car disappear around the corner just before the police pulled into the lot with sirens and lights. "Damn her," she muttered.

The police took her statement and a copy of the picture she'd taken of the dumpster with Wendy's note painted on it. There wasn't much they could do except take notes and file a report. She thanked them and called Kate after they left.

"She warned you to leave me alone?" Kate's voice rose as she spoke.

"Yep. But the police are going to make a few passes daily to check on the place and they have a growing list of complaints against her now. They have to catch her in the act at some point."

"I'm so sorry. Short of a police escort everywhere I go, I don't know how to catch her. Maybe you should stay away from me." Kate sobbed.

"Oh no. I'm not going to let her scare me away. I care about you, Kate. I want to be in your life, and I hope you feel the same."

"I do. But I don't want you hurt."

"We'll be careful. We'll start taking pictures if we see her. At least we can prove she was there."

"That would be something, I suppose."

Kate sounded more settled, and Leslie relaxed slightly. "How's Portia?"

"She's good. She loves her pumpkin. She points and giggles and pretty much talks nonstop now about the carving experience."

"I'm glad she had a good time. We'll have to plan some other fun activity soon."

"The dance on Saturday is a go. I'm looking forward to it."

"So am I. Especially the part where I get to hold you in my arms while we dance."

"Yeah. Me, too."

"I have other news. Mom and Dad are going to Hawaii for their anniversary next month. They told me tonight."

"That's great. They deserve a vacation."

"Yeah, they do. Get some sleep tonight, and I'll talk to you tomorrow."

"Good night, Leslie."

Leslie made a cup of tea. The situation with Wendy was getting serious. Kate might be right about needing police protection. A restraining order obviously wasn't keeping her away. She sighed in frustration while considering what type of security to add to the restaurant. She made a few notes for the morning and went to bed.

The next morning, Leslie woke to the sound of rain on her bedroom window. Rainy fall mornings were meant for snuggling in bed with a lover. She rolled over and suppressed her yearning. She had work to do. She made herself a cup of coffee and settled at her computer to search for security systems. At least she could make sure the doors and windows were alarmed in case Wendy tried to break in. But what could she do to help Kate?

CHAPTER TWENTY-FIVE

The daycare parking lot was full when Kate pulled in. She parked and went inside to find the group of children seated at three long tables. Various crayons and paints were spread across them, and each child looked totally engrossed in an art project. Portia saw her and crawled over the bench seat to run to her.

"Mommy, come see." She grabbed her hand and pulled her to the table to show off her handiwork. "This is you, me, and Lelie." She pointed to three stick figures with yellow and green scribbles surrounding them.

"Very nice, honey. You're a good artist." Kate smiled at Portia's inclusion of Leslie. She'd obviously made an impression on her, and it might be hard on her if she had to distance herself because of Wendy. She'd have to figure out a solution soon. "Let's go home now." She gathered all of Portia's drawings and paintings and let her say good-bye to her friends before leading her to the car. She'd made a good choice with this daycare. The owners were retired teachers, and it showed with the progress Portia was making in both her vocabulary and her interactions with other children. She'd informed them that she was having a problem with a stalker, and to please watch for anyone who might try to get close to Portia. They'd understood completely and it helped her relax, knowing that they were aware and would be on guard.

One of her biggest worries about all the moving had been how Portia would relate to other kids, and seeing her today hugging her friends good-bye, helped ease her concerns. She pulled out of the parking lot and checked the area for Wendy. She checked her rearview mirror several times and went around the block twice before pulling into her driveway and triggering the security light. They rushed inside and Kate breathed a sigh of relief. This had to stop. She set a cup of milk on the table for Portia and let her pile her drawing paper in front of her while Kate made dinner.

"Are we going to see Lelie?" Portia asked.

"You want to show her your picture, don't you?"

Portia nodded and looked at her expectantly.

"Maybe we'll go on Friday. Why don't you draw a few more pictures and you can take them all at the same time." Kate set two bowls of macaroni and cheese on the table and sat to eat while Portia took a bite then went back to drawing.

Kate settled on the couch with a glass of wine after dinner to call Sharon. Portia sat next to her engrossed in the *Finding Nemo* movie.

"Hi, Sharon. Would you be available to sit with Portia on Saturday evening?"

"Sure. What time do you need me?"

"I'll confirm it tomorrow, but I'm thinking from four until about eleven. We're hosting a dance at the LGBTQ center."

"It sounds fun. I don't have any plans so let me know what time to be over."

"Thanks. I appreciate it. By the way, my couch folds out to a bed, so if you'd rather not drive home late, you're welcome to stay here."

"I'll keep that in mind. Thanks."

Kate disconnected the call and tamped down her growing excitement. The dance was something she'd been looking forward to since the fundraising committee brought up the idea. She hadn't wanted to make it a Halloween theme, but she'd been outvoted so she expected most people would be in costume. She'd prefer no costumes between her and Leslie when they danced. She chuckled at herself. Maybe Leslie'd wear a genie outfit and those full breasts would press out of the skimpy top. Kate could trace their outline with her fingertips and dip between the cleavage. She shook off the fantasy and concentrated on Portia and the movie.

"Time for bed, young lady." Kate turned off the TV when the movie was over and settled Portia in her bed. She returned to the couch to watch the news and finish her wine before heading to bed.

Kate couldn't remember the dream that pulled her from sleep, but her clit throbbed, and her nipples tightened. Bits and pieces floated to awareness featuring Leslie in a starring role. She rolled over and checked her alarm clock. Plenty of time. She began the exploration to finish what her dream woman started, and as her orgasm surged through her, she cried out Leslie's name. She stretched and rose from bed to start her day, ignoring her lingering arousal.

"Come on, Portia. Mom has to go to work." Kate watched Portia fill her Disney backpack. She helped her zip it closed and let her carry it to the car. She raced ahead of her when they got to the daycare building and Kate grinned at her enthusiasm. "I'll see you this afternoon, honey." Kate kissed her good-bye and went to work. Her mind wandered to her sexy dream and Leslie off and on throughout the morning, and at lunch time she went to her car to call her.

"Hi, Kate. Is everything okay?"

"Yes. I wanted to hear your voice."

"I'm glad. I like hearing yours. I hired another cook today."

"Great. He and Paul will be able to take over while your dad is gone."

"She and Paul. She's been running a kitchen at a sizeable restaurant in Traverse City and recently moved here. I was lucky to get her."

"I told Portia we might stop in on Friday for dinner." Kate wasn't sure why, but she needed to see this new woman who'd be working with Leslie every day.

"Great. I'd love to see you."

Kate relaxed. "I'd love to see you, too. Don't forget about the dance Saturday."

"I won't, believe me. I'm looking forward to it. I'll see you Friday."

"Yes. See you Friday." Kate smiled for the rest of the afternoon.

Portia was in the same seat Kate had found her in every day. Another benefit of having retired teachers at the daycare was their understanding of the importance of consistency for children. Portia could count on having a daily area of her own. She had watercolor paintings scattered in front of her on the table.

"Look, Mommy." She held up a paper with blobs of different colors.

"Beautiful, honey. I love the different colors."

Portia beamed and put all her papers in a neat pile before packing them into her backpack and taking Kate's hand to walk to the car. "Are we going to Lelie today?"

Kate hesitated for a moment. They didn't have to wait until Friday. "Yes. Let's surprise her."

Portia clapped and wiggled in her car seat.

Kate drove through the parking lot twice keeping an eye out for Wendy's car before she parked in the front and took Portia inside. Trish brought her a cup of coffee and Portia a glass of milk. She didn't see Leslie. "Is Leslie in tonight?" she asked.

"Yeah. She's in the back with our new cook, Ronda." Trish took their order and retreated to the kitchen.

Ronda. Kate disliked the name without even meeting the woman. She took a deep breath, realizing she was being silly. She checked her reflection in the metal napkin holder and wished she'd used her rearview mirror. When she glanced up Leslie was striding toward her. Her welcoming smile chased away Kate's uncertainty.

"I asked Ronda to come out to meet you as soon as she's done with your order." Leslie turned to Portia. "Thank you for coming with your mom today, Princess. I see you have your throne."

Portia giggled.

"She wants to show you her artwork." Kate pulled the drawings and painting out of Portia's backpack. "She's quite the artist."

"Oh my. These are wonderful. I can tell you had fun making them." Leslie fussed over them, and Portia continued to giggle.

"Hello. You must be Kate." A stout gray-haired woman set their plates on the table. "It's nice to meet you."

"Thank you. It's nice to meet you, too. I hope you like working here." She relaxed. Ronda was no threat.

"Oh, I love it. I was in a super busy restaurant up north, and I'm not anywhere near retirement, but I wanted a more relaxed atmosphere. This is perfect." She laughed and went back to the kitchen.

"Do you have time to sit for a minute?" Kate asked.

Leslie slid onto the seat next to her. "Yep."

Kate shifted so her thigh rested against Leslie's, pleased to hear her quick inhale. "I plan to be at the center by four to help set up for the dance. Do you want to go with me, or meet me there, or I can pick you up?" Kate heard herself babbling and stopped talking.

"Any one of those things." Leslie grinned. "But I suppose it would make sense for me to meet you there. At four?"

"Yeah. I'll put you to work."

"Sounds perfect."

Kate tamped down her excitement. "I need to tell you the dance committee decided it's going to be a Halloween dance."

Leslie frowned. "Do I have to dress up?"

Kate laughed. "I'm not planning to."

"Good. I won't either. Although, I haven't told you what we're doing here for Halloween. We're all dressing as 1950s waitresses."

"That sounds like fun, but I like a dance to be a dance. To me, a Halloween party is where I'd put on a costume and stand around drinking and chatting." Kate checked the time, surprised how quickly time went when she was with Leslie. She glanced at Portia who was squirming in her seat. She'd finished her meal and was ready to leave. "I suppose we better get home."

Leslie stood and lifted Portia off her booster seat. "I'll see you soon. Thank you for showing me your art."

Portia wrapped her arms around Leslie's neck and Leslie hugged her before setting her on the floor.

Kate took her hand and walked to her car. She strapped Portia into her car seat and turned to get behind the wheel when Leslie grabbed her hands and pulled her into a hug.

"I look forward to Saturday," Leslie whispered in her ear and kissed her quickly.

"I'm looking forward to it, too." Kate slowly moved away and slid behind the wheel. She drove around the lot once and headed toward the exit. She'd almost reached the street when Wendy's car stopped in front of her. Wendy jumped out of the car and ran toward Kate's driver side window. Kate backed up and spun her tires as she raced out of the lot, ignoring Wendy's screams.

"You're mine. You can't get away!"

Chapter Twenty-six

L eslie?" Trish called from the dining area. "Hurry!"
Leslie rushed to see why Trish sounded upset and watched as Kate raced out of the parking lot. Wendy stood ranting and waving her arms but jumped into her car and drove away before Leslie could call the police. She did anyway, so they'd have another report. "Thanks, Trish. That woman is Kate's ex-wife."

"She looks kind of crazy."

"She is." Leslie locked the doors before helping Trish clean the room. "I'll send out an email for a group meeting tomorrow."

Trish nodded and left out the back door.

Leslie checked all the doors were locked and made a final walk-through of the building before engaging her new alarm system and going home. She checked her phone several times hoping for a call from Kate. She finally gave in to her concern and called her.

"Hi, Leslie."

"Hey. I saw Wendy outside when you left. Are you all right?"

"Yes. She tried to get to me again, but I got away. I took a roundabout way home and I lost her, so at least, she doesn't know where I live now."

"You and Portia are welcome to stay with me if you need to."

"Thank you. Portia is thriving in her new daycare, and I'm settling in, and I really don't want to move again if I don't have to."

"I'm having a group meeting with our employees tomorrow, and I'm going to ask them to keep an eye out for Wendy, as long as you're okay with it." She waited, hoping Kate would agree. Keeping people in the dark wasn't a good idea.

"I think it's a good idea. I made another report last night."

"Good. Get some sleep tonight and give Portia a hug for me."

"I will. Good night, Leslie."

Leslie went to her computer to compose an email to her employees.

The next morning, Leslie woke early and went to talk to her parents.

"Good morning, honey. You're here early. Is everything okay?" Her mother looked concerned.

"It is. I wanted to let you know I'm having a meeting with our employees today." Leslie organized her thoughts, not wanting to concern her parents. "Kate is having trouble with her ex-wife. That's the main reason I had the new alarm system installed. I want to tell everyone to let me know if she shows up here."

"Has she threatened you?" Her father looked angry.

"Honestly, she's warned me to stay away from Kate a couple of times, and I think she graffitied our garbage bin, but I worry more about her hurting Kate or taking her little girl."

"Do you want us to cancel our trip?"

"No way. You guys deserve a dream vacation. You go and enjoy yourselves. I'll let you know if anything serious happens. But I'm sure it won't. I'm just taking precautions."

Her parents looked at each other and appeared to come to an agreement. "Okay, but you be very careful."

"I will. I promise." She left them to relax for a while, but she felt better. Now that they knew, they could also watch out for their own safety. Was she making a mistake, getting involved with a woman who had this kind of baggage?

No. Kate was worth it, and some nut job who couldn't take no for an answer wasn't going to ruin something good.

The next morning, Leslie set five place settings on one of the tables and waited for Trish and the others to arrive. She made notes while she waited.

"Hi, Leslie." Trish sat at the table with her.

Ronda, Paul, and Carla arrived five minutes later and settled at the table with them.

Leslie poured them each a cup of coffee and set a plate of baklava on the table. "Thanks for coming in early. I don't want to scare anyone, but the woman I'm dating, Kate, has an ex-wife stalking her. She's shown up here a few times to warn me away from her, so I wanted all of you to be aware of it." She described Wendy to them and told them what kind of car she drove and included the fact that she'd threatened her with a knife. "If you see her on the property, call the police. There's a restraining order against her, and she could turn violent, so don't approach her. Do you have any questions?"

"I do. If I see her and punch her lights out, will I get in trouble?" Ronda grinned.

"I believe the police would call it something like 'defense of a third party,' but we'd all have to agree we felt our lives were threatened by her." Leslie laughed. "I'm not sure what she's capable of, so if you see her just call the police and don't put yourselves in danger."

Nobody else spoke so Leslie went over the work schedules and the group dispersed. She went to check on her parents and found them in the kitchen helping Paul and Ronda.

"Your parents are amazing," Ronda said. "I've been in this business for years, but I've learned several shortcuts this morning. And I'm putting together a recipe book with their Greek dishes."

"Thank you, Ronda. I've often thought of doing that." Leslie hugged her parents and went home to update the schedule in her computer. She finished the update and checked the time. Kate would be at work. She hesitated for a second then dialed her number. She could hear her voice on her voice mail if nothing else.

"Hi, Leslie. Is everything okay?"

"Yes. I wanted to say hello. I had the meeting with everyone this morning and told them about Wendy. We'll all keep an eye out for her. Are you and Portia okay?"

"We are. I don't think Wendy has found out where we live, and I hope it stays that way."

"Good. I won't keep you."

"I'm glad you called. Take care."

"You, too." Leslie put her phone away and concentrated on the new design for the dining room. She moved tables and added separation walls, and then rearranged everything. She picked out new upholstery and tested various color schemes. She saved her work and made a mental note to show it to Kate. Once her thoughts went to Kate, she gave up on any more work and went to help Trish and Carla in the dining room.

"Hi, Leslie," Joy and Nat called from one of the booths.

"Hey, how're you two doing?"

"Great. We didn't feel like cooking tonight so here we are." Nat barely looked up from the menu.

"I'm glad you came."

"Are you going to the dance tomorrow?" Joy asked.

"I am. Kate's on the planning committee, so I'll be there at four to help her set up."

Nat tipped her head and smiled. "It sounds like you and Kate have become an item."

"An item? We're dating, if that's what you mean." She tilted her head. "I think we are, anyway. Kind of. You know how complicated it is."

"I think it's great. What are you wearing?"

"I don't know yet. If you mean a costume, we're not."

"But it's a Halloween theme. You have to wear a costume." Nat looked appalled.

"Kate doesn't want to wear one either. I don't know. Maybe I'll think of something."

"Our costumes are going to be a surprise," Joy said.

Leslie went to the kitchen to retrieve their order and tried to ignore various skimpy costumes she'd love to see on Kate. Maybe she would think of something they could wear after all. She finished out the day and went home to consider an idea. The ring of her phone startled her until she saw the readout. "Hi, Kate."

"Hey. How's everything?"

Leslie stretched out on her bed. "Everything's good. Nat and Joy stopped in for dinner tonight. They'll be at the dance tomorrow."

"It'll be nice to see them."

"Yeah. They said to say hi to you. They told me their Halloween costumes will be a surprise."

"Huh. That'll be fun."

"Yeah. I have an idea about costumes for us, if you're up for it." Leslie paused to wait for Kate's response.

"Okay. What's your idea?"

"Remember the disco dancing era? What if we found disco diva outfits?"

"Disco divas, huh? It could be fun, but where do you find those?"

"Trish is getting 1950s waitress costumes for us for the restaurant. I'll ask her if she can find the divas."

"Okay. Let's do it."

Leslie relaxed. "I guess I'll see you there tomorrow." Something about this didn't sit right with her. "Unless I come and pick you up." She struggled not to hold her breath.

"I'd love it if you came to pick me up, but I promised to stay and help take down all the decorations we'll be putting up."

Leslie released her breath. "I could help with that, too." She winced at the pause in Kate's voice. Something was off. "Is everything okay with you? With us?"

"Yes...No. Sorry, I'm concerned about Wendy. I don't want you hurt, and I'm not sure it's wise to get involved with someone until this is resolved."

"Don't worry about me." Leslie wished she could wrap her arms around Kate. "I'll be fine. We've got an alarm on the restaurant now, and I've started carrying pepper spray like yours. We've filed several reports against her, so they'll catch her." Leslie began to pace. "Please give us a chance."

There was a long moment of silence. "Okay. I'll try to put her out of my mind, but I think we should take two cars. She might leave you alone."

Leslie didn't think which cars they took would matter. "Whatever makes you comfortable. I'll meet you there then. And, Kate?"

"Yes?"

"I'm looking forward to this."

"Me too. Good night."

Leslie sent a text to Trish about looking for costumes and logged on to her computer to research disco divas. She'd come up with the idea off the top of her head, so she needed to find out what she'd gotten herself into. The bell-bottoms wouldn't be too bad, and she could deal with the sparkly shirt. She hoped Kate would choose the low-cut top. She closed down her computer for the night and went to bed.

The next morning, Leslie did the daily walk around the building she'd begun since Wendy's note on the garbage bin. Satisfied things were secure, she went to ready the dining area for customers.

"Good morning." Trish came in carrying a large box. "I've got costumes." She set the box on a table and pulled out the waitress uniforms. "The disco outfits will be in tomorrow. What are they for, anyway?"

"Kate and I are going to a Halloween dance."

"Oh, how fun!"

"Yeah." Leslie smiled and suppressed her fantasy of Kate's skimpy top and tight pants.

CHAPTER TWENTY-SEVEN

"A," Portia said clearly and distinctly as Kate held up the flash cards. She made it to the letter E before hesitating.

"Good job, honey." Kate had been working with her every evening to test her letter recognition. She gave a silent thanks to the daycare center for their support in her expanding vocabulary. Her thoughts strayed to Leslie. She had been so sweet trying to come up with an idea for the dance. Kate wouldn't care if they had costumes, but the more she thought of it, the more it sounded like fun. The pall of Wendy hung over them and had begun to cause her to question everything she did with Leslie. And it was getting old. She had to figure out a way to convince Wendy to move on with her life. She turned on the news and watched Portia carefully color inside the lines of her coloring book characters. Kate cringed at the thought she was raising a child with obsessive-compulsive disorder. She relaxed when Portia gave up and scribbled colors all over the page. The ring of her phone startled her.

"Hi, Leslie. What's up?"

"I'd like to come over, but I don't know where you live. Can I?"

"Okay." Kate gave her the address. "Any particular reason you're coming over?"

"I need to see you, and I have something I want to show you."

"Then I'll see you when you get here." Kate took Portia to bed before picking up her work clothes from the floor and tossing them into her laundry basket. She put her tea pot on the stove and sat back on the couch to contemplate what Leslie had to show her. She peeked out the peephole in the back door when the security light went on, but she didn't see Leslie's car. She grabbed her phone and pepper spray and swallowed back her rising panic. She opened the door a crack to see better and took a settling breath when Leslie stepped into view. She unfastened the chain lock and let her inside. "Where's your car?" she asked as soon as Leslie was safely inside.

"I parked in the shopping center lot and walked here."

"Ah. Thank you."

Leslie took her hands in hers. "We *will* catch her."

"I hope so. What did you bring to show me?"

Leslie held up a bag and followed her to the living room. Kate turned and waited for her to open the bag.

"Wow." Kate held up the sparkly top. "I like it."

"I thought we should try these on to make sure they fit."

"Good idea. There's hot water on the stove, and I left the tea out. Help yourself while I change."

"Thanks."

Kate checked herself in her full-length mirror after she put on the outfit. "Not bad," she whispered and went to find Leslie who had also changed and stood in the living room holding out her hand. She took her hand and they danced. She laughed when Leslie began to sing "Staying Alive." She plopped onto the couch after a few minutes and pulled Leslie down next to her. "We know the outfits work well." She grinned. "I'm glad, but I suppose we should take them off so we don't have to wash them before the dance."

"You're right. Let's change and have some tea." Leslie squeezed her hand and went to the bathroom to change.

Kate changed and found Leslie in the kitchen with two mugs of tea. She handed her one and followed her to the living room couch. "I was only a baby when disco music was popular."

"Yeah, me, too. I think it would've been fun to have grown up with it."

"I'm glad you came over tonight," Kate said.

"I wanted to be sure the costumes fit, and I needed to see you." Leslie stretched one arm along the back of the couch.

Kate automatically leaned into her and sipped her tea. She allowed herself to relax into the warmth of Leslie's body. Fears of Wendy faded away as she basked in the refuge of Leslie. "It feels good to have your arm around me."

"It feels good to have it around you. Do you have to work tomorrow?"

"I'm going in for a few hours. We've got a surgery patient coming in."

"I won't keep you any later then." Leslie stood and took her cup to the kitchen.

"Be careful driving and let me know when you get home." Kate opened the door a crack and looked outside for any sign of Wendy before turning to Leslie. She held her gaze for a heartbeat then grabbed the front of her shirt and pulled her into a kiss. She broke the connection and leaned her forehead against Leslie's. "I've wanted to do that since you got here."

"I'm so glad you did." Leslie stroked her cheek and glided out the door.

Kate took a deep breath and released it, locked the door, and turned out the lights before going to bed. At some point she hoped she wouldn't be doing it alone for much longer. But concerns about Wendy made that hope a slim reality.

Kate woke early and dropped Portia off at daycare on her way to work. She managed to keep her excitement about the dance to a minimum as she picked Portia up from daycare on her way home and rushed home to change.

"Thanks for coming over early, Sharon."

"No problem. I totally love that outfit!"

Kate grinned and twirled. "Thanks. Leslie came up with the idea."

"You're going to have a ball, and I want to hear all about it." Sharon set crayons and coloring books on the table and sat with Portia.

Kate checked her rearview mirror and watched the intersections and parking lots closely as she drove. She finally relaxed when she pulled into the center's lot and saw no sign of Wendy. *Maybe she finally gave up.* She carried the box of decorations into the building and began putting them up. She turned back to the box and laughed as Leslie strode in and tugged her onto the dance floor. She twirled and stepped to music Leslie sang for a few minutes before going back to hanging streamers, ribbons, and paper pumpkins.

Leslie whispered in her ear, "I'll be right back." She left and returned with two cups of apple cider. "I thought we might need to hydrate before all our dancing begins. I saw Joy and Nat by the refreshments. They want us to sit at their table."

"Sounds good. The decorations are done. They look nice, don't they?"

"They do. And so do you." Leslie took her hand and led her to their table.

"You two look amazing!" Joy stood and hugged Leslie.

"You guys are pretty hot yourselves," Kate said. "I love those Roaring Twenties costumes."

"We are going to have a ball!" Nat straightened her super skinny tie.

Kate grabbed Leslie's hand and began what she'd been looking forward to for days. Dancing with her. She twirled and spun and did whatever they thought would be disco moves. The DJ slowed down the pace and Kate moved into Leslie's arms as if they'd been doing it forever. She'd loved to dance since she was a kid, and Leslie shared her fondness for it. She was out of breath by the time they returned to the table.

"I'll get us some cider," Leslie said to everyone at the table.

Kate relaxed with Joy and Nat and enjoyed watching the dancers while they waited for Leslie to return with their drinks. She appreciated the different costumes and laughed at a few outrageous ones. They'd made a good decision to dress up. She watched Leslie as she juggled four cups of cider without spilling a drop.

"If anyone wants donuts, I'll go back to get them," Leslie offered.

"I think we're good. Thank you." Kate spoke for them after checking with Nat and Joy.

"Shall we dance?" Leslie reached for her and Kate took her hand.

"That's what we're here for." She waved at Nat and Joy to join them.

The music slowed and Kate eagerly enveloped herself in Leslie's arms. She caught glimpses of Nat and Joy as they moved about the dance floor wrapped in each other's arms. They held each other with a tenderness and familiarity born from years of intimacy. Kate smiled at her friends as a wave of longing washed over her. It's what she'd always hoped for and thought she'd found with Wendy. She'd been so wrong about her, how could she trust herself with anyone else?

She shook off her musings. They were only dancing.

"Is everything all right?" Leslie whispered in her ear, and her warm breath sent a shiver through her.

"Fine, why?"

"You stiffened in my arms and now you're trembling." Leslie drew her tighter against herself.

Kate rested her head on Leslie's shoulder and immersed herself in the shelter of her embrace. The song was over way too soon for Kate's liking. She held Leslie's hand as they walked back to the table and grinned at Joy and Nat snuggled together. She suspected they'd be leaving soon to go home and tear each other's clothes off. Happiness for her friends warred with envy. She turned her thoughts to Portia and her friends and family and focused on gratitude.

"Would anyone like more cider?" Leslie asked.

Her question pulled Kate from her reverie. "I'll go with you." She walked with Leslie to the refreshment area and hoped the cider was cold enough to lower the heat of the desire burning in her belly. "This dance turned out better than I expected. I'm thrilled we had such a huge turnout."

"It's the best one I've ever been to." Leslie squeezed her hand. "Because I'm here with you."

Kate turned away as she felt the heat rise up her neck to the face. She looked across the room and terror gripped her throat. Wendy leaned against the wall, glaring at them.

CHAPTER TWENTY-EIGHT

Wendy stomped toward them, and Leslie stepped in front of Kate. Her cell phone was in the pocket of her jacket hanging on her chair.

She heard Kate from behind her. "Leave us alone, Wendy." She stepped around her and continued. "Go home and make a life for yourself."

"You're mine and I'm not leaving without you." Wendy moved closer. "You've carried on like you're single long enough. It's time to come home."

"Wendy, we're divorced. We're over and you need to move on."

Leslie saw Nat approach out of the corner of her eye. "Our friend has called the police. They'll be here any minute." She turned toward Nat and waved.

"Kathryn is mine and you need to leave her alone or you'll be sorry." Wendy glanced toward Nat and began to back away. "You'll see, Kate. We're meant to be, and I'll make you understand how wrong it is that you're letting someone else touch you." She turned and slammed open the door so it hit the wall, and then she was gone.

Kate dropped into a nearby chair and held her face in her hands. Leslie stood behind her and rested her hands gently on her shoulders before she spoke. "She's gone. I'm going to get my phone and make a report."

Kate tipped her head back and Leslie wiped tears from her cheek. "I'll do it." She stood and took a deep breath. "She's my problem."

Leslie took Kate's hand to walk back to the table, unsure how to help her. All she could do was be there for her. She watched as Kate went away from the crowd to make her call to the police. She sipped her cider and waited.

"One more report added to the others." Kate slumped in her chair when she returned to their table. "I don't know what to do."

"Can we do anything to help?" Joy asked.

"Thank you, but she's my problem, not anyone else's. I'm just sorry she's messing things up for other people." Kate swiped at a tear rolling down her cheek.

"We'll catch her." Leslie kissed Kate's hand.

Kate gave her a sad smile but remained quiet.

"It's the final dance. Let's make it last." Leslie tugged Kate onto the dance floor, grateful it was a slow song. She held her close and poured all the positive energy she could in her touch. If she held her close enough maybe she could chase away Kate's fears. The music ended way too soon for Leslie and the dim lights brightened. The dance was over.

"I need to stay and help clean up. You can go home." Kate stepped out of her arms.

"No way. I'll help clean up." Leslie hugged Joy and Nat good-bye and began collecting empty cups off the tables. She watched them hug Kate and talk for a moment before leaving. She finished cleaning tables and took the garbage bags to the bin before looking for Kate. "I took out the garbage bags. Are you saving the decorations?"

"Yes. I'll help the rest of the committee take them down. You go home."

Leslie placed her hands on Kate's waist and leaned into her. "I was sort of hoping we'd have time for a good night kiss later."

"I'm sorry, Leslie. I care about you too much to keep putting you in the middle of my mess with Wendy." She kissed her lightly. "You go home and stay safe." Kate turned and started to walk away.

"Wait, sweetheart, please don't shut me out. We can work together to catch Wendy. We can figure something out. Please." Leslie's throat tightened and she forced back tears.

"I'm so sorry, but I can't let you be hurt." Kate didn't look back as she walked away, but Leslie heard the pain in her voice.

Leslie drove home in a fog. She took off the Halloween costume and hung it up to be washed in the morning, moving on autopilot as she reviewed their night. She dropped onto her bed and let the tears fall. She'd thought she and Kate were headed for something serious. Their connection was strong, as were her feelings for Kate. She thought it was reciprocal, so how could she send her away? She answered her own question by recognizing her own sense of protectiveness when it came to Kate. She'd do anything to protect her, and that was exactly what Kate was trying to do. Protect her from the wrath of Wendy. She had to find a way to convince her to let her help. She fell into a restless sleep.

The next morning, she woke to a sense of emptiness. She got up, took a shower, and walked to the restaurant. She shook off her despair and focused on what she had to do. She checked the kitchen and managed a smile for Paul before heading to the dining area to ready it for the day. She checked the condiments were on the tables and wiped them down as well as the chairs. The mindless work kept her from obsessing over her loss and wondering what Kate was doing. She finished and went to check on her parents.

"Hi, honey. How was the dance?" Her mother's excitement increased Leslie's pain as she recalled how Kate had walked away.

"It was a lot of fun, and we had a great turnout. Is everything good here?"

"Oh yes. We were busy but your dad and I enjoyed helping out. It's nice not to be completely in charge anymore."

"Great. Are you ready for your trip?"

"We are." Her mom looked at her dad who was grinning ear to ear.

They needed this vacation. Leslie couldn't remember the last one they'd been on. "Let me know if you need anything besides the ride to the airport." She went back to the kitchen and wandered to the storage room aimlessly. She checked the supplies and made a list of needed items then went to check on Trish and Carla.

"How was the dance?" they both asked at the same time.

"It was great. We had a huge turnout." That was all Leslie could manage to say.

"Cool. You guys had the best costumes," Trish said.

"They were good. Thanks again for picking them up." Leslie watched Trish and Carla glance at each other and walk away. She'd never had a good poker face and probably didn't now. She had to get herself together. She left them to their jobs and went home. She washed the outfit she'd worn to the dance and hung it to dry then lay on her bed and buried her face in her pillow. Memories of Kate in her arms as they danced, the feel of her lips when they kissed, and her smile, and her laugh, and her hair all came together in the woman she'd fallen for. She had to find a solution to the Wendy problem or somehow let Kate go until she felt like she could open herself to someone again. She decided to quit torturing herself and got up to work on the new design for the restaurant. She worked for an hour comparing color combinations and rearranging tables. She sent a few emails to get price quotes and then shut down her computer. She'd get the staff's opinions and incorporate Kate's ideas into a final draft soon. She went to see if her parents needed any help.

"Are you all right, honey?" her mother asked as soon as she walked into the kitchen.

"Sure, why?"

"You're usually here early bustling around."

Leslie could feel her mother scrutinizing her. "I'm not used to staying out late anymore. I'm a little tired." She knew as soon as she spoke, her mother didn't believe a word of it.

Her mother wrapped her arms around her. "I'm here if you want to talk, honey." She kissed her cheek and stepped away.

Leslie helped Trish and Carla for a couple of hours before checking on her dad. It was unlike him not to show up to help in the kitchen. She found him reading the paper seated on the couch in her parents' living room with his feet up on the coffee table. "Morning, Dad."

"Good morning, honey." His huge smile relaxed Leslie's initial concern.

"You look comfortable," she said.

"I'm practicing for our vacation." He grinned.

"I see that. You and Mom are going to have a wonderful time."

"Yes, we are. We've worked hard our whole lives, and this will be a special gift to your mother." He turned toward her and set aside the paper. "Are you all right? You look sad."

Leslie smiled at her father. "How did you know Mom was the one you wanted to marry?"

"I'm not sure where that question is coming from, but it's a good one. Would it be shallow to say because of her baklava? We were only eighteen when we met and her parents were very protective, so I'd go to her house and have to get past her father to be able to see her. I almost gave up until one summer evening we were sitting on their porch swing." He smiled, lost in memories. "I put my arm across the back of the swing, and when she turned toward me, we kissed. That was it. I was hooked from that day forward. It wasn't just a great kiss, mind you. It was…well, she was *everything*. Smart, full of fire, kind. She made me laugh. We married a year later because I couldn't imagine a single day without her by my side. There's a lesson I hope we've taught you, honey. If there's something or someone you want, don't give up on trying."

"Thanks, Dad." Leslie kissed her father's cheek and went home. She hurt to her core when she thought of losing Kate, but was some of that pain because she'd given up on her? Kate had a crazy ex pursuing her. She needed support, not someone wallowing in self-pity because they couldn't have what they wanted from her. Leslie hurt. She acknowledged that pain and needed time to heal, but she couldn't give up on Kate. She'd help her in any way she'd allow her to.

CHAPTER TWENTY-NINE

D id you pack your backpack?" Kate supervised the packing Portia insisted she do herself.

"Why are we going to Aunt Deanna's?" She stuffed her coloring book and crayons into her backpack as she spoke. It seemed all her questions were *why* lately.

"We're invited to visit. Don't you want to go?" Kate frowned. Her motivation to leave for a while had more to do with missing Leslie than visiting her sister. Memories of Leslie on her couch, of her singing as they danced in her living room, and memories of the blistering kiss they shared before she left plagued her. Getting away might help her forget. At least that's what she told herself.

"Can we go see Lelie?"

Kate flinched at the question. "Leslie is busy at the restaurant. Do you remember the restaurant?"

Portia nodded and continued to try to stuff all of her toys into her overstuffed pack. "I like her."

"I know, honey. I do too." Kate forced back unshed tears. She'd made the right decision to keep Leslie safe. She wished it didn't hurt so much to live with it. She filled two suitcases with some of their clothes and put them in her car.

"Mommy, I don't want to go." Portia sat on the floor and Kate's throat tightened at her sad pout.

"It's just for a visit, honey. We're not moving again. Okay?"

Portia stood and picked up her backpack. "Okay." She hung her little head and hugged her teddy tightly.

Kate put Portia in her car seat and checked the area before pulling onto the street. The ride was uneventful except for her constant alertness for signs of Wendy.

Marta met them in the doorway. "Welcome back." She took Portia's hand and led her into the house. "I've got chocolate chip cookies baking."

Portia was quiet and Kate could tell she wasn't a happy kid. Mention of cookies of any kind always brought a smile and giggle. It was confirmed. She was the worst mother, the worst girlfriend, worst wife, probably the worst person ever. She quit chastising herself and took their suitcases upstairs. She only planned to stay a week. Just long enough to put some time and space between her and Leslie. A few days to distract herself from memories of Leslie's touch. Her kisses. Her smile. Hopefully, a week with her sister wouldn't put them at risk, but she desperately needed the cocoon-like peace she got with her family. She curled into a ball on the bed and let the tears come. She didn't know exactly how long she lay on the bed, but she rose when she smelled dinner cooking. She looked for Portia, but her bed looked untouched. She went downstairs ready to beg forgiveness for showing up and abandoning her child when she saw her looking content with her coloring book and crayons and a plate full of cookies in front of her.

"Mommy." Portia slid off her chair and ran to hug her.

"I'm right here, sweetie." She picked her up and danced in a circle, pleased to hear her laugh. Maybe she wasn't the worst mother in the world. She set her down and Portia climbed back on the chair to resume her coloring. "Thanks for keeping an eye on her, Marta. Sorry I fell asleep upstairs."

"Mommy needed nap time," Portia said from her seat.

"Deanna will be home soon, and I'm sure she'll be glad to see you," Marta said. "Here." She pulled a bottle of Kate's favorite wine from a cabinet. "She asked me to pick this up for you."

"Thanks. I'll wait till she gets home to open it."

"Mommy, look!" Portia held up her latest coloring handiwork.

"Oh, that's beautiful, honey." She held up the paper for Marta to marvel at the scribbles of color covering the page.

"It is. You're very talented."

Portia grinned ear to ear and began another design. Kate checked the time. "I think I'll open the wine after all and wait for Deanna in the den." She took her glass and settled on a chair to enjoy the fireplace.

"There you are," Deanna said as she walked into the den and sat next to Kate.

"Yep. Thank you for having us again. It'll only be for a week."

"You can stay as long as you need to."

"Thank you. I appreciate it."

"So, what's up?" Deanna leaned back in the chair and sipped her wine.

Kate took a moment to collect her thoughts. "I told you Leslie and I were dating. Well, Wendy has been showing up all over the place. She followed Leslie's car and showed up at the restaurant. I'm worried she'll hurt her, so I told Leslie we couldn't see each other anymore."

"I imagine Leslie didn't agree."

"No, she didn't. But she doesn't need to put up with Wendy. She's my problem."

"Do you believe Leslie cares about you?"

Kate smiled at memories. "Yes, she does."

"Then I presume she's ready to try to help you get rid of Wendy."

"I don't want her hurt because of me. And there's literally nothing she can do to help."

"I know. Maybe in this case, two heads are better than one. And isn't stopping seeing her exactly what Wendy wants?" Deanna drank her wine and remained quiet.

Kate finished her wine and watched the fireplace in companionable silence with her sister. She cared about Leslie too much to involve her in her Wendy dilemma any more than she already had. But she missed her and Deanna had a point, except Wendy wanted her back. Hopefully, if Wendy went looking for her and didn't find her with Leslie, she'd leave Leslie alone. She sighed with gratitude when Marta called out that dinner was ready, and Kate followed Deanna to the dining room. She listened to the conversation around the table and absorbed the peace of being surrounded by family. After dinner, she carried their empty dishes to the kitchen and took Portia upstairs. She allowed the gush of tears she'd been holding back to flow once she got to their room.

"Why are you crying, Mommy?" Portia wrapped her arms around Kate's neck.

"I'm sad, honey. I miss my friend."

"I miss Lelie, too."

Kate shook her head in disbelief. Portia was smart, but her sensitivity amazed her. "You go to sleep, honey." She kissed Portia's forehead and went to bed, but sleep eluded her for a long time. Deanna's point about doing exactly what Wendy wanted her to, stung. There was truth in it. But how did she balance Leslie's safety with the desire to be with her?

The next morning Kate woke and sat up disoriented. She plopped back onto her pillow and turned to her side while her tears fell. Her life was a mess, and she missed Leslie. She took a deep breath and wiped away her tears. She had Portia to think about. She got up and checked on her sleeping daughter before going to the shower and getting ready for work.

Portia was still asleep when she finished dressing, so she went downstairs for breakfast.

"Good morning." Marta's smile was a welcome sight.

"Morning. Thank you, again, for caring for Portia today. Tomorrow will be daycare." Kate finished a bowl of oatmeal and went to work.

By the end of the week, Kate still missed Leslie, but her fountain of tears had stopped, and she felt more settled, so she packed to go home. Portia raced to the car after hugging everyone good-bye and remained quiet in her car seat. "We'll be home soon, honey." She watched for Wendy's car everywhere as she drove and went around the block twice before parking behind her building. She rested her head back on the seat, closed her eyes, and took a deep breath. She couldn't maintain this level of stress for herself or for Portia. She took Portia inside before going back to get their suitcases and sighed with relief at no sign of Wendy. Portia raced to her room as soon as they reached the door. She obviously felt safe here and had claimed her space.

Kate locked the door and made herself a cup of coffee before she settled on the couch and turned on her phone to listen to the missed call. "Hi, Kate. It's Leslie. Please leave me a message or a text letting me know you're okay." Kate replayed the voice mail three times to hear Leslie's voice. She tossed her phone on the couch and began to pace. She checked on Portia who was busy emptying her toy box and refilling it. What was she doing to her kid when packing and unpacking became her favorite game? If she was trying to protect Leslie it would be for the best to cut herself off completely from her. The one week away had been a healing time with her family but had also given her enough time to recognize the huge void in her life without Leslie. Somehow, she'd allowed her to become a significant part of her life, and the vacuum left by her absence hurt. Wendy knew where Leslie worked, and she might've figured out where she lived. Wendy would probably keep harassing her until she got Kate back, and that would never happen, but would staying away from Leslie make a difference? She sat back on the couch with too many questions spinning through her mind. She decided some mindless task would help, so she unpacked their suitcases and loaded the washing machine. She settled back on the couch and hovered her finger her phone for a moment. *Portia and I are okay, tx.* She forced herself to stop and hit send. She didn't think too much about her decision but noted the settling of the ache in her chest as she grabbed Portia's coat and loaded her in the car.

Twenty minutes later, she pulled into the restaurant parking lot and scanned the area before getting out of the car. Portia held her hand and tugged her toward the door. Kate took a breath to settle her nerves before she opened the door and they walked in. She sat in the booth next to the door and waited.

"Hi, Kate. I haven't seen you in a while. What can I get you?" Trish smiled at Portia.

Kate gave her their order and hoped Leslie would step out of the kitchen.

Trish returned with their order and filled Kate's coffee cup. "Leslie will be sorry she missed you. She went to meet someone for lunch. Let me know if you need anything else."

Someone for lunch. Like a date? Did Leslie turn back to the dates from the speed-dating event? After only a week? If so, it was her own fault. She'd pushed her away and into someone else's arms. Kate moved the food around on her plate and managed a smile at Portia who finished her meal and drank a glass of milk. "Ready to go home?"

"Where's Lelie?"

"She's not here today, honey."

Kate left money on the table and led Portia to their car. She checked the lot for any sign of Wendy's car and saw Leslie pull into a spot by the building. She watched her check the area before getting out of the car and walking to the door. She stopped before opening it and seemed to be listening to something before she turned and met her gaze. She started toward her and hesitated when she got close, a question in her eyes. Kate smiled and Leslie came to her driver's window.

"I missed you," Leslie said.

"Yeah. I missed you, too. I think I panicked. No. I did panic." Kate rested her fingers over Leslie's where she leaned on the open window and felt an instant sense of calm. "I don't know how to get away from Wendy and it's making me crazy." Kate winced at the uncertainty that crossed Leslie's face, and she hoped she had the courage to change it.

CHAPTER THIRTY

A re you and Portia able to come for lunch or dinner tomorrow? We're all dressing as 1950s waitresses." Leslie was pushing, but she feared if Kate left now, she wouldn't come back. She'd been thrilled to see her in the parking lot and willing to talk to her but sensed her hesitancy.

"I forgot tomorrow is Halloween. I promised Portia I'd take her trick-or-treating with Deanna's boys." Kate didn't offer more, but the sadness in her eyes spoke volumes.

"We'll be here if you can." Leslie stepped away from Kate's car. She wouldn't push her. It would have to be Kate's choice to want her in life, and she planned to be there if she did.

Portia waved to her from the back seat as Kate drove away. "Bye, Lelie!"

She blinked back tears and trudged back to the building and willed herself to muster enthusiasm for their Halloween plans. She'd picked up ingredients for her mother's Halloween cookie recipe, so she concentrated on mixing the dough and pushing Kate out of her thoughts. If Kate didn't feel the same way about her as she did then there was nothing she could do except move on. She finished mixing the cookie dough and put it in the refrigerator to set overnight.

"We're busy tonight," Trish said as she brought a tray of used plates into the kitchen.

"Good. Let me know if you need me to help out."

"I will. So far, Carla and I are keeping up pretty well."

Leslie went home and concentrated on the revised design plan she'd reviewed with the architect she'd met for lunch. She'd pointed out a few options Leslie hadn't thought about, and the upgrades to the aging building were going to cost more than she anticipated. After an hour of fiddling with the budget, she headed back to the restaurant.

"Hey, Leslie. I'm glad you're back. We could use your help now. People were standing in line a few minutes ago."

"Sure." Leslie worked until closing, grateful for the distraction from her constant thoughts of Kate. "You two go home. I'll clean up tonight, and thanks for working so hard today." Leslie smiled as Trish and Carla waved and hurried out the door. She wiped all the tables and chairs and refilled the condiments on the tables before mopping the floor. She checked the doors were locked and walked through the kitchen to the back exit. She noticed the bright red painted message as she tossed the garbage bag into the bin. This time Wendy had painted the wall.

I warned you. You'll be sorry.

Leslie groaned. She was tired and didn't want to spend time washing the bricks, but she didn't want to scare Paul who usually took out the garbage, so she dragged out the power washer after she took a picture. The only good thing about this incident was it gave her an excuse to call Kate. Unfortunately, it also gave Kate another excuse to push her away.

She loaded the picture onto her computer and emailed it to Kate, noting the time and place and the presumption it was the work of Wendy. She closed down her computer before she obsessively checked for a reply and then went to bed without one.

The next morning Leslie tried hard to work up enthusiasm for the planned Halloween day. Kate and Portia wouldn't be there, so she hoped Trish's and Carla's enthusiasm would rub off on her. She checked the time, put on her jeans and sweatshirt, and headed to the kitchen. She made sure everything was ready for the day and walked through the dining area. She mopped the floor and went home to change. Trish and Carla were in the building when she returned. They giggled like little girls and twirled with their skirts, bobby socks, and saddle shoes. Maybe this would be fun. She turned on the playlist of fifties music she'd created and waited for the first diners of the day.

Leslie took the order of the first group to enter. It was a family of four dressed as a mama bear, papa bear, and two baby bears. She waved at Joy and Nat when they arrived dressed in their Roaring Twenties outfits, and finished taking an order before heading to say hello. "I'm glad you guys made it today."

"It looks like your idea was a good one. Is Kate here?" Joy asked.

"No." Leslie checked Trish and Carla had things covered and sat next to Joy. "Remember her ex you saw at the center?"

"We sure do."

"She's made threats against both of us, so Kate's afraid she'll hurt me. She pretty much told me to stay away from her for my own safety."

"I can understand that," Nat said. "Put yourself in her position. Wouldn't you want to protect someone you cared about?"

"But she's not giving me a say in it at all. She pushed me away." She winced at how petulant that probably sounded.

"I'd be terribly upset if Nat wouldn't let me help her in that situation. I couldn't let her go through it alone." Joy kissed Nat's hand.

Leslie grinned at her friends. Their opposing opinion was exactly what constantly ran through her mind. "I'm not giving up on her, but I won't force myself on her. God knows she's had enough of that in her life."

"Let us know if there's anything we can do to help," Joy said.

"Thanks. It's good to have you as friends." Leslie went back to work. If she stayed busy enough, she could ignore thoughts of Kate for a little while.

Leslie breathed a sigh of relief at closing time. Their costume idea turned out to be a huge success, and she yearned to share her day with Kate. She helped to clean up and went home. She reclined on her bed with her laptop and rearranged tables and chairs on her new design for the dining room but quit after a few minutes when thoughts of Kate kept interrupting her concentration. She set her computer aside and gave in to her need to hear Kate's voice.

"Hi, Leslie," Kate answered on the third ring.

"Hey. How'd the trick-or-treating go?"

"We're still out. How was your day?"

Leslie tried not to hold her breath. Kate sounded willing to talk to her. "It went well. I'm exhausted, but Trish and Carla came in dancing and left dancing."

"Great. I got your email. I made another report, and I need to give you a copy of the restraining order. If she gets caught there, you'll need to show it to the police."

"When?" Leslie barely contained her excitement. Was she going to see Kate?

"I don't know."

"Kate!" Leslie pushed down her frustration. "Wendy already knows about us, so what difference does it make if we see each other?" Leslie's stomach churned.

"That's true, but—

"We can meet somewhere other than here or at your place. Maybe a store?"

Kate was silent for a few moments. "Okay. How about the grocery store by Deanna's? Do you know where it is?"

"I do. When?"

"Half an hour?"

"I'll see you there." Leslie hung up and rushed to her car.

Kate was waiting for her at the far end of the parking lot when she arrived. The darkness and isolated location fit the mood of their clandestine meeting. Kate stepped out of her car and looked around before hurrying to hand her the papers. "Keep these with you at all times. I'm so sorry I got you into this mess. Please stay safe." Kate leaned and brushed her lips over hers before she dashed back to her car and drove away.

The whole event was over before Leslie could speak. She swallowed her disappointment, put the restraining order papers into her glove compartment, and drove home. If that's the way Kate wanted to end things, she'd have to accept it. Maybe Wendy would give up if she didn't see them together anymore, which was likely what Kate was thinking would happen. *She'll think she won.* Leslie plodded from her car to her house, weighed down by the disappointment of the result of their meeting. She swallowed her unhappiness and resigned herself to accept Kate's withdrawal.

The next day Leslie ordered material to begin the first phase of upgrades to the restaurant. She immersed herself in the work, matching colors and patterns. She went over her choices with Ronda for a second opinion but wished it were Kate. "I'm going to close the place for a couple of days for the renovations. I think it's going to be a nice update." Leslie put away her plans and called Joy.

"Hi, Leslie. What's up?"

"I wanted to find out about the next Meetup event."

"This Saturday. We're hiking at the Maybury State Park. Are you going to join us?"

"Yes. I'll be there."

"We look forward to seeing you."

Going to the park would remind her of Kate, but everything did, so she might as well spend time outside with friends.

Saturday morning, Leslie made sure everything was under control at the restaurant and left for the day. She joined the group and walked the trails enjoying being out in the crisp fall air. She avoided the area where she and Kate had met and walked with Joy and Nat.

"Have you talked to Kate?" Joy asked.

"She gave me a copy of the restraining order for Wendy the other day, but she still feels I'd be safer if we're apart." Leslie shrugged.

"I get it." Nat shrugged. "Nothing is in her control, so she's trying to do what she thinks is best."

Joy shook her head. "Going through something like this alone isn't right. But I suppose I get where she's coming from, even if I don't think it's the right option." She bumped Leslie with her shoulder. "We've invited a few people over for cider and donuts this afternoon. Why don't you join us? Maybe it'll help take your mind off her."

Leslie appreciated her friend's attempt to distract her. "Sounds good. Thanks."

She followed the line of cars to Joy and Nat's, surprised by how many of the women on the hike were invited. Maybe she could find a distraction in the crowd. She sipped her cider and talked to several different women, forcing herself not to compare them to Kate. She excused herself after a couple of hours. She lost herself in thoughts of Kate as she drove home and panicked when she arrived to find a police cruiser in the parking lot. She looked past the car and saw the large front window of the restaurant had been broken. Shards of glass covered the cement next to where Trish and Ronda stood talking to the officer. She jumped out of her car, and hurried to the building. "What happened?" She addressed the officer.

"It appears someone threw a large rock through this window." He held up a plastic bag with the rock in it.

"I'm Leslie Baily, the owner. Do we know who it was?" She suspected Wendy.

"No," he answered.

"It happened before noon. I was in the kitchen," Trish said.

"We'll see if we can get any prints off it and let you know."

Leslie gave him her contact information and showed him the restraining order before cleaning up the broken glass. She considered whether to let Kate know about this escalation in Wendy's assaults. She'd be using it as an excuse to hear her voice, but the stab of sorrow that thought brought convinced her she'd be torturing herself. Kate made it clear she wanted to distance herself, and Leslie didn't want to make it harder on her. The police documented the event and maybe they'd get lucky and get Wendy's prints, but she doubted it. She finished boarding up the window and went to her office to call the insurance company.

CHAPTER THIRTY-ONE

The ride home wasn't long enough for Kate's tears to stop. She had a kind, caring, sexy woman call her sweetheart, and she'd pushed her away. *Damn Wendy.* Kate sat for a few minutes to collect herself before getting Portia from the back seat and going inside. Why she didn't think to give Leslie a copy of the personal protection order already she didn't know, but she had one now. Would she call her anymore if Wendy showed up at the restaurant? She paced in front of her couch willing a solution to materialize. Wendy had already found Leslie's restaurant, so sending her away might not be helping. But Wendy couldn't know she wasn't seeing her anymore, so was she torturing herself and Leslie for nothing? Her thoughts spun out of control, and she closed her eyes against the growing headache. No answers emerged from her muddled thoughts, so she went to read Portia a bedtime story.

"Ugly Duck, Mommy." Portia held up her favorite children's book and Kate sat next to her on her bed to read. Portia barely managed to stay awake until the ugly duckling turned into the beautiful swan. Kate kissed her forehead and covered her with a light blanket before she settled on the couch with a glass of wine. She had no solution to her dilemma with Wendy but losing Leslie because of her was unthinkable. She finished her wine and went to bed.

Kate woke to her phone ringing on her nightstand. "Hello." She glanced at the clock.

"I'm sorry to call so early but Wendy was here last night. We saw her on the cameras in the backyard." Deanna sounded more annoyed than frightened. "Rob went outside to confront her, but she was gone before he could get to her."

"This has to stop, but I'm not sure what more to do. I gave you a copy of the restraining order, didn't I?"

"Yes, and I called the police before I called you. I thought you'd like to know."

"Thanks, Deanna. I'm keeping track of the many reports filed against her. I wish I could figure out a way to trap her so she couldn't get away. I'm sorry you have to put up with her."

"Take care of yourself and be careful. I worry she'll try to hurt you or Portia."

"Yeah. Me, too." Kate disconnected the call and climbed out of bed. She made herself coffee, brought her laptop to the couch, and updated her growing list of Wendy sightings. She considered what she knew. Wendy had tracked her to Deanna's, to Leslie's, and to the LGBTQ center, but where was she living? She'd probably lost her job to have so much time. She could be living out of her car for all Kate knew. This had to stop. No way was she going to raise Portia in this environment of fear and constant moves. She put her laptop away and checked on her daughter sleeping peacefully. She vowed to make sure she always would.

She had an hour before she had to get ready for work, so she reviewed her finances and picked a date for her holiday trip to visit her parents. They'd always been a supportive presence in her life, and she missed them. She'd let them know she was leaving Wendy and the divorce was pending, but the time since she left Wendy had flown by and it was past time to update them on everything going on. That is, if Deanna hadn't already done it. She wrote herself a note and left it on her kitchen counter before checking that Portia was still asleep. She showered quickly and dressed for work before checking on her again. She sat on the bed talking and gesturing to her stuffed animals.

"How do scrambled eggs sound for breakfast, honey?"

Portia nodded enthusiastically, and they finished breakfast and Kate dressed her for the day before leaving.

She grumbled at her automatic perusal of the area around her car before she seated Portia in the back seat and pulled out of the parking area.

She checked the parking lot at work for any sign of Wendy and parked in a different spot than usual. She began her day with a string of pre-op hip replacement X-rays. Many of the clients at the orthopedic clinic where she worked were elderly and had replacement surgeries scheduled. She worked steadily until lunch when she took a break and called her parents.

"Hi, Mom. I'm at work, but I've been thinking of you and wanted to say hello."

"Are you still living at Deanna's?"

Kate cringed knowing she'd been avoiding telling her parents about her constant moves since the divorce. "No. Portia and I have our own place not far from Deanna's."

"I've been worried about you since you told us about the divorce. Is everything okay?"

"Lots has happened, but I don't have time to talk about it now. I'm planning a visit around Thanksgiving, so let me know when's a good time."

"Anytime you can make it is perfect. We'd love to see you and we have no plans to go out of town. We can celebrate Portia's birthday when you come."

"Sounds good, Mom. I'll get my holiday work schedule and let you know."

"Take care, honey. We love you."

"I love you, too." Kate felt more settled after talking to her mother. She had something to look forward to now. As quickly as that thought emerged, fear replaced it. Wendy knew where her parents lived. She could be putting them in danger by leading her to them if she went to visit. This was definitely getting out of hand, and she had to figure out a solution. She finished her workday and headed to pick up Portia. Her anxiety rose the closer she got to the daycare center. She'd let them know about the situation when she enrolled Portia, but she still struggled with fear Wendy would show up and try to snatch her. Her fears evaporated when Portia ran to meet her at the door.

"Mommy, look." She pointed to a lopsided Popsicle stick house on the table in front of Portia's chair.

"It's beautiful. Did you build it yourself?"

"I helped Ms. Brady."

"You did a good job." She hugged Portia and led her to the car.

Kate tried to pretend her life was normal. She'd talked to her mom, went to work, and picked up Portia from daycare. Her fantasy shattered when she got home and automatically checked for Wendy lurking around. She hurried into the building and locked the door behind her then reached for her phone to call Leslie and share her day. She shook off her imaginary notions and faced reality. She made dinner and helped Portia practice letter recognition before putting on *Snow White and the Seven Dwarfs*. Portia fell asleep toward the end and Kate carried her to her bed and then settled back on the couch and turned on the news. She grinned at her Leslie imaginings coming to life when her phone rang. "Hi, Leslie."

"I'm glad you answered."

Kate stood and began to pace. "Did Wendy show up again?"

"Yes, but I needed to hear your voice. I miss you."

"Did she show up at the restaurant?"

"I got back from an outing and found the police there. Someone threw a rock through the front window. The police are checking for fingerprints, but I'm doubtful they'll find any. My money's on Wendy. Do you think we could get together and talk about it?"

Kate couldn't deny she wanted to see Leslie. Her fear of Wendy dulled under the comfort of Leslie's voice. She argued with herself long enough that Leslie spoke again.

"I hope you're doing well. I'll leave you alone if that's what you want."

"Wait. I would like to talk about it." A sense of calm covered her like a warm blanket on a winter night knowing she'd see Leslie again.

"Friday night? We could meet at the bistro."

"Okay. About six?"

"I'll be there."

Kate refused to think too much about what a bad idea it was to keep Leslie involved in her Wendy drama. But she was already involved, so she allowed herself the anticipation of seeing her again. Good idea or not. She filed the broken window incident in her computer as a probable Wendy event.

Kate couldn't quell her anticipation at seeing Leslie, and the days dragged until she picked up Portia from daycare on Thursday and called Sharon.

"Hi, Kate. Everything okay?"

"Yeah. I'm going out with Leslie tomorrow night, and I'd like to know if you're available to stay with Portia."

"I sure am. What time do you need me?"

"About five thirty until nine."

"No problem. I'll see you tomorrow."

"Thanks, Sharon." Kate hung up and went to see what bedtime story Portia wanted. After finishing the story of *The Boy Who Cried Wolf*, Portia mumbled about bad wolfs and baby sheep, so Kate put that story aside for when she got a little older. She kissed her lightly on the cheek and got ready for bed.

Kate rolled over and checked her bedside clock for the fourth time. Thoughts of her life and the situation with Wendy raced through her mind, and she couldn't find the off switch. She got up, made herself a cup of chamomile tea, and tried to relax on the couch. She turned on the TV and watched a ridiculous comedy show for a few minutes before surfing through channels and shutting it off. If only getting rid of Wendy could be so easy.

CHAPTER THIRTY-TWO

"Thank you." Leslie waved to the workers as they drove away after replacing the front window of the restaurant. She admired the glass, glad she'd gone to the extra expense of tinting.

"Hey. That looks great," Trish said as she arrived for the day.

"It does. I think it'll look nice with the new shades I ordered."

"Oh. Let's put them up right away." Trish hurried inside.

Leslie admired the view from outside a minute longer and went in to help Trish. She grinned at her enthusiasm. "I think Mom and Dad will be pleased when they get back."

"When are they due back?" Trish asked.

Leslie chuckled. "Whenever they 'tire of sunshine, mountains, and crystal clear water.' Those are their words from the postcard I got yesterday."

"I'm glad they're enjoying themselves. I like your parents." Trish stepped back to admire their work and began to ready the dining area for the day.

Leslie mopped the floor and made sure the kitchen was ready for Ronda and Paul before she went home to order paint and supplies. She finished updating her records and noted the date of the new window, grateful her insurance covered most of the cost. She turned her thoughts to Kate and their date, if that's what it was. She hoped to convince her to let her help get rid of Wendy, although she wasn't sure how it would happen. She only knew Kate was special to her, and she wanted time to discover what they might have together. It would be up to Kate, and she'd support her in any way she'd allow. She checked everything was going smoothly at the restaurant and went home to decide what to wear for her evening with Kate.

Leslie helped Trish and Carla a few hours in the afternoon before she changed and left for the bistro. Questions scrolled through her mind as she drove. Would Kate send her away again, or would she let her try to help? She gave up speculations and enjoyed the anticipation of spending time with her. She automatically checked the area as she pulled into the parking lot. It was getting old for her. It must be exhausting for Kate. She acknowledged an overwhelming sense of protectiveness, but one of many reasons that drew her to Kate was her strength and independence. She checked the area for Wendy one more time before going into the building. She searched the room and enjoyed the surge of arousal when she spotted Kate. She almost looked relaxed as she leaned back in her chair with one hand wrapped around a glass of wine. She wore a soft looking button-down sweater Leslie ached to unbutton. She waved when Kate looked up and their gazes locked. She took a deep breath and released it as she joined her at the small table. "I hope you haven't been waiting long."

"No. I got here a few minutes early to fortify myself." She held up the glass.

Leslie ordered a cup of tea before speaking when the server stopped at their table. "I had the window replaced today. Have you had any more Wendy sightings?" She mentally slapped herself at the topic of Wendy being the first thing out of her mouth. But it was what this meeting was supposed to be about.

"Not since after your window incident, then her lurking at Deanna's. I'm afraid she's not going away." Kate leaned her elbows on the table and wrapped her hands around her wineglass.

"How's Portia doing?" Leslie sipped her tea.

"Great. She loves the daycare center. I'm planning a trip to see my parents in a few weeks and we'll celebrate her birthday. Can I buy you dinner? I'd like another glass of wine, but I haven't eaten since lunch."

"They have an excellent bean stew here." Leslie relaxed after her initial surprise at the question. It seemed Kate wasn't going to send her away just yet. "I'd love a bowl."

"How are your parents doing?" Kate asked between spoonfuls of food.

"I got a postcard yesterday indicating they love it and won't be home for a while."

"That's great. They're hard-working people. They deserve a break."

"Where in Ohio do your parents live?" Leslie ached at the thought of Kate being so far away.

"Just outside of Cleveland."

"That doesn't sound like too far a drive. How long will you stay?"

"I don't know yet. I haven't made definite plans. I have to see what the work schedule is like." Kate finished her bowl of stew and took a sip of wine. "What life is like."

Leslie finished her food and wrestled with the decision to mention Wendy again. They were supposed to be discussing her, but she couldn't bring herself to spoil their evening. She decided to let Kate bring her up. "I ordered paint for the restaurant today, and we put up some new blinds."

"Great. I'm sure it's going to be lovely." Kate sounded defeated.

"Bring Portia anytime to see it." Leslie hoped by mentioning Portia, Kate would cheer up.

"I should probably get home." Kate looked at her watch. "Sharon is staying with her."

"I'm glad you agreed to meet me tonight." Leslie stood, unsure what else to say. "I hope you and Portia come by the restaurant soon." Kate looked so sad and Leslie didn't want to leave her. "Why don't you stop by tomorrow? You can see what I've done so far."

Kate stood and swiped a tear from her cheek. "Take care of yourself, Leslie. I'm sorry about tonight. I didn't mean to lead you on and…if something ever happened to you…" Another tear rolled down her other cheek.

Leslie took her hands in hers. "I appreciate you're trying to keep me safe, but Wendy already knows about me. She's seen us together, so if she can't get to you directly, it makes sense she'll try to get to you through me. And she'll do that whether you're around or not, so you may as well be around. Please let me try to help you." Leslie wanted to wrap Kate in her arms and kiss away her fears, but she stood still, stroked Kate's hands with her thumbs, and waited. It had to be Kate's choice to let her in.

"I don't know what to do." Kate tipped her head back with her eyes toward the ceiling.

"What if our only contact was by phone? We could call and text to stay in touch and Wendy would never know." Leslie squeezed her hands gently. "I'll miss touching you, but at least that's something, right?"

Kate withdrew her hands but held her gaze. A small smile lifted the corners of her beautiful mouth. "We could do that."

Leslie followed Kate out the door and they checked the parking lot for a sign of Wendy before leaving. She drove home smiling. At least she'd have contact with Kate even if she couldn't be with her. Over time, maybe they'd find a way to be together for real. She parked and checked the building before going home and lying on her bed with her phone. She waited half an hour to allow time for Kate to get home before dialing her number.

"Hi, Leslie. I presume you got home safely."

"I did, and I presume you did, too."

"Yes. Sharon left and Portia's busy with her new LEGO blocks."

"I love those things. I wanted to make sure you got home safely."

"I appreciate it."

"I'm going to do my walk-through of the restaurant. Can we talk tomorrow?"

"Yes. Same time?"

"Sounds good. Good night, Kate." Leslie put her phone in her pocket and went to make sure everything was locked up. She left out the back door to check the bin that had been Wendy's favorite drawing board.

You will be sorry! It looked like she'd used the same red paint as before.

Leslie grumbled about having to drag out the power washer again and cleaned it after taking a picture to send to Kate to add to the file. She put the washer away for what she hoped was the last time and went home. She tossed and turned for half an hour after going to bed. This latest evidence confirmed she wasn't going away, and she was pissed. They had to do something more than report her. They needed a plan to catch her.

Leslie sat at her kitchen table the next morning to watch the first snow flurries of the year. If they didn't turn into a heavier snow, it wouldn't keep the diners away. She finished breakfast and drank a cup of coffee while she watched the morning news. Trish and Ronda were already in the restaurant when she arrived. "Good morning," she said as she mopped the floor.

"Morning," Paul called from the kitchen.

"Morning." Carla arrived and waved to everyone. "The roads are getting a little slick out there."

Leslie put all her cleaning supplies away, grateful for the employees she'd found. "We may not be too busy this morning. Give me a call if you need me." She went home and gave in to her urge to text Kate.

Hi, Kate. Are you at work today? Leslie squashed a tiny twinge of guilt at possibly interrupting Kate's workday. Kate's reply only took a minute.

Hi. No. I'm off this Saturday. What're you doing?

Thinking of you.

Ah.

I won't lie to you. You stir something in me. Not the most poetic line, perhaps, but true.

I think about you, too.

The admission made her smile, keeping that little flame of hope alive. *Sorry to spoil the mood, but I suppose I ought to tell you Wendy left another message for me painted on the garbage bin.*

Another?

She winced. *Maybe I didn't tell you about the other one on the wall. She's not happy with my interest in you, but we know that already and she's not scaring me away.*

I'm so sorry, Leslie.

Leslie responded that it wasn't her fault, but there was no return message. With a deep sigh, she set her phone aside and turned to her coursework for a distraction.

CHAPTER THIRTY-THREE

K ate plugged her phone in to charge and checked her emergency supplies on the kitchen counter next to a copy of the restraining order. She'd collected items for protection in case Wendy found her and tried to break in. She had an aerosol can of hair spray, which she'd read sprayed in the face could burn, an extra pepper spray, and a flip phone she'd connected to one of the emergency response companies. Her brother-in-law had offered her a 12-gauge shotgun, but she wasn't comfortable with firearms around Portia. She didn't think she could ever shoot anyone anyway. Dialing 911 was her defense.

Leslie made a good point when she said it was too late, that Wendy already knew about her and had seen them together, but Kate's protective instinct urged her to push her away. Wendy would go after anyone she deemed a threat to her *property*. And Kate believed that was exactly the way Wendy thought of her. She owned her and no one else could have her. She poured herself a cup of coffee and settled on her couch to read. She put the book down after rereading several pages. It seemed impossible to concentrate on anything besides her Wendy problem.

She checked on Portia who was busy with three new coloring books and contemplated an extreme option she'd been wrestling with. She deliberated long and hard before coming to the conclusion it might be the only way to protect Leslie. Wendy would think she'd won. She'd deleted Wendy's number from her contacts after getting the restraining order, but she still had her number in an old address book she'd kept for Portia. She'd hold off on her final decision overnight. She knew she and Portia couldn't live this way, and she cared too much about Leslie to have her and her livelihood threatened. She'd have to go back to Ohio. She tried reading again, but the page blurred through her tears. She swiped her face, took a sip of coffee, and called Deanna.

"Good morning."

"Hi. Are you busy?"

"Nope. I'm enjoying a morning off by sitting in the den with my coffee watching the snowflakes fall. What's up?"

"I needed to hear a friendly voice."

"Is Wendy still stalking you?"

Kate hesitated to reveal her plan until her final decision was made. "Yes, she is, and she's threatening Leslie by vandalizing her restaurant. I'm scared, Dee."

"She's pretty good at ignoring the restraining order and avoiding capture. I'd be scared, too. Is there anything I can do to help?"

"I'm afraid I'm on my own with this." Leslie's words of being in it together brought more tears, and she sniveled.

"You sound terrible. Why don't you and Portia come back here for a few days? Maybe Wendy will get tired of following you back and forth."

"Thanks for the offer. I'll think about it." She knew Wendy wasn't going to give up until she got what she wanted or was arrested.

Her pacing calmed her enough to think more clearly and she found Portia asleep on her bed when she went to check on her. Her coloring books were stacked neatly on her new play table with the crayons scattered across it. Kate covered her gently with a light blanket and returned to the couch. Portia would be better off. Safer, staying with her sister and her family, but she wasn't sure she could leave her behind. She was certain Wendy would prefer Portia stayed with Deanna, but she couldn't abandon her. She wouldn't let Portia grow up thinking she'd been tossed aside because her mother didn't want her anymore. If she decided to go back with Wendy, Portia would go with her. She lay on the couch and curled her knees to her belly hoping answers would come.

The ringing of her phone startled Kate awake. She grabbed her phone but didn't get off the couch. "Hi, Leslie."

"Is everything all right?"

"Yes."

"You sound awful. Please tell me what's wrong? Is it Wendy? Did she hurt you?"

Kate decided she'd better talk or Leslie would show up in person. "No. I haven't heard from Wendy."

"What's wrong, sweetheart? Please talk to me."

Kate sat up and held back tears. "I'm so tired of running from her. I can't do this anymore." She couldn't hold back any longer and hung up as her sobs took over. She blew her nose and made her decision. She considered her options and retrieved paper and pencil to make a list. She needed to leave a message for her boss at the clinic. She could request an extended leave, and she could call the daycare once she was on the road to let them know Portia wouldn't be back. She had no idea what to expect from Wendy, and fear suddenly gripped her throat making it hard to breathe. Wendy was cruel and abusive. Although she'd never threatened Portia, she worried how the tense environment was affecting her. She'd make up a story about having to go away for work for a while and drop her off at Deanna's on the way. Somehow, she'd find a way back to her, eventually. The sob caught in her throat at the idea of having to leave her beautiful little girl behind in order to save her from the bad choice Kate had made. She could only pray that Portia would forgive her one day.

She retrieved Wendy's number and called her.

"Have you come to your senses?" Wendy sounded drunk.

"I give up, Wendy. You win. I'll go back to Ohio with you." Kate forced her voice to stay steady.

"It's about time. You saved me the trouble of burning down your bitch's restaurant. Where are you?"

Kate scrambled for a reply. She didn't want Wendy here. "I'll collect my stuff and drive to the Ohio house."

"There is no house. The fucking bank took it. Where are you?"

"What? Didn't you make the payments?" Panic settled in the pit of her stomach.

"It doesn't matter. I've got an apartment. Where are you!"

"I'll meet you at the entrance to the expressway. I'll follow you from there."

"If you're not there in an hour, that restaurant is ashes. And don't even think about leaving the kid behind. She comes with you or no deal." Wendy hung up.

Kate immediately called Wendy back as her plan began to fall apart.

"You better be on your way."

"I want to leave Portia here. There's no reason for her to be uprooted again."

"You will bring her or that restaurant and your sister's precious house will be burned to the ground. Get it? I don't want you to think you've got a reason to take off again, and if I have to come back and get her myself, I will."

Kate swallowed the lump in her throat. There was no way in the world she'd leave Portia alone with Wendy. "Okay. I'll leave as soon as we're packed." She slumped into a chair and covered her face in her hands as the tears flowed. What had she done?

Kate took a settling breath and quickly sent a text to Leslie. It wasn't fair and it wasn't enough, but it was all she could manage. She couldn't leave without at least a good-bye. She composed the most difficult text she'd ever written.

I care too much about you to let Wendy hurt you. I'm leaving today, and you'll be safe. Take care of yourself, Leslie.

She packed their suitcases as full as possible and loaded Portia's toy box and chair into the car with whatever else she could fit. She pinched the bridge of her nose to force away a stress headache. They'd be starting over again only this time, with Wendy. She clung to the hope she'd somehow find a way to escape again and find Leslie. She leaned against the doorframe in her kitchen. It wouldn't change anything. They could get in her car and escape to Oregon, and Wendy would burn down Leslie's restaurant and probably

Deanna's house. Maybe Wendy would get tired of them once she got them back. That thought made her chuckle, but not in a happy way. No chance.

"Where are we going, Mommy?" Portia said from her car seat.

"We're going back to Ohio, honey."

"Why?"

"Wendy is sorry she wasn't nice to us before. She wants us back." Kate hoped her explanation would satisfy Portia. But Portia gripped her teddy hard, holding it to chest and looking at her shoes. Kate spotted Wendy's car on the side of the road before the entrance to the expressway. She took a deep breath and followed her. They arrived in their old neighborhood and Wendy pulled into an apartment complex Kate had never liked. She parked next to her and waited.

"Well? You coming?" Wendy glared at her.

"This is it?" Kate checked the back seat, grateful Portia slept soundly.

Wendy grumbled and came to the driver's side of her car, so she lowered the window. "Yeah. You coming in or do I have to go back and do some burning?"

Kate nodded, got Portia out of the back seat, and followed Wendy to her apartment. "She needs to use the bathroom." Kate led Portia to where Wendy pointed and sent a quick text to Deanna to let her know where she was and why while Portia sat on the toilet. She hoped Deanna would understand the seriousness of Wendy's threat to burn down Leslie's restaurant. She quickly told her of the other threat Wendy had made to her house. She had no idea what came next. Wendy's apartment was a small two-bedroom with one bathroom and a galley kitchen. The few pieces of furniture she had looked to be secondhand, and Kate sent a prayer of thanks she'd grabbed Portia's sleeping bag. She'd have to shop for a bed tomorrow. She retrieved the items she'd packed from the car and steeled herself for the coming evening and night. She cringed at the double bed when she set her suitcase on the floor in the bedroom. She brought in Portia's toy box and chair and set it up in her bedroom.

"Mommy? Why are we here?"

"We live here now with Wendy." She laid out a blanket from her car on the floor and put her sleeping bag and pillow on top of it. "It'll be like camping tonight."

Portia didn't respond but looked sad.

"I'm getting you a bed tomorrow, honey." She kissed her cheek. "Come on. Let's get some dinner." Kate hoped there was something in the refrigerator beside beer. She searched the cupboards and found two boxes of macaroni and cheese. She went to the living room and found Wendy on the couch finishing her second beer. "I'm making some macaroni and cheese."

Wendy toasted her with her beer bottle and turned back to whatever she was watching on TV.

Kate had given in to what Wendy wanted and she would have to live with it until she found a way out. She inventoried the contents of the refrigerator and made a shopping list. At least the milk still had a couple of days before the expiration date. She made sure Portia was fed and filled two bowls. She set one next to Wendy and ate the other one before making sure Portia was cleaned up and comfortable. She sat in the worn recliner and held Portia in her lap. "What're we watching?" Kate decided she might as well try to engage Wendy if for no other reason but to remind her they were there. She glanced at her limp posture. The empty beer bottle slid out of her hand to the floor, and her chin rested on her chest. Memories flooded back of her snoring, slack-jawed head leaned against the back of a couch. Nothing had changed except the house Kate had mostly paid for was gone, and she'd have to make do with this apartment. At least she probably wouldn't have to put up with her in bed. She'd most likely be in the same position in the morning as she was now. Kate rose to get Portia settled for the night and to check for clean sheets.

CHAPTER THIRTY-FOUR

No, no, no!" Leslie yelled, picked up her pillow, and threw it back onto the bed. She began a text to Kate and erased it and began another one and erased it. "What the hell is she doing?" She put her phone away and took deep breaths to calm down. She forced herself to reread Kate's text calmly. She needed to figure out where she was and go convince her to return. All she said was she was leaving today, and she'd be safe. Where would she go? And what did she need to protect Leslie from? It had to be Wendy. She paced in her living room and forced back tears. She needed to concentrate. She had to find her. Maybe Wendy finally got to her, kidnapped her, and sent that text from her phone to make her think it was from Kate. She had to figure this out. She put on her coat and left. Maybe she could find a clue at her flat.

Leslie knocked on the door and peered in the windows, but it was dark inside and no one looked to be home, and her car was gone. She was certain Wendy had something to do with this, and she had to figure out what. She didn't have Kate's sister's number, but she knew where she lived. She checked the time and sent a note to Trish before getting on the road toward Deanna's.

She pulled into the circular drive and sprang out of the car.

The door opened right away, and Marta stood smiling at her. "It's good to see you, Leslie. Come in."

"Hi, Marta. Is Deanna home yet?"

"She's in the den. I'll tell her you're here."

Leslie paced in the hallway waiting for Marta to return.

"Do you remember where the den is?" Marta asked.

"Yes, thank you." Leslie took the stairs two at a time and calmed herself before reaching the room.

"Hi, Leslie. I'm not surprised you're here. Sit and we'll talk." Deanna sipped on a glass of wine. "Would you like a glass?"

"No, thank you. You know why I'm here?"

"I think so. It's Kate, isn't it?"

"Please, do you know anything about what happened" Leslie barely managed to hold back tears. "I got a text from her telling me she was leaving so I'd be safe."

"I got a text, too. She said Wendy threatened to burn down your restaurant and my house if she didn't go back to Ohio with her. You know about all the other threats Wendy has made, and this one pushed Kate to the limit. She gave in and agreed to go back with Wendy so she wouldn't set fire to your place and mine. She took Portia with her. If she'd have told me before she left, I would have suggested she leave her with me."

"Do you know where in Ohio they are?"

"I'm sorry. I know her old address, but Kate said they were in an apartment somewhere because Wendy lost the house."

"God. What am I going to do?" Leslie stood and sat back down. She didn't need to take out her frustration on Deanna. She was probably just as upset about losing her sister.

"I can't tell you what to do, but if you can, take a day and clear your mind. It's easier to find solutions to problems when the anger and pain lessen. She obviously still has her phone and Wendy hasn't hurt her. We'll exchange phone numbers and if either one of us hears anything we can talk about it."

"Thanks. You're right, Deanna. Wendy probably won't hurt her, for a while, anyway, since she went to all the trouble to travel around stalking her. But I remember Kate told me she did hit her once, but never Portia." Leslie groaned. She stood after she put Deanna's number into her phone and gave hers to her. "I'm sorry to have barged in on you like I did, but I care very much for your sister, and this is…" She gave up holding back her tears and sobbed into her hands. "I'm sorry." She sniffled.

"I know Kate feels the same way about you. That's why she couldn't let Wendy hurt you. Do you want a cup of tea or something before you go?"

"No. Thank you for being here and talking with me."

"Anytime, Leslie. I'm worried about her, too. Be careful driving home."

Leslie sat in her car a few moments to collect her thoughts. Deanna gave her more information and now it was time to formulate a plan to rescue Kate. She went home to consider options. She automatically watched for Wendy as she drove and checked the parking lot when she got home. She shook her head and smiled for the first time since getting Kate's text. Wendy had what she was after. Kate had sacrificed her freedom so she wouldn't show up here again. She didn't take any solace in knowing that.

She found Trish and Ronda in the kitchen talking when she arrived at the restaurant. "How're things tonight?" she asked.

"How are you? Trish rested her hand on her shoulder.

"I'm fine."

Trish looked concerned. "You're usually in and out all day and checking on things. We haven't seen you all day. We worried a little since the roads were icy."

"I appreciate your concern, but I had some personal business to take care of."

Ronda and Trish shared a look before Ronda spoke. "We were concerned it might have something to do with Kate and her idiot stalker."

Leslie almost forgot she'd warned her staff about Wendy. Suddenly exhausted, she dropped into a nearby chair. "Wendy has Kate." She told them about getting her text and talking to Deanna and Wendy's threat to burn down the restaurant. "I'm not sure how, but I'm going to find her and bring her home." She stood and began her pacing until Trish rested her hand gently on her shoulder.

"What can we do to help?" Trish asked.

Leslie swallowed back any more tears, even ones of gratitude. She needed to focus. "Thank you. Both of you. I'm not sure what to do yet, but I'll figure something out. I refuse to let Kate spend the rest of her life with that nasty woman because of me."

"We're here. Let us know if you need anything." Ronda went back to the kitchen and Trish began cleaning the dining area.

She went out the back door and checked the garbage bin for any red paint. She walked past it and considered how it made her feel. What must Kate be feeling? She shuddered at the thought of what Wendy might be doing to Kate. Leslie had never considered herself violent or vindictive, but she couldn't be certain what she would do if she found out Wendy had hurt Kate. She waited until after ten in hopes Wendy was asleep and composed a text to Kate. She refused to consider Wendy forcing Kate to share her bed.

I talked to Deanna today. You don't need to do this. We can figure out a way to catch Wendy together. Please come back to me. L

Leslie turned the volume on her phone to as loud as possible and put it on her nightstand. She tossed and turned while she waited for a reply and finally got up and began making a list. She wrote down what she knew. The act gave her something to focus on instead of her fear. Wendy showed up when Kate lived in Ferndale. She must have followed them when she picked her up to go to Nat and Joy's and saw them together. Then she must have followed Kate to the restaurant and seen them together there. She tossed the list aside as an effort in futility. It didn't matter when or where Wendy first showed up. She needed to get Kate back and make sure Wendy could never show up again. She put the copy of the restraining order on her dresser and went back to bed. She grabbed for her phone when it dinged.

Portia and I are safe. Wendy is drunk most of the time, and I try to stay away from her. I don't want to take a chance she'll retaliate more severely if I leave her again. I'm sorry.

Leslie got up and wandered around her house. She remembered the first time Kate and Portia were over and Portia's glee at finding her beanbag chair. She still had the nearly full bottle of wine she'd bought for Kate in her refrigerator. She mentally relived the kiss in her kitchen when Kate grasped the front of her shirt and pulled her into her. Their first life-changing kiss would be imprinted in her mind, and heart, forever. There had to be a way to get her back and she would find it. She crawled back into bed and finally fell asleep.

Leslie threw herself into cleaning the restaurant for the next week. Her parents planned to be home from their vacation before Thanksgiving, and she wanted everything to be running smoothly. The extra work did nothing to help take her mind off Kate. Every night at ten thirty she sent Kate a good night text along with a plea to return. She only received one reply assuring her they were still safe but too frightened to return. On Sunday, Leslie called Deanna and went to talk to her. She arrived before noon and Marta indicated the den where Deanna sat before the gas fireplace.

"Hi, Leslie. How're you holding up?" Deanna turned to face her.

"I'm a mess. I came to see if you've heard anything new."

"Sorry. I'd have let you know if I did. Kate did send me a text once telling me she and Portia were okay."

"Yeah. I got one, too. But she's still too terrified about Wendy's rage to come back. You said you had Kate's old address. Could I get that from you?"

"Sure, but I told you they're in an apartment somewhere, didn't I?"

"Yes. I thought it would give me a place to start looking at least." Leslie had never been to Ohio and had no idea where in the state the address was. She just felt a tiny bit closer to Kate having it. She clutched the note with the address on it like a lifeline, as if she held a small piece of Kate.

CHAPTER THIRTY-FIVE

Kate left the clinic and hurried to pick Portia up from her babysitter. She'd been thrilled to find a position in a clinic close by. She left the financial mess Wendy had gotten herself into up to her to resolve. They were no longer legally married and that's the way it would stay. She made enough to pay the rent and keep food on the table for Portia. Wendy used most of her earnings as a bagger at the local grocery store for beer. If she weren't so nervous Wendy would chase her, she'd have snuck out in the middle of the night while Wendy snored, drunk, next to her. But she couldn't possibly begin the whole process all over again. At least this way she had a modicum of control. She knew where Wendy was, and she wasn't constantly looking over her shoulder. It wasn't much, but it was something. If there was anything she could be grateful for Wendy's excessive drinking, it was she passed out before reaching for her in bed. She loaded Portia into the car and stopped at a local deli for dinner. Wendy could figure out her own meal. She wanted Portia to have a healthy diet, and she loved the tuna salad.

"Mommy?"

"Yes, honey?"

"When are we going home?"

Kate cringed. She thought Portia was settling into a new routine. Obviously, she was wrong. "This is our home now."

"Is Lelie going to come here?"

"No. Leslie lives in Michigan. Remember I showed you the map?" Kate held back tears at her daughter's sad expression.

"You can have some ice cream after you finish your tuna salad." The mention of ice cream seemed to brighten Portia's spirits. Kate wished it could be so easy for her.

"Where've you been?" Wendy slurred her words when they arrived back at the apartment.

"At work, then I fed Portia. Why?"

"I came home early so I could spend time with my family, and you weren't home." Wendy weaved as she spoke.

"I have a job, remember? So we can pay rent and buy food?" Kate took Portia into her room before Wendy began a rant. She suspected she'd lost another job due to her drinking.

"I brought home macaroni and cheese. The kid likes it, doesn't she?" She tossed two boxes on the counter.

"Yes. Thank you. Her name's Portia, remember?" Kate couldn't believe she needed to keep reminding Wendy of Portia's name. More than likely, she didn't bother to remember it. Or her brain was so pickled from booze she couldn't. She tried hard not to look to a future anymore. She'd do her best with Portia and make sure she felt safe and loved. That was the plan that kept her sane whenever memories of sweet and gentle Leslie surfaced, which was often.

"I'm going to get some supplies." Wendy staggered out to her car.

A sliver of guilt passed over Kate for letting Wendy drive drunk, but she remained quiet. She'd be back with beer, no doubt. She set Portia up at the table with crayons and her coloring books before making the macaroni and cheese Wendy may or may not eat when she got back. Her phone pinged with a text message, and she didn't have the emotional strength to ignore it.

Please let me know you're okay.

Emotionally drained, and weary, Kate replied.

We're okay. Tired, but okay.

She wanted to add so much more but stopped herself and turned back to the wretched life she'd chosen. She mixed the powdered cheese into Wendy's dinner and put the final product into a Tupperware container for her. It could be hours or minutes before she stumbled back into the apartment.

"How about bath time?" She smiled at Portia expecting a gleeful response.

She climbed off her chair, her shoulders slumped. "Okay."

Kate took her hand and led her to the tub. She added bubble bath and Portia finally smiled. She was laughing by the time she was in the water tossing the bubbles in the air, and Kate breathed a sigh of relief. She dried her off after bath time and put on her new butterfly pajamas. Kate hadn't bothered with another toddler bed but found a twin frame at the resale shop and bought her a new mattress. Portia seemed to like the openness of it and she hadn't fallen out, so Kate figured she'd be fine.

"Ugly duck?" Portia picked out her book from the shelf Kate had made from boxes.

"Okay." Kate settled on the small accent chair she'd gotten the same time as the bed frame.

Portia looked to be fighting to stay awake until the end. "Butaful swan."

Kate kissed her forehead and pulled the covers over her before she went to sit up in bed and read. The ring of her phone surprised her. "Hi, Deanna."

"Is everything okay there?" Deanna sounded worried.

"It's as okay as it can be. What's up?"

"I've spoken to Leslie several times. She's falling apart. Are you sure you won't change your mind and come back?"

Kate wanted to shout yes, pack Portia up, and leave before smelly drunk Wendy got back. "If I leave her again, I have no doubt she'll follow up on her threat to burn down Leslie's restaurant. And what if she targets your house after that? And wherever I go after that? I can't do that to any of you, and I can't keep living that way." Kate took deep breaths to keep from breaking down.

"Well, I told her I'd try. I hope things work out for you."

"I keep thinking we could move across country, but it wouldn't change Wendy's threats. She's vindictive enough to follow through on them no matter where I am."

"I love you, and I get that you're in a no-win situation, but I hope you'll reconsider," Deanna said. "Think about talking to Leslie,

Kate. Maybe you two could come up with a solution together." She emphasized her last word.

"Thanks. I'll think about it. I love you, too." Kate hung up and plugged her phone in to charge. She read a few more pages and checked the time. Wendy usually stumbled in before this. Not that she missed her. It meant she could have more time before she had to pretend to be asleep. She got up and made herself a cup of chamomile tea and put the macaroni and cheese into the refrigerator. She carried her cup to the bedroom and indulged in a fantasy she was waiting for Leslie to join her. They'd cuddle and talk and finish the tea before making love leisurely and drifting to sleep in each other's arms. She put her book away and considered what Deanna had told her. She would call Leslie someday, but it would be easier for her to forget her if they had no contact. That thought unleashed her pent-up tears and they soaked her pillow when she tried to muffle her cries. She fell into a restless sleep plagued by dreams of Wendy stalking her.

Kate woke to Portia mumbling about pumpkins and paint. She rolled to her back and realized Wendy wasn't there and it didn't look like she had been. She put on her robe and went to check on Portia. "Good morning, honey." She picked her up and danced around the small room until Portia giggled. "Ready for breakfast?" She hoped they wouldn't find Wendy passed out on the living room floor again. The route to the kitchen was clear and Kate couldn't find any sign of Wendy having been there. She'd have rejoiced except the main reason she divorced Wendy was because she'd stay out all night and come home reeking of alcohol and perfume. She didn't know what condition Wendy would be in, but she'd be back. She made a pot of oatmeal and sat to eat with Portia before getting her dressed and taking a shower. She left a note for Wendy in case she found her way back and went to work.

Kate stopped at the food mart before she went to pick up Portia. Wendy had been relatively sober for two days and demanded they have dinner together so Kate picked out items she knew Wendy liked and would still be healthy for Portia. She didn't care what she ate. She drifted through her days with nothing more than her daughter's welfare in mind. Her clothes hung on her, and she wore her hair in a ponytail. Haircuts were a luxury she saved for Portia. She carried the bag of groceries in one arm and held Portia's hand to the apartment. Thankfully, Wendy wasn't home. It meant they'd have a few minutes of quiet time.

"Ugly duck, Mommy?"

"It's not bedtime yet, honey." Kate winced at Portia's request. It was the fifth time in three days she'd asked to be taken away from the reality of their life. Living in the world of ducks and swans had become preferable. Something had to change. She took advantage of the peace without Wendy and sat in Portia's room to read to her. Before she began, she took a deep breath and sent a text to Leslie.

I hope you're well. I miss you.

It wasn't fair, and Kate's resolve to keep Leslie safe didn't waver. The strength it took for her to keep doing so did. Leslie's reply came within minutes.

I miss you so much, Kate. I have an idea how to catch Wendy. Please come back to me.

Kate reread the text several times and admitted her curiosity at what idea Leslie had. Broken-spirited and disheartened, she replied.

I'm scared. I'm not sure what Wendy is capable of, and I don't want you hurt, but I'm not sure how much longer I can put Portia through this.

You don't have to. I think I have an idea that could work and we could catch Wendy, but I need your help. Can you call me later? Or tomorrow? Anytime, please?

I will.

Like a mama bear protecting her cub, Kate wrapped Portia in her arms and allowed a sliver of hope to seep through her fear.

Chapter Thirty-six

Kate's text sounded defeated and sad, and it took all of Leslie's resolve not to get in her car and go look for her. She still had Kate's old Ohio address, but she'd probably end up driving in circles. She clung to Kate's text and hoped she'd gotten through to her. She turned her phone volume as high as it would go and slid it into her pocket before going to the restaurant to talk to Ronda. She found her scrubbing the stove. "Hi, Ronda."

"Leslie." She turned to face her. "I'm glad to see you smiling again."

"I finally got Kate to reply to a text. It's a start."

"Is she okay?"

"She said she is, but she's worried about Portia. I hope I've convinced her to come back. We'll see."

Ronda surprised her by wrapping her in a hug. "I've found things in life work out as they're supposed to." She released her and went back to cleaning.

"Thanks, Ronda. I'll be leaving to pick up Mom and Dad from the airport in half an hour. Let me know if you need anything before I go." She did a walk-through of the dining area and let Trish know she was leaving before going home. She checked for a message from Kate, but her phone remained silent. The trip to pick up her parents only took an hour, and their stories and enthusiastic description of the island helped distract her from her constant worry about Kate.

"How're Kate and Portia doing?" her mother asked.

Leslie deliberated how to tell the truth but not worry her too much. "They're okay. Kate's visiting out of town for a while." She told herself it wasn't a complete lie.

"I hope you two are still dating." Her mother studied her but didn't press for a reply.

Fortunately, they pulled into the restaurant parking lot so she didn't have to respond.

"The place looks great. You changed the lighting and painted, didn't you?" her father asked when they walked through the restaurant on their way home.

"I did. I have a few new tables coming in tomorrow, and I plan to have all of the seating recovered. Whenever you want, I'll show you what I chose."

"Tomorrow, honey. It's been a long flight and we're both hungry."

"Let's get you settled." Leslie carried their suitcases into their house and set their kitchen table for two. She grinned and responded to the knock on their door.

"Special delivery." Ronda stood holding up two bags. "Freshly made moussaka with salad and blueberry pie."

"Thanks, Ronda." Leslie introduced her parents before she and Ronda left them seated at their table. She went home and hesitated only a moment before she composed a text to Kate. *Mom and Dad got home from Hawaii today. Are you able to find a way to sneak away? My plan to catch Wendy includes your help. We can do it, Kate.* Leslie sent the text and went back to waiting for a reply. The dining room was full when Leslie returned to check on things. Trish and Carla passed each other carrying trays as if performing a choreographed dance, so she took over operating the register. The steady stream of patrons helped her concentrate on her job and distract her from worries about Kate.

"Thanks for covering the register," Carla said as she passed with a tray full of empty plates and cups.

"No problem." Leslie waved and made mental notes to work on designs for a padded bench seat for the waiting area. When the flow of customers slowed, she went to check on her parents.

"There you are." Her mother hugged her and held her at arm's length. "Do you need us out there?" she asked.

"Things are winding down for the day so I think we're good. You guys relax and get settled back in."

"We will, honey. Our trip was fantastic, but coming home is…" her mother sighed, "coming home."

"You certainly did an excellent job hiring. Ronda is great and Trish and Carla are worker bees," her father said.

Leslie chuckled. "They are efficient. And Paul is a whiz on the griddle. I think he'll be relieved to have you back. It'll give him another male presence amid all us females."

"We're so proud of you." Her father put his arm over her shoulder and led her into their kitchen. "We brought you something." He pointed to their refrigerator. The door was completely covered in a variety of tiny Hawaii shaped magnets. "Pick whatever you want."

Leslie laughed and hugged him. "Thank you. I'll have to come back and shop." Her parents looked to be struggling to keep their eyes open. "Why don't you two go relax and get over your jet lag. I'm going to help clean and lock up for the day. I'll see you tomorrow but call if you need anything."

"Leslie?" her mother called.

"Yes?"

"We love you."

"I love you, too." A little of Leslie's anxiety lessened at having her parents' home. Now she had to figure out how to get Kate here safely. She went home and reviewed the plan to catch Wendy and decided to start the process and hope Kate would contact her soon. She went to bed thinking about the next step in her plan. Leslie checked the time before she reached for her chiming phone. Five a.m. She didn't recognize the number on the readout. "Hello?"

"Leslie, it's me. I don't have much time."

"Kate. Are you all right?" She sat up ready to dress and go wherever Kate needed her. "Where are you?"

"I'm getting ready for work. Wendy took my phone, so this is my new number."

"Damn. Did she see our texts?"

"No. I got into the habit of deleting them in case this happened. I'm sorry."

"Please, stop apologizing and get back here."

"What do you have planned? I'm not sure anything will work."

"I'm having security cameras that record installed around the restaurant and my house. When you come home, I expect Wendy'll follow you, and we'll have proof when she shows up."

"But what if she hurts someone?"

"We'll get her on camera before that happens. So will you try to get away from her?"

"I have to plan it. Portia...I'll let you know what I come up with." Kate disconnected the call.

Leslie put her phone away and got out of bed. She had work to do. She made an appointment with the company who'd installed her alarm system to set up cameras and called a meeting for her parents and the staff.

"What's going on, honey?" her mother asked.

"I'm having surveillance cameras installed around the building. They'll be recording, so I needed to let you all know. My intention is to deter any break-ins, and it'll lower the insurance premiums. That's all except to tell you they'll be installed today. Does anyone have any objections to this?"

Everyone shook their heads.

"Okay. Thanks." Leslie followed her parents home to talk in private.

"This is about Kate's ex, isn't it?" her mother asked.

She gave them a rundown of everything that had happened in their absence. "Wendy threatened to burn down the restaurant, so Kate went back to Ohio to appease her and protect me. I've talked to her recently and told her about the cameras. She's going to try to sneak away from Wendy to come back and we'll catch her on camera when she tries to do something truly harmful. That's it. That's the plan."

"I'm sorry you're going through that," her father said. "Let's hope your plan works and doesn't get out of hand."

"It's been tough, but I hope we can catch her soon." She rubbed at her temples. "We have to do *something*."

"When is Kate coming?"

"I don't know. As soon as she can safely get away. I'm going to meet the installer, so the cameras are positioned where I want them. See you later." Leslie checked her phone for a text from Kate and put it in her pocket, her dad's question rolling through her mind. *When will you come back to me, Kate?*

Leslie closely watched the camera installation and kept the company representative long enough to be comfortable with their operation. She spent an hour after they left practicing replaying what was recorded. She went home to send a text to Kate, which came back undeliverable. She must have changed phones again. At least Leslie hoped that was the case. She paced for a while until she realized it wasn't calming her and went to help clean the restaurant. She mopped the floors and wiped tables before dimming the lights. She checked the doors were locked and the new cameras were activated before going to her parents to say good night.

"Hi, honey. We didn't expect to see you again until tomorrow. Come sit. We're watching TV." Her mother patted the seat next to her. "You're worried about Kate, aren't you?"

"I am. She said she had to plan her escape. Something about Portia. I haven't heard anything more since." Leslie hugged her parents and went home. She checked that her phone's volume was as high as it would go and heated a cup of milk. She settled on her bed and tried to dispel the feeling of despair that had taken hold of her since Kate left. She couldn't know where their relationship was headed but she knew without a doubt, if Kate came back to her, she'd do everything in her power to keep her safe.

CHAPTER THIRTY-SEVEN

Come on, honey, we're going for a car ride." Kate pushed aside her exhaustion and checked the clock for the third time. Little sleep and the constant stress of Wendy's drunken rants had her frazzled and worried about the toll it was taking on Portia. The plan Leslie devised could work. She held on to hope, and at six a.m. she wrote a note for Wendy to let her know she planned to stop at the grocery store after work. It would give them extra time. She tossed garbage bags of clothes and toys into the trunk of her car, buckled Portia in her car seat, and headed for the expressway. And Leslie. Once she was far enough away to feel relatively safe, she pulled into a rest stop and used the new phone she had hidden under the seat of her car to call Leslie.

"Hello?"

"I'm on my way." Her hands shook and her voice trembled.

"I'm so glad. I was worried about you."

"We're all right. Just exhausted."

"I'm going to open my garage door. You pull into the garage as soon as you get here and the button to close it is by the door. There's fresh milk and juice in the refrigerator. Do you know about how long it will be?"

"I'm guessing an hour or a little longer. I'll see you soon." Kate put the phone in her jacket pocket and concentrated on driving. She took a deep breath and continued to check and recheck her rearview mirror. She pulled into Leslie's garage and rushed out to close the door before collecting Portia.

"Lelie," she exclaimed as they went into the house. She raced to the living room and threw herself onto the beanbag chair. "Where's Lelie?"

"We'll see her soon, honey. First let's have something to eat." Kate looked through the cupboards and found a box of cereal. "Would you like some Cheerios?"

Portia sprinted back and climbed onto the chair at the kitchen table like she'd been doing it for years. Almost instantly, she was back to the happy child she'd been before they left, and a small part of Kate's terror fell away.

Kate made herself a bowl of cottage cheese with chunks of pineapple she'd found in the back of the refrigerator. She smiled at Leslie's thoughtfulness. After they finished eating, she sent a short text to Deanna to let her know she was back and would update her later.

"Mama needs a nap. Let's lie down for a while and wait for Leslie to get home." She put their empty bowls in the sink and took Portia's hand, intending to rest on Leslie's bed. She passed the extra bedroom and saw a twin bed with a soft pastel quilt and a Disney Princess chair and play table like the one she'd had to leave behind. "Well, it looks like you've got your own room." Kate hesitated for a moment. She and Leslie hadn't discussed living arrangements as part of their plan, but this felt right, so she went with it for now. She laughed when Portia ran past her and climbed onto the bed. She covered her with the beautiful quilt and kissed her forehead before heading to take her own nap. She sent a text to Leslie first to let her know they'd arrived and fell asleep minutes after lying down. Kate dozed and shifted into the comfort of a warm body and the security of an arm embracing her. She clutched her arm and snuggled back into Leslie with a contented sigh. "Hi," she murmured.

"Welcome home." Leslie hugged her tighter.

Kate rolled to her back to confirm what her body was telling her. Leslie held her in her arms, and she was safe. "I hope you don't mind I fell asleep on your bed. I was exhausted. Portia's probably still sleeping."

"She is. I checked on her before I came in here and found you. I like you in my bed." Leslie placed a light kiss on her lips.

"Mm. I like you holding me. I was so afraid Wendy was right behind me that I kept checking my rearview mirror the whole way. I set the cruise control and counted the miles. I was exhausted by the time we got here."

"I was frantic she'd hurt you. How long do we have before she realizes you're gone?"

"She'll start to suspect by six tonight, probably. I told her I'd stop for groceries on my way home to buy us some time."

"That's good. I'll leave you to rest some more. Then I'll show you the cameras."

"No. I'm okay. I can't wait to see them and say hello to your mom and dad." Kate stood and stretched. She winced at the pain in her back caused by the tension of driving clenched in fear.

"Do you think Portia will like lamb? Mom's making braised lamb with mushrooms tonight. We're all invited to dinner."

"It sounds great to me, and Portia usually eats anything. I've never offered her lamb, however."

"We'll figure something out for her if she doesn't like it."

Kate reached for Leslie who looked uncertain. She grabbed the front of her shirt and kissed her. Fear and doubt melted in the warmth of her embrace. She never should have left.

Leslie's passionate response ignited the craving she'd held back for too long. She gently eased her back onto the bed and pressed their bodies together while deepening the kiss. "I've missed you so much, sweetheart. I was petrified I'd never see you again."

Kate held her close and whispered in her ear. "She didn't hurt us, and I would've found my way back to you somehow, from anywhere, love." She kissed her with no restraint, no questions, and no fear between them.

"We better get up, or we'll miss dinner. And breakfast." Leslie was breathing hard.

"Yeah. Portia will come looking. She's already asked about you."

"She did?" Leslie grinned as if given a great gift.

"Lelie!" Practically on cue, Portia ran into the room and crawled onto the bed.

"I'm so glad to see you." Leslie hugged her and winked at Kate.

"I'm going to take a shower before we go," Kate said and slid off the bed. "We're going to dinner with Leslie tonight, honey."

Portia stood and began to jump until Kate grabbed her. "Do you remember me telling you no jumping on the bed?"

"Yeah." Portia's sullen expression turned into giggles when Kate began to tickle her.

"You go ahead and shower. Portia and I will entertain ourselves until it's my turn." Leslie picked up Portia and carried her like a sack of potatoes to the living room.

Kate shook her head and smiled as she searched through her garbage bag for her toiletries. She took her time using her lavender and cinnamon body wash. Desire flared when she thought of Leslie's hands smoothing it over her breasts and down her belly. She fantasized about them together under the spray, gliding their bodies against each other, their legs entwined and desire building between them. She quickly finished washing, found a towel in the bathroom cabinet, and went in search of some clothes. She dumped the bags she'd hastily packed on the floor and found clean underwear and a totally wrinkled blouse. She put on her jeans and laid the blouse on the bed to press out the wrinkles with her hands before putting it on and going to the living room. Portia sat on the beanbag chair, and Leslie sat cross-legged on the floor next to her reading aloud from one of her books. Leslie looked up when she entered the room and gave her a look that made her pulse race.

"Your turn. Come on, Portia. Let's get dressed to go to dinner."

She hopped off the chair and hugged Leslie before racing to the room she'd obviously claimed as hers.

Kate dumped her garbage bag of clothes on the bed and sorted through them. She chose a pair of jeans and a sweater and dressed her quickly.

"Ready?" Leslie stepped out of the bathroom in a pair of khaki pants and a long-sleeved navy blue Henley shirt.

Kate wiped her mouth, certain she was drooling. Leslie's full breasts filled out the front of the shirt and the pants were tight enough to show her curves but loose enough to be comfortable. She took Portia's hand and followed Leslie out the back door toward her parents' house. Leslie turned to lock the door and grasped Kate's free hand as they walked. The feeling of rightness brought tears to her eyes. This morning she was running away from a precarious situation and tonight she was holding hands with Leslie and going to dinner with her parents.

Leslie pointed to where the cameras were located as they walked. "We'll check them all after dinner. If Wendy comes looking for you tonight, we'll be ready."

"I'm so sorry for—"

"No more apologies. You are not responsible." Leslie kissed her and squeezed her hand. "Let's go eat."

"Kate!" Leslie's mother hugged her as soon as they walked in the door. "Come sit." She bent and whispered to Portia.

Portia ran to the table and waited until Leslie's mother brought a booster seat shaped like a throne.

"For the princess." She lifted Portia onto the seat.

"Thanks for inviting us to dinner," Kate said.

"We're excited you're okay. Leslie told us a little about your situation. I hope you don't mind. We'd like to help if we can."

Kate relaxed in the presence of Leslie's parents. They were good people. She looked at Leslie before she spoke and caught her slight nod. "Thank you for being so wonderful. I'm still not sure this is the wisest idea, but I don't want to live in fear anymore. I can only pray that no one gets hurt."

"Sometimes you have to take a big risk to get the results you need," her mom said. "We'll be right beside you."

"I appreciate your support. I feel like I've gained a family." Kate smiled as she watched Portia giggle and shove a spoonful of food in her mouth. When she'd woken that morning, flooded with fear, she wasn't sure she could go through with their plan, but Leslie had made it sound so possible that she'd clung to the hope it had generated. And here they were seated with her parents sharing a meal. They still had the final event of capturing Wendy to accomplish, but she smiled as she wiped away tears of gratitude.

CHAPTER THIRTY-EIGHT

"Do you think she'd drive all this way this late?" Leslie snaked her arm around Kate's shoulder and pulled her close when they returned from dinner and settled on her couch after putting Portia to bed.

"I wouldn't put it past her. I think it would depend on how much she'd had to drink."

"How long is the drive?"

"Just over an hour. If she's drunk, I don't know." Kate looked sad and scared.

Leslie raised their joined hands and kissed Kate's. "We'll catch her. Come on. I'll show you the camera monitor." She led the way to her office where she pointed to a monitor showing views from each camera. "These two are by the garbage bin on which she'd painted. And these show the perimeter of the building. They're all set up to record any motion day or night. Put this number into your phone." Leslie gave her the security contact number. "I'll get notification on my phone of motion on the camera, and then we contact the police. If Wendy shows up, we'll catch her."

"I'd like to believe that," Kate said.

Leslie got up to make a cup of tea and slid a pillow gently under Kate's head. She settled on the end of the couch when she returned, rested Kate's feet in her lap, and softly massaged them. She sipped her tea and allowed her thoughts to wander. Part of her hoped Wendy would show up soon and they'd be done with her, and part of her felt the uncertainty of what came next. Would Kate stay with her, or would she move to a place of her own? Maybe in Ohio near her family. She'd called her love. That meant something. She was in love with Kate. She was certain, but for now she put everything out of her mind except the task at hand. Catching Wendy. She'd talk to Kate in the morning and find out where she stood. She shifted out from under Kate's feet and looked in on Portia before she checked the camera monitor. Then she changed the sheets on her bed as if clean sheets would convince Kate to sleep next to her.

"Where'd you go?" Kate looked sleepy, a bit disheveled, and sexy as hell.

"I checked the camera monitor and put clean sheets on the bed." She waited for Kate to respond.

"Are you coming back to the couch?"

"I'll be right there." She refilled her cup and made one for Kate and carried them to the living room.

Kate sat with her feet up on the coffee table. "Thanks for the tea." She took a sip. "Are we going to stay up all night waiting for her?"

"We don't have to. I can turn the volume up on my phone, and I'll hear the alert."

"Good." Kate stood and held out her hand to pull her off the couch. She didn't let go until they got to the bedroom. "Does your bedroom door lock?"

"Yes." Leslie rushed to lock the door and returned to stand in front of Kate seated on the bed.

"Sometimes Portia gets up in the night and she might come looking for me."

"Will she be nervous in a strange place?"

"I don't think so. She knows this house and you, and she likes it here."

"Do you?"

Kate stood and pulled her onto the bed on top of her. "Oh yeah." She claimed her lips and rolled over so Leslie was under her. She wrapped one leg over Kate's and pressed their centers together.

Memories of their first kiss, so good, paled in comparison to the emotion boiling over and passion building between them. Need overshadowed thought and she squirmed. Unable to get close enough. Kate sat up and began slowly unbuttoning her blouse. Breathless, Leslie heard her own heartbeat like an echo in her chest. She rested her hands on Kate's waist and battled the urge to reach for the last button. Kate finally stopped the gentle torture, unfastened the final button, unclasped her bra, and tossed them aside. Leslie whimpered when her breasts spilled out. She cupped them in her hands and flicked each nipple with her tongue while Kate threw her head back and pushed against her mouth. She sucked on one and stroked her bare waist and back before rolling over to pin Kate beneath her. She sat up to yank off her own shirt and bra and trembled at the first caress of Kate's fingers on her breasts. She stood and tugged Kate to stand in front of her. "I need you."

She unzipped her jeans, pushed them off along with her underwear, and kicked them aside. Kate inched her jeans down her legs and stepped out of them before she turned and arched back against her chest. Leslie accepted the invitation and cradled her breasts from behind while she nuzzled her neck. Kate reached back with one arm over her shoulder and used the other hand to clasp Leslie's hand and move it across her belly to the waistband of her panties. Leslie skimmed the silky skin under Kate's waistband and crept her fingers toward her heat. Kate's breasts rose and fell with the pace of her breath and her quiet murmurs morphed into needy pleas. Leslie pulled Kate tighter against herself and used both hands to slid Kate's panties down. Kate stepped out of them and turned to face her.

Once they stood with nothing between them, Leslie drew her into a searing kiss, and they tumbled back onto the bed. Leslie traced Kate's naked body with her fingertips, memorizing every curve, every spot that elicited a sound from her beautiful lips, and every place that caused her to rise to meet her touch. Kate responded with touches of her own and soft kisses across her belly and stomach. She cradled her breasts and took each nipple into her mouth. Leslie whispered in Kate's ear, "Come with me?"

Leslie slid her hand slowly down Kate's abdomen to her wetness and felt Kate's fingers stroke her at the same time as they surged into orgasm together enfolded in each other's arms. An overwhelming sense of protectiveness was the last thing Leslie remembered before sleep overtook her.

Leslie woke to the alarm on her cell phone, disoriented for a second by Kate's warm body spooned against her back. She smiled at the memory of their lovemaking but recognized the alarm from the security cameras. She gently shifted away from Kate and searched for her clothes.

"Are you getting up?" Kate sat up and stretched.

"It's the cameras." Momentarily distracted by the rise and fall of Kate's bare breasts, Leslie continued. "I got an alarm."

Kate sprang out of bed and found her clothes. "I'll meet you at the monitor."

Leslie went to her office and watched the recorded images. The view of Wendy spray-painting a warning note, then starting a fire in the garbage bin was clear. She called the police to report the event and urged them to hurry over to catch her in the act.

Kate stepped behind her and wrapped her arms around her. "Did you see her?"

Leslie replayed the images for her. "I called the police, but I'll bet Wendy is gone." She covered Kate's hands with hers. "Portia still asleep?"

"Yeah. She's obviously comfortable here. Thank you." Kate kissed her neck igniting her desire. "What about the fire?"

"It burned itself out inside the bin, but I'll check. The police will be here soon, I think we better stay dressed." She grinned and kissed her. She saw the police on the monitor and they went to meet them at the door. Leslie played the video of Wendy lighting a rag stuffed into a bottle and tossing it into the bin. They filled out a report and promised to send a patrol car to look for her.

"I hope they find her." Kate frowned and rested her hands on her shoulders.

Leslie's heart ached at Kate's unspoken apology. "They will, love." She prayed for truth to her words and checked the time. Three a.m. "I'll wait until it's light outside to look at the bin. Shall we try to get some more sleep?" She stood and took Kate's hand to lead her to the bedroom. She nestled into Kate's embrace when they got back to bed as if she'd been doing it for years. Everything about being with Kate was new, yet familiar. She didn't question the feelings Kate evoked. She thanked whatever forces had brought her into her life.

Later, Leslie disentangled herself from Kate, surprised by the light filtering into the room through the blinds. She rarely slept past five in the morning. She lay still for a moment to appreciate her good fortune to have Kate in her life and in her bed. Future plans raced through her mind like a movie, and she hoped Kate's matched her own. Portia would grow into a well-adjusted, loving young woman, and she'd be a part of teaching her about life. Her throat tightened at the responsibility she was about to take on. She'd never considered what raising a child could be like, but she looked forward to learning from Kate. Her life was about to change drastically, and she couldn't wait. She kissed Kate lightly and pushed aside her desire to trace her body in search of all the spots that ignited her passion. Her soft murmurs of pleasure still echoed in her mind from the night before. She rose and collected the clothes she'd tossed aside when they'd returned to the bedroom. Desire drew her attention to Kate who slept in her bed, but she had work to do. She left a love note on the nightstand on what she now considered Kate's side of the bed and went to check on the restaurant.

"Good morning," Trish called from the dining room.

"Good morning. Thanks for making the coffee." She poured herself a cup. "I have something to tell you."

Trish stopped what she was doing and turned to her. "Okay."

"Wendy was here last night. Well, early this morning, and she tossed what I'll call a firebomb into the garbage bin. I don't know where she is now, but I worry about what she's capable of, so please keep an eye out for her and call the police if you see her."

"I will and Carla will, too, I'm sure."

"There's something else." Leslie couldn't stop the grin spreading across her face. "Kate and Portia are here and will be a part of my life now."

Trish surprised her by rushing to hug her. "I'm so happy for you." She held her at arm's length.

"Thanks. I'm happy, too." Leslie set her coffee cup in the kitchen and went out the back door. She checked the area for any sign of Wendy before retrieving the power washer and cleaning off Wendy's note.

If she's not with me, she's not with anyone. You'll both pay for this.

CHAPTER THIRTY-NINE

Kate woke and immediately missed Leslie's presence. She didn't question how it could happen so quickly. She only knew she missed her. Leslie represented the good in her life. She represented love. She'd finally made the right choice in a lover, and she relaxed in the feeling. Memories of Wendy's early morning appearance rushed back flooding her with fear. She reminded herself of their plan to catch her. She'd managed to escape, and she and Portia were safe. She rose and sorted through the pile of clothes she'd dumped out of the garbage bag onto the floor but didn't find her robe. She noticed Leslie's hung neatly on a hook on the door, so she slipped it on and fantasized about her arms around her. She resolved to make an effort to stop leaving her clothes on the floor when she opened Leslie's closet and saw everything hung neatly on matching hangers. She closed the door and went to find out what Portia was mumbling about in her room.

"Mommy!" Portia ran to her, and Kate picked her up and did their dance around the room until she giggled.

"Did you sleep okay, honey?" She pushed Portia's hair out of her face. They both needed haircuts.

Portia nodded. "I don't like the other house. I like Lelie's house."

"I know you do. I do too." Kate hesitated. Would it be too soon for her next question? Should she talk to Leslie before making any promises? She decided to wait until she and Leslie could have a serious discussion. It would be a huge life change for her to add a

<blockquote>• 243 •</blockquote>

toddler into her life. "Let's go see what we can find for breakfast." Kate poured a glass of juice for Portia and fixed two bowls of cereal before making herself a cup of coffee.

"Good morning, Princess." Leslie came into the kitchen from the back door. She winked and Kate caught her hesitation when she started to offer her a kiss. They needed to talk.

"Hi, Lelie." Portia raised her spoon to wave before going back to eating.

"How's everything outside?" Kate waited for what she hoped was good news.

"It's good. I cleaned her note off the bin and saw no sign of her. I brought you both breakfast, but if you'd rather eat cereal that's okay."

Kate stood and grabbed the food out of her hand. "It smells wonderful."

"Dad made us all omelets and bacon this morning."

Kate set plates on the table and dished out the food, surprised when Portia finished her cereal and took a mouthful of omelet. Apparently, she'd raised a kid with a healthy appetite. "We'll thank Mr. Baily later," she told Portia. Kate finished her meal and sipped her coffee while playing footsie with Leslie under the table.

"Mom invited us for lunch. She's making homemade vegetable soup and grilled cheese sandwiches."

Grilled cheese was one of Portia's favorites. "That sounds fantastic, doesn't it?" She looked at Portia whose eyes lit up and she nodded several times before going back to chewing on bacon. She wouldn't miss the macaroni and cheese in a box one little bit, and she swore to herself never to make it again. "Do you have to work in the restaurant today?" Kate asked.

"I need to check on supplies and be on call if I'm needed. It's nice having reliable employees. Why?"

Leslie's simmering look had her squirming in her seat. "I'd like to talk." She didn't want to get too specific in front of Portia.

"Whenever you want, I'm available. Mom and Dad are planning lunch for noon. I'm going to check on the supplies. I'll see you later, Princess."

Portia giggled from her seat at the table and mimicked her words. "See you later."

Kate considered her options for the day. She didn't want to risk driving somewhere and Wendy seeing her, but she couldn't hide inside Leslie's house forever. She'd talk to Leslie tonight after Portia went to bed. She washed the few dishes they'd used and started a grocery list. She checked Leslie's refrigerator, as neatly organized as her closet, and then surveyed the cupboards which were nearly bare. Portia sat quietly coloring while Kate rummaged in the kitchen. The domestic scene would have been calming if it wasn't overshadowed by the fear of Wendy returning. She reminded herself they had the cameras now, and it gave her a tiny bit of peace. She finished her grocery list and left Portia coloring at her new table to go hang up her clothes. She didn't find any extra hangers, so she picked up her pile from the floor and folded everything, and then went to Portia's room to fold the clothes she'd dumped on the floor there. Her work for the day was done and it wasn't even noon. The conversation she would have with Leslie later would begin with Kate going back to work. She found a vacuum cleaner in the hall closet so she vacuumed the whole house. Portia seemed content to color and play with her LEGOs so Kate picked one of Leslie's romance novels and stretched out on the couch to read. She was drawn from sleep by warm lips pressed against hers. "Mm. What a nice way to wake up." She pulled Leslie on top of her on the couch. She laughed and Leslie grunted when Portia climbed on top of her to join the fun.

"Mom and Dad have lunch ready," Leslie squeaked out the words.

Portia climbed off the pile and Leslie stood and reached for Kate's hand. She took it and was pulled into Leslie's arms. Portia wrapped her arms around Kate's legs, and Kate absorbed the sense of correctness at the scene.

"We better go before the soup gets cold." Leslie led the way out the back door to her parents' house.

Kate hesitated before stepping outside. She checked both directions and jumped when Leslie turned and reached for her hand.

"It's okay, Kate." Leslie wrapped her arm around her waist and supported her.

"I'm okay. She inhaled deeply and drew strength from Leslie's presence. She checked the area for Wendy's car as they proceeded across the parking lot. Would she ever get over the fear? She settled down once they got into the house and finally relaxed when they sat in Leslie's parents' kitchen.

"We're so happy to have you two here." Leslie's mom hugged them all and her father had a huge grin on his face.

"Thank you for having us. I understand you had a wonderful vacation." Kate's breathing returned to normal as her minor panic attack faded away. Kate listened to Leslie's parents tell them about their Hawaii trip and was grateful for the distraction from her Wendy mess. It could have been a normal day in a normal life that wasn't that way at all. Portia ate two pieces of baklava and Kate hoped she wouldn't be bouncing off the wall all night. She had plans for Leslie that didn't include her beautiful child. They walked back to Leslie's hand in hand with Portia hanging on to Leslie's. As hard as she tried not to, she thought of Wendy and her total disinterest in Portia. This was what life was supposed to be like. She lifted Leslie's hand to her lips and kissed it.

Kate tucked Portia into her bed for a nap when they returned to the house. "Shall we nap, too?" she asked Leslie.

"That sounds perfect, but I have to check in with Trish first."

"I'll go with you. I'm not used to being home all day." She followed Leslie and when they got close to the building, she smelled the gasoline at the same time as Leslie.

"Go back to the house and check the monitors. If you see Wendy, call the police, and tell them to hurry. I'm going to make sure everyone is okay." Leslie ran to the back door of the restaurant.

Kate shouted for her to be careful and watched the monitor as Wendy tossed gasoline against the wall of the storage area of the restaurant where Leslie kept crates and boxes. She called the police just as Wendy lit a match and the flames crawled up the wall. They assured her they were on the way, and she watched in horror as Leslie's supplies burned. If the fire department didn't get here soon the fire would envelop the building. She let out a breath when she heard the sirens. The fire department got there first and moved quickly. She saw Wendy stop and listen before she flung the container with gasoline at the door of the storage room and ran.

Kate continued to watch the monitor trying to figure out which way she'd gone and found her on a camera at the side of the building exactly where the police had pulled in. She held her breath as Wendy tried to run past the police cars and one of the officers grabbed her and restrained her with handcuffs. The fire crew managed the flames, which quickly turned to white smoke.

Kate dropped into the desk chair, covered her eyes, and released tears of relief, allowing herself a moment to collapse before she rushed outside to check on Leslie. She met her in the parking lot talking to the police and showing them the restraining order. They finished taking her statement and took Wendy into custody after requesting that Kate send all the documentation she'd been keeping on her computer over in an email so they could add it to the list. The officer kindly assured her that she was safe now.

"Are you all right, love?" Kate's voice shook. Leslie gathered her in her arms and held her until she stopped shaking.

"I'm okay. It's over, sweetheart. Wendy is going to jail for willful and malicious arson on top of felony stalking."

"Is the restaurant okay? Did she do much damage?"

"The fire department put out the fire and no one was hurt. I'll assess the damage in the morning. I sent everyone home and we'll be closed tomorrow. Come on. Let's go home."

Kate held Leslie's hand as they walked back to her house. She checked on Portia as soon as they got in the door. She was busy drawing pictures and had missed the whole event. Kate sighed with relief. "Can we lie down for a little while?"

"Come on." Leslie tugged her to the bedroom and gently removed her pants and shirt before covering her with her quilt and taking off her own and sliding under the cover next to her. She gathered her in her arms and rocked her. "I love you, you know." She kissed her lightly and continued to rock her.

"I do know. And I love you, too." She kissed her with all the emotions bubbling inside her. "We haven't talked about what's next."

Leslie pulled back a little so she could look her in the eye. "I know it's been crazy, and we've hardly had a lot of time to do the dating thing. But we can go out and call it a date anytime we want to and come home and snuggle and do whatever we want to. I'd love it if you moved in with me."

Kate swallowed hard, her heart racing. "Do you mean that? You're ready to take on a child, too?"

"I'm ready to have you and your amazing daughter be the rest of my life, yes." She kissed Kate's knuckles. "I think she likes me, and my parents are going to be thrilled to have a grandchild to spoil rotten." She searched Kate's eyes. "Are you sure you're ready to do it?"

Kate let the tears fall. "I've been lost and alone for so long. I don't want to leave your side, and if you let me, we'll stay here and be the family I've always wanted."

Their kiss was slow, unhurried, and full of promise.

The nightmare was over. Life could be what she wanted it to be from here on out. She curled into Leslie's arms, safe and loved. What had started so long ago with a magnificent kiss had turned into something she had only been able to dream about.

Epilogue

That looks great, sweetheart." Leslie watched Kate hang various photos and prints on the wall of the restaurant. Kate had a good eye for color and space, so Leslie finished the last of the painting and left the wall hangings to Kate. She stood back and admired the renovated dining area. Her mother came out from the kitchen and wrapped her arm around her waist. "It's lovely, honey."

"Thanks, Mom. I'm glad you approve. I want to keep the cozy atmosphere but update a little."

"You did a great job. I love the photos and artwork. We never considered putting up pictures, but it adds interest to the place."

"Do you like the theme I came up with?"

"I love it. I'm glad we saved all our old photos of the place when we first opened. You did a great job putting together the array of changes throughout the years."

"You can thank Kate for that. She's got an artist's eye."

"I can't believe it's been a year since the fire," her mother said.

"I know. Portia's going to kindergarten this year." Leslie loved watching Portia grow up, inquisitive, headstrong, and happy. Just like her mother.

"And you and Kate have a one-year anniversary soon. Do you have anything planned?"

Leslie wasn't about to tell her mother about the sexy plans she had for Kate later that night. "Not really. We might go out to dinner."

"You let me know if you want us to watch Portia for the evening. We love having her with us."

"Thanks, Mom. I'll let you know after I talk to Kate."

"I'll see you later, honey. Your dad and I are going to watch our show now."

Leslie smiled. Her parents were happy and healthy and considered themselves semi-retired, Kate and Portia were settled in with her, and the restaurant was doing well financially, in part thanks to her finishing her university course and understanding the nuances of business ownership better. Wendy was in jail for the next decade, and their lives were calm. Kate loved her new job working with orthopedic patients in recovery from strokes, and between work and family and her new position as volunteer at the LGBTQ center, all the fear she'd lived with had slipped away like seaweed pulled back into the ocean. She went to wrap her arms around Kate's waist from behind and nuzzled her neck.

"Mm, this is nice, but I have one more picture to hang." Kate turned and kissed her quickly. "And I need to call Deanna and update her on the new developments. She'll be thrilled to hear that Wendy's out of our lives for good."

"I need you," Leslie whispered in her ear. "Soon."

"We have work to do. There'll be time later believe me. I need you, too."

"Okay. Let's finalize the plans for the new outdoor space." Leslie took Kate's hand and led her to what used to be the storage room. She'd had the burned walls removed and secured a new roof to create a covered outside eating area. "I think we're ready to open up this area with two outdoor heaters in the corners. What do you think?"

"Yeah. It might be better to get four. One for each corner. It'll be nicer on cool evenings."

"I'll send in the order for the heaters and the table and chairs today." Leslie took Kate's hand and led her to one of the inside corners of the area and kissed her. "You had a great idea to transform this area into usable dining space."

"Thanks. I see it as justice. It might've stayed a storage room forever if *she* hadn't destroyed it. Now, it'll be a pleasant seating area."

"Yep. I'm glad something positive came out of all the anguish. By the way, Mom offered to take Portia for the evening. Would you like to go out or something?"

"Yes. I choose the 'or something.'" Kate walked Leslie back to push her up against the wall and kissed her. "It's a date."

About the Author

C.A. Popovich is a hopeless romantic. She writes sweet, sensual romances that usually include horses, dogs, and cats. Her main characters—and their loving pets—don't get killed and always end up with happily-ever-after love. She is a Michigan native, writes full-time, and tries to get to as many Bold Strokes Books events as she can. She loves feedback from readers.

Books Available from Bold Strokes Books

#shedeservedit by Greg Herren. When his gay best friend, and high school football star, is murdered, Alex Wheeler is a suspect and must find the truth to clear himself. (978-1-63555-996-5)

Always by Kris Bryant. When a pushy American private investigator shows up demanding to meet the woman in Camila's artwork, instead of introducing her to her great-grandmother, Camila decides to lead her on a wild goose chase all over Italy. (978-1-63679-027-5)

Exes and O's by Joy Argento. Ali and Madison really only have one thing in common. The girl who broke their heart may be the only one who can put it back together. (978-1-63679-017-6)

One Verse Multi by Sander Santiago. Life was good: promotion, friends, falling in love, discovering that the multi-verse is on a fast track to collision—wait, what? Good thing Martin King works for a company that can fix the problem, right...um...right? (978-1-63679-069-5)

Paris Rules by Jaime Maddox. Carly Becker has been searching for the perfect woman all her life, but no one ever seems to be just right until Paige Waterford checks all her boxes, except the most important one—she's married. (978-1-63679-077-0)

Shadow Dancers by Suzie Clarke. In this third and final book in the Moon Shadow series, Rachel must find a way to become the hunter and not the hunted, and this time she will meet Ehsee Yumiko head-on. (978-1-63555-829-6)

The Kiss by C.A. Popovich. When her wife refuses their divorce and begins to stalk her, threatening her life, Kate realizes to protect her new love, Leslie, she has to let her go, even if it breaks her heart. (978-1-63679-079-4)

The Wedding Setup by Charlotte Greene. When Ryann, a big-time New York executive, goes to Colorado to help out with her best friend's wedding, she never expects to fall for the maid of honor. (978-1-63679-033-6)

Velocity by Gun Brooke. Holly and Claire work toward an uncertain future preparing for an alien space mission, and only one thing is for certain, they will have to risk their lives, and their hearts, to discover the truth. (978-1-63555-983-5)

Wildflower Words by Sam Ledel. Lida Jones treks West with her father in search of a better life on the rapidly developing American frontier, but finds home when she meets Hazel Thompson. (978-1-63679-055-8)

A Fairer Tomorrow by Kathleen Knowles. For Maddie Weeks and Gerry Stern, the Second World War brought them together, but the end of the war might rip them apart. (978-1-63555-874-6)

Holiday Hearts by Diana Day-Admire and Lyn Cole. Opposites attract during Christmastime chaos in Kansas City. (978-1-63679-128-9)

Changing Majors by Ana Hartnett Reichardt. Beyond a love, beyond a coming-out, Bailey Sullivan discovers what lies beyond the shame and self-doubt imposed on her by traditional Southern ideals. (978-1-63679-081-7)

Fresh Grave in Grand Canyon by Lee Patton. The age-old Grand Canyon becomes more and more ominous as a group of volunteers fight to survive alone in nature and uncover a murderer among them. (978-1-63679-047-3)

Highland Whirl by Anna Larner. Opposites attract in the Scottish Highlands, when feisty Alice Campbell falls for city-girl-about-town Roxanne Barns. (978-1-63555-892-0)

Humbug by Amanda Radley. With the corporate Christmas party in jeopardy, CEO Rosalind Caldwell hires Christmas Girl Ellie Pearce as her personal assistant. The only problem is, Ellie isn't a PA, has never planned a party, and develops a ridiculous crush on her totally intimidating new boss. (978-1-63555-965-1)

On the Rocks by Georgia Beers. Schoolteacher Vanessa Martini makes no apologies for her dating checklist, and newly single mom Grace Chapman ticks all Vanessa's Do Not Date boxes. Of course, they're never going to fall in love. (978-1-63555-989-7)

Song of Serenity by Brey Willows. Arguing with the Muse of music and justice is complicated, falling in love with her even more so. (978-1-63679-015-2)

The Christmas Proposal by Lisa Moreau. Stranded together in a Christmas village on a snowy mountain, Grace and Bridget face their past and question their dreams for the future. (978-1-63555-648-3)

The Infinite Summer by Morgan Lee Miller. While spending the summer with her dad in a small beach town, Remi Brenner falls for Harper Hebert and accidentally finds herself tangled up in an intense restaurant rivalry between her famous stepmom and her first love. (978-1-63555-969-9)

Wisdom by Jesse J. Thoma. When Sophia and Reggie are chosen for the governor's new community design team and tasked with tackling substance abuse and mental health issues, battle lines are drawn even as sparks fly. (978-1-63555-886-9)

A Convenient Arrangement by Aurora Rey and Jaime Clevenger. Cuffing season has come for lesbians, and for Jess Archer and Cody Dawson, their convenient arrangement becomes anything but. (978-1-63555-818-0)

An Alaskan Wedding by Nance Sparks. The last thing either Andrea or Riley expects is to bump into the one who broke her heart fifteen years ago, but when they meet at the welcome party, their feelings come rushing back. (978-1-63679-053-4)

Beulah Lodge by Cathy Dunnell. It's 1874, and newly engaged Ruth Mallowes is set on marriage and life as a missionary…until she falls in love with the housemaid at Beulah Lodge. (978-1-63679-007-7)

Gia's Gems by Toni Logan. When Lindsey Speyer discovers that popular travel columnist Gia Williams is a complete fake and threatens to expose her, blackmail has never been so sexy. (978-1-63555-917-0)

Holiday Wishes & Mistletoe Kisses by M. Ullrich. Four holidays, four couples, four chances to make their wishes come true. (978-1-63555-760-2)

Love By Proxy by Dena Blake. Tess has a secret crush on her best friend, Sophie, so the last thing she wants is to help Sophie fall in love with someone else, but how can she stand in the way of her happiness? (978-1-63555-973-6)

Loyalty, Love, & Vermouth by Eric Peterson. A comic valentine to a gay man's family of choice, including the ones with cold noses and four paws. (978-1-63555-997-2)

Marry Me by Melissa Brayden. Allison Hale attempts to plan the wedding of the century to a man who could save her family's business, if only she wasn't falling for her wedding planner, Megan Kinkaid. (978-1-63555-932-3)

Pathway to Love by Radclyffe. Courtney Valentine is looking for a woman exactly like Ben—smart, sexy, and not in the market for anything serious. All she has to do is convince Ben that sex-without-strings is the perfect pathway to pleasure. (978-1-63679-110-4)

Sweet Surprise by Jenny Frame. Flora and Mac never thought they'd ever see each other again, but when Mac opens up her barber shop right next to Flora's sweet shop, their connection comes roaring back. (978-1-63679-001-5)

The Edge of Yesterday by CJ Birch. Easton Gray is sent from the future to save humanity from technological disaster. When she's forced to target the woman she's falling in love with, can Easton do what's needed to save humanity? (978-1-63679-025-1)

The Scout and the Scoundrel by Barbara Ann Wright. With unexpected danger surrounding them, Zara and Roni are stuck between duty and survival, with little room for exploring their feelings, especially love. (978-1-63555-978-1)

Bury Me in Shadows by Greg Herren. College student Jake Chapman is forced to spend the summer at his dying grandmother's home and soon finds danger from long-buried family secrets. (978-1-63555-993-4)

Can't Leave Love by Kimberly Cooper Griffin. Sophia and Pru have no intention of falling in love, but sometimes love happens when and where you least expect it. (978-1-636790041-1)

Free Fall at Angel Creek by Julie Tizard. Detective Dee Rawlings and aircraft accident investigator Dr. River Dawson use conflicting methods to find answers when a plane goes missing, while overcoming surprising threats, and discovering an unlikely chance at love. (978-1-63555-884-5)

Love's Compromise by Cass Sellars. For Piper Holthaus and Brook Myers, will professional dreams and past baggage stop two hearts from realizing they are meant for each other? (978-1-63555-942-2)

Not All a Dream by Sophia Kell Hagin. Hester has lost the woman she loved and the world has descended into relentless dark and cold. But giving up will have to wait when she stumbles upon people who help her survive. (978-1-63679-067-1)

Protecting the Lady by Amanda Radley. If Eve Webb had known she'd be protecting royalty, she'd never have taken the job as bodyguard, but as the threat to Lady Katherine's life draws closer, she'll do whatever it takes to save her, and may just lose her heart in the process. (978-1-63679-003-9)

The Secrets of Willowra by Kadyan. A family saga of three women, their homestead called Willowra in the Australian outback, and the secrets that link them all. (978-1-63679-064-0)

Trial by Fire by Carsen Taite. When prosecutor Lennox Roy and public defender Wren Bishop become fierce adversaries in a headline-grabbing arson case, their attraction ignites a passion that leads them both to question their assumptions about the law, the truth, and each other. (978-1-63555-860-9)

Turbulent Waves by Ali Vali. Kai Merlin and Vivien Palmer plan their future together as hostile forces make their own plans to destroy what they have, as well as all those they love. (978-1-63679-011-4)

Unbreakable by Cari Hunter. When Dr. Grace Kendal is forced at gunpoint to help an injured woman, she is dragged into a nightmare where nothing is quite as it seems, and their lives aren't the only ones on the line. (978-1-63555-961-3)

Veterinary Surgeon by Nancy Wheelton. When dangerous drugs are stolen from the veterinary clinic, Mitch investigates and Kay becomes a suspect. As pride and professions clash, love seems impossible. (978-1-63679-043-5)

A Different Man by Andrew L. Huerta. This diverse collection of stories chronicling the challenges of gay life at various ages shines a light on the progress made and the progress still to come. (978-1-63555-977-4)

All That Remains by Sheri Lewis Wohl. Johnnie and Shantel might have to risk their lives—and their love—to stop a werewolf intent on killing. (978-1-63555-949-1)

Beginner's Bet by Fiona Riley. Phenom luxury Realtor Ellison Gamble has everything, except a family to share it with, so when a mix-up brings youthful Katie Crawford into her life, she bets the house on love. (978-1-63555-733-6)

Dangerous Without You by Lexus Grey. Throughout their senior year in high school, Aspen, Remington, Denna, and Raleigh face challenges in life and romance that they never expect. (978-1-63555-947-7)

Desiring More by Raven Sky. In this collection of steamy stories, a rich variety of lovers find themselves desiring more, more from a lover, more from themselves, and more from life. (978-1-63679-037-4)

Jordan's Kiss by Nanisi Barrett D'Arnuck. After losing everything in a fire, Jordan Phelps joins a small lounge band and meets pianist Morgan Sparks, who lights another blaze, this time in Jordan's heart. (978-1-63555-980-4)

Late City Summer by Jeanette Bears. Forced together for her wedding, Emily Stanton and Kate Alessi navigate their lingering passion for one another against the backdrop of New York City and World War II, and a summer romance they left behind. (978-1-63555-968-2)

Love and Lotus Blossoms by Anne Shade. On her path to self-acceptance and true passion, Janesse will risk everything—and possibly everyone—she loves. (978-1-63555-985-9)

Love in the Limelight by Ashley Moore. Marion Hargreaves, the finest actress of her generation, and Jessica Carmichael, the world's biggest pop star, rediscover each other twenty years after an ill-fated affair. (978-1-63679-051-0)

Suspecting Her by Mary P. Burns. Complications ensue when Erin O'Connor falls for top real estate saleswoman Catherine Williams while investigating racism in the real estate industry; the fallout could end their chance at happiness. (978-1-63555-960-6)

Two Winters by Lauren Emily Whalen. A modern YA retelling of Shakespeare's *The Winter's Tale* about birth, death, Catholic school, improv comedy, and the healing nature of time. (978-1-63679-019-0)